OF THE

GRANDE DAME HOTEL

A NOVEL SET AT THE BREAKERS OF PALM BEACH

DEBY EISENBERG

This one is for my loving inspirations, Skylar, Jace, Laken, Sage, Makenzie, Jayden, Payton, Reese and Daryn. I am hoping that they will find and pursue their passions in life.

Chapter 1

PALM BEACH 1942

Two in the afternoon was the exact time of day Addie most loved to stroll along the ocean shore, seeking the little treasures that the vibrant waves of high tide would magically churn out onto the sand before retreating for the next swell. But on this day, Addie was only hoping to find her intriguing new friend, Natalie Evington, who she knew would be having her Saturday run. When Natalie came into view, Addie darted toward her with a great intensity, fueled by anger and insult.

"Do you think I have a cruel heart?" she asked Natalie as she caught up with her to run in tandem.

Natalie turned toward the voice and smiled. "Hardly, Addie. I don't believe anyone would think you had a cruel heart."

"My mother thinks so," Addie insisted.

"Your mother?" Natalie shot back, with a dubious voice. "She's too sweet to have ever said a mean word to you."

"But she did now," Addie insisted. "She said that my heart was . . . I don't quite remember . . . unsympathetic, and something else . . . and she sounded so disappointed." Already Addie, not in the same athletic shape as the older girl she admired, was struggling to keep up with her pace. At five foot three, she could hardly emulate the long strides of someone taller and leaner than herself, someone blessed with the perfect feminine body proportions of length and curves that turned every masculine head in their direction while they made their way past the sunbathers. As always, Natalie appeared oblivious to her magnetic attraction, to the conversations she halted, the books that were quickly set aside, the footballs that were no longer being tossed around but instead held in crooks of arms, as they passed one group after another.

By her friend's side, Addie self-consciously pulled down on the skirt bottom of her swimsuit and rounded her shoulders to hide the newly emerging contours of her bustline. But Natalie, though she slowed down to run at Addie's pace, seamlessly continued with their conversation, her head held high, her broad shoulders arched back to maintain her perfect posture, with no concern that she was accentuating the very attribute that Addie tried to obscure.

"Now, Addie, what, exactly, did you say to your mother that brought that on?" Natalie questioned.

"I said I was upset that the cute young men will all be going off to war." Addie stopped running, bent her knees and rested her hands on her thighs, as she tried to catch her breath. She was glad when Natalie glanced around over her shoulder with an understanding smile and backtracked a few yards.

"I know what I said was selfish. I know they will be fighting for 'a greater good.' We hear that phrase all the time." She paused again for a deep breath. "But did it have to be now? Did it have to be right now, when I am just about to turn sixteen and become part of the real world –your world – with opportunities to go to dances, and maybe even on dates?"

This was to have been Addie's year, her glorious, wonderful year of attending events, instead of just watching balls from behind curtains. In years before, she had longingly observed as, one after another, the society girls coming down from New York brought their suitcases and travel trunks stuffed with beautiful debutante gowns for one more wear in the winter season. She had even helped her mother arrange for those gowns to be altered just so much here or there, adjusting a sleeve or collar for comfort and practicality in the heat of the Florida sun. Ever since she was thirteen, she had often been the one to return the clothes to the guest rooms. And when she hung them in the closets, she would linger there, gazing at, touching, sometimes even smelling the bouquet of dresses that she saw. The guests didn't know who she was, really, and would often order her around as if she were merely a young hotel maid and not the daughter of the assistant manager of the grandest resort in America, The Breakers of Palm Beach, Florida.

Natalie finally stopped running, and she turned to give Addie the full attention she craved. At almost twenty years old, she spoke to her like a wizened older sister. "Well, you know what I am wondering? Was the word your mother said 'foolish'? Did she say that you had a 'foolish heart'? That would be more believable." She paused, momentarily, adding, "And it's true, and I do agree."

"Agree with my mother?"

"No, I agree with you," Natalie answered, shaking her head with the same frustration of her young friend, realizing that so much of the joy of her envisioned future would be placed on hold because of circumstances beyond their control. "Makes me sad. Right now, right at my time, too, how did it happen that all the men are gone? I thought this next year could be my escape."

Addie was surprised at this admission. She saw Natalie only as the most perfect, stunning, and self-confident person, and felt so lucky that they had recently become friends, occasionally spending time together at the beach when Addie was out of school on the weekends. Natalie, having finished three semesters at Bryn Mawr, the women's college in Pennsylvania that had been her mother's alma mater, finally admitted to her father that she wasn't really happy there. When Natalie was fifteen, her mother lost her fight to cancer. Although Natalie tried to follow in her mother's educational footsteps, her own prints were ground deeply in the Florida sand. She had enjoyed her classes and done well, but she had tired of the all-girl environment and the cold northeastern winters. She was anxious to return to her sunny hometown. For the past few months, she had been freelancing articles on Palm Beach life for a local tourist magazine owned by one of her father's friends, and she planned to apply to the University of Miami for the fall term.

"Escape from what, Natalie? From your wonderful life in your huge home? I don't think I exaggerate when I say you live in a beautiful mansion."

Natalie shook her head and skirted Addie's gaze, as if searching for her words in the cloudless sky. "You could say it's a mansion, yes. But I don't feel at home there anymore. Not for some time now." There was a sadness in this answer that Addie could recognize, but not truly understand. Before she could question it, Natalie challenged her. "How about you? You are one to talk – actually living at The Breakers Hotel."

"A hotel though," Addie replied quickly. "Not quite a home."

Each girl looked at the other curiously, thinking that there would be a wealth of conversations ahead, when they heard the loud and low-toned pitch of a boy's voice calling out from a distance. "Addie . . . hey, Addie, wait up!"

"Oh my God, that's Nathan Bernstein. I don't even have to turn to recognize the voice," Addie said.

The girls shaded their eyes and squinted in his direction. "You must know him. He looks pretty tall and handsome from here," Natalie said.

"Oh, I know him. But you're wrong. He is gawky, and he follows me everywhere. I think he spies on me, because it's too coincidental to run into someone so many times. But never on the beach. You'll see. He's a shade lighter than pale. He doesn't look like someone who can take the sun. Just continue walking – ignore him. He's such a child."

"Obviously, he has a crush on you," Natalie laughed. Addie waved her comment away with the gesture of an overzealous fly swat, but Natalie persisted. "I don't know. I see already that he has a cute mop of dark hair. And I don't think he is quite a child. I say our age, maybe a year older. You should go with it," she instructed. "Remember – our choices are limited now."

"Well," Addie said, as she paused to consider it. "I guess I can't argue with that. But I wish he were even a little older, and then he could go to war." She looked up at Natalie with a smirk on her face, triumphant with her remark. And then she thought about her words. "Oh no, I didn't mean that. I didn't mean anyone should have to bear the awful risks of war." She was working hard to retract her statement, with great regret.

"Exactly what I told you, earlier," Natalie said, laughing and putting her arm around the younger girl. "No one would ever say you had a cruel heart."

"And I know why he wants to hang with me," Addie continued. "It's the commonality. I understand it. I feel it, too – another Jewish person around here. That is a rare find. I know him from our temple. But still . . . just ignore him when he comes up. You don't even have to look at him."

Natalie just shook her head and laughed at Addie. "You are so silly. I have a feeling that someday . . . someday soon . . . you may feel differently."

Addie was grateful to see that Nate had stopped along the way to toss a ball around with some younger children who were playing catch, allowing the girls more time alone to talk. "Well then, could you teach me?" Addie pleaded to Natalie. " – teach me how to act when someone acceptable might be interested? Before the guys started leaving, I saw how they all wanted to be with you." Suddenly, Addie felt shy to say what was on her mind, so she took in a deep breath first. "I've never been kissed, you know."

"Sweet sixteen and never been kissed?"

"It's true. Well, not sixteen quite yet, so there is still hope." Addie looked intently at Natalie now. "How about you, when was your first kiss?"

Natalie thought for a moment and shook her head. And then she smiled. "I think it was seventh grade – just playing spin the bottle – it had nothing to do with romance."

"Oh no, I want my first real kiss to be so memorable," Addie cried. And then she thought about it. "I guess I should feel sorrier for you than me. It's not like I could actually go out with the boys, the men, who are off to the army. I'm not old enough for them. But this could be my year of dating the high school boys."

At this point, Nathan appeared at their backs, surprising them with a "Hey, Addie, I could be your first date."

When she turned to his voice, this time Addie focused on the thick brown hair that Natalie had complimented and, to Nate's surprise, she was less dismissive of him than ever.

He couldn't believe it. Addie was looking right at him and doing so without rolling her eyes. She never did that. She actually seemed to be looking into his eyes, and so he took it as an invitation to do the same, to study her beautiful brown eyes, incredibly intriguing and disproportionately large for her petite frame. He was in heaven. That was, until he realized that she was not looking at his eyes, but more so, at his hair. "Oh my God," he said, "Is there a bug crawling around up there?" He made a quick jerking motion, and then rifled his fingers through his thick curls and shook his head so that his waves danced from side to side and would release any errant creature.

"See what I mean," Addie whispered to Natalie, who started to laugh at the comedy of it. "Could you please try to act normal?" Addie whined at Nate. "I want to introduce you to someone. This is my friend, Natalie." Nate, who had been nervously sneaking peeks at Addie in her swimsuit, had not even noticed the girl standing beside her, who he now saw looked like a fashion model, and he would later berate himself for his overreaction.

"Wow! Pleased to meet you," Nate said, eying Natalie from head to toe.

"Down, boy," Addie cautioned. "You'd have to stand in line for her."

Natalie smiled at him and gave Addie a surreptitious wink of approval. "Pleased to meet you, as well," she said, extending her hand to Nate to set him at ease.

They all began walking the shore together, coming up to an area where the smooth beach sand gave way to a rocky patch. Addie bent down to pick up a perfect seashell of formidable size, bearing not even the slightest chip and roaring the ocean's voice when she placed it close to her ear. She held it out briefly to show them, and then she gingerly laid it back on the sand. "Let some excited eight-year-old tourist find that one – I'm well over those. I'm only looking for the most interesting items possible."

"Yeah, Addie," Nate said, mockingly, "You want to be the one to find a message chiseled into a board from a shipwrecked vessel which floats its way to our shore. 'I've been trapped on

Jupiter Island since 1912 – Please send help!'" He leaned into her and laughed, and she slapped at his arm.

"No, something more interesting," Addie insisted. "Jewelry from an old ship crushed by the rocks in the last century, maybe." Then she shook her head, laughing at herself, and suspended the reverie. "Anyway, Nate, what are you doing over here?"

"Have you heard it? That's what I came to ask you."

"Heard what?" the girls asked, simultaneously.

"I don't know. It's like I've been hearing sounds in the distance. They almost sound like explosions to me."

"Well, it would certainly be the far distance," Addie shrugged. "You don't have to worry about that. You can't hear the fighting in Europe from here."

"I know that, but . . . it's almost like I've felt vibrations with it. The first one was late yesterday, and I can't stop thinking about it."

"Maybe you're imagining it. We've all had nightmares since Pearl Harbor, Nate," Natalie added with an almost motherly concern.

"That's for sure. But I don't think it's just in my mind. I've always had a very acute sense of hearing."

Now Addie did roll her eyes, addressing her comments to Natalie. "He's told me that before. He thinks because of his poor eyesight that his other senses have become more heightened." As Addie said this, Nate self-consciously pushed his glasses higher on the bridge of his nose. "The truth is, I think he just wants to be a part of it, pretend that he is part of the war effort."

The three continued walking with an easy camaraderie, until Addie ran to a shiny object that turned out to be a compass. She placed it in the small backpack she always carried, dangling from one shoulder. It often held a potpourri of items she would discover on any beach walk, sometimes coins or unique shells, sometimes rings or bracelets that she would later drop off at the hotel's lost and found.

"Well, I do." Nate suddenly interjected, touching Natalie's shoulder to gain her attention. "I'm just seventeen, but I do want to be part of the war effort." He stopped walking and stood with his head down. "The men in my family are all involved, and it's scary." He coughed out the last word, as if stifling a slight cry. "My brothers have gone to training camps, ready to ship out soon. My dad's away with his engineering firm's government contracts. And now, I feel like I have to do something, but I'm too young to enlist."

He tried to stand taller again, facing Addie, and then turning slightly to direct his words to Natalie. "I know that Addie rejoices in making fun of me for that – well, really for everything. But I like to be a part of things going on. I have a need to understand things."

"Addie, you should reconsider your criticism," Natalie admonished her. "Those are good traits in a person."

"And I really have an interest in the construction of things," Nate continued. "Got that from my dad. I might have an easy explanation for the sounds. Maybe they're doing blastings to make sandbars and add rocks to stop the waves before they come to shore and batter the buildings. Think about your hotel name, The Breakers. Maybe it's –"

And then there was the truly unmistakable sound of an explosion. Nate abruptly stopped talking and they all turned to the north and watched as a plume of fire and smoke rose from the water, well before the horizon.

Instinctively, they started running in that direction, their eyes focused on what they had just witnessed, their hearts pounding in their chests. Nate, with the lean build of the high school runner that he was, led the way, followed by the impressive strides of Natalie.

They did not realize that Addie was not with them. A strange pile of objects in the direction of the sidewalk had caught her attention. As she ran toward it, she had slipped in a sunken patch of an oily substance. Her fall had sent her into an area cluttered with foliage, where a recent storm had uprooted palm trees and bushes and displaced them. She had not actually hurt herself. But she was about to cry out for attention, when she became engrossed in the objects surrounding her. An almost intact dark wooden dresser and a pile of clothing were strewn about. She worked for a minute trying to extract something wedged in one drawer that was keeping it partially open. When she yanked on what turned out to be a wide white trouser, like a sailor might wear, the object was released. It was a picture frame, holding a barely discernable, water-soaked photograph that might be of a young woman and a baby. She couldn't believe it. She wondered if she had hit her head and was in a dream. And then nothing could contain her excitement. "Nate, Wait. Natalie, hold up," she cried out.

Nate was the first to hear her over the crashing of the waves and the whoosh of the slightly strong wind. He touched Natalie's arm next to him and they both looked back. Addie was running toward them, waving her arms wildly, while holding up objects that looked like flags from the distance. As she caught up to them, she stopped to catch her breath.

"What have you got there?" Nate asked. "Looks like a shirt and a uniform jacket of some type."

"Yes, don't you see? It's incredible. There are treasures right back there." She pointed in the direction. "They were soaked from the sea, just like I imagined, washed by the waves and caught in the heavy brush."

Suddenly Natalie gave out a gasp. "Addie, are you okay? Do you know your leg . . . your leg is bleeding?"

"I don't think so," Addie said calmly. "I don't feel anything. What do you mean?" But when even Nate began pointing, wide-eyed, at some red substance spotting her leg from her calf to her toes, she began screaming, touched the apparent wound, rubbed her leg, and yelled again. And then she stopped. "I don't seem to have any cut."

As if scripted, in unison, they turned toward the pile of items and ran back. Nate was the brave one, working to move some of the largest palm fronds to clear part of the area at the end of the blood trail, while the girls could barely do more than shield their eyes. But when he moved a last heavy branch covered by mounds of slimy seaweed, their mutual screams were enough to alert dozens of people from the nearby hotel beach cottages.

And soon a small crowd was gathering around them. The body of a man, dressed in the torn attire of a merchant seaman, his face so scraped and bloodied that his age was indiscernible, had made its way to shore. He lay in the shallow red pool of his own blood as if he were murdered on the spot he was found, instead of, more likely, a casualty from the explosions Nate had heard the previous evening. The onlookers were frozen around the site, until a few of the yard workers took off their caps in a gesture of respect.

Suddenly, something propelled Nate to move closer to the body, and he knelt down. Then he looked up quickly, surveying the crowd. When he saw one man with the proper attire, Nate called out to him. "Sir, please, I need your belt as quickly as possible." The man understood immediately and came forward. "The blood is coming from this leg wound," Nate told him, as he indicated the point on the body. "It is still pulsing out," he insisted. And then he paused to take in a breath. "This man is alive." he said in his strongest voice. He applied the tourniquet belt as he had learned from his Boy Scout days, while others ran to summon help.

Nate held his position by the injured sailor, until a short time later, when there was a convergence of police and firemen to the area. After attending to the man, the emergency team placed him on a stretcher to move him from the beach to the ambulance waiting at the street level. He was now conscious enough to begin moaning. One of the attendants turned to Nate. "You saved a life today, young man. You should be proud of yourself. Your parents will be proud of you."

Like the other onlookers, Nate was still reeling from the shock of the event. Addie and Natalie were hugging him from either side, patting his back, and smiling up at him, with teary eyes. But Nate was still trying to process all that had just happened. He kept his head down, feeling both sad and humbled. And then, abruptly, he grabbed the hand of each girl and led them to catch up with the stretcher.

"Just a question, sir," Nate said, tapping the closer aide on his shoulder. The men turned to him and slowed their pace. "How is it possible, though, that he survived in the ocean when he was so badly injured?"

The man holding the rear handles answered with no hesitation, as if he had been reconstructing the scenario himself. "Best guess? He was a lucky guy and then an unlucky guy. Damn Nazis have submarines right out there, German U-boats, right off our coast, and they've started torpedoing Allied merchant ships. We've just had reports of oil spills coming to shore. And yes, bodies and body parts, too, of those less fortunate. Your guy, here, was probably thrown clear in last night's explosion, maybe barely conscious, but he hung on to objects or floated to shore with them, almost riding the waves of the tide, until he was deposited in this area. We've seen this before in peacetime shipwrecks. Surprisingly, the ocean may have been his friend, but the shore did its damage. Probably the rocks and shells battered his face and something on the sand cut him badly. My partner picked up a huge piece of bloodied broken glass in one of those bushes." He nodded his head in the direction, and then both stretcher bearers continued walking more briskly.

Emotionally and physically exhausted, Addie, Natalie, and Nate gave final hugs and then separated, continuing individually to their homes.

As she walked, Addie could hardly stop shaking, trying to process all she had just witnessed. She was horrified to have seen, firsthand, a casualty of war. A phrase which had only been a concept now had a face to it. She could not rid herself of the image of the battered and bleeding man. She wondered if the photograph she discovered in the drawer could have been of his wife and baby. But if not, it undoubtedly belonged to some other sailor on the destroyed ship. Tears welled in her eyes as she thought of so many families who would soon receive unbearable news. When she reached her apartment at The Breakers, her parents listened to her story and comforted her as best they could. But as she lay in bed that evening, the only thing that calmed her was focusing on Nate's heroic action. Intermingled with her depressing thoughts was one elevating emotion. She felt an emerging admiration and pride for her friend.

Over the following weeks, Addie replayed the scene in her head. She began to realize how self-centered she had been. Just a short time ago, she was the most innocent girl, worried about childish things, boys, and dating. She had bemoaned her world, so recently becoming devoid of its young men. What she could never have anticipated was that within months, her area would become one of the most active centers of military activity in the nation. The war had come to the American continental coast-line, and with it, tens of thousands of young men and women would be serving their country on the home front, right at her doorstep in Palm Beach County, Florida.

Chapter 2

MANHATTAN 1975

Beth Morgan was still trying to process just how much her life had changed over the past weekend. On Friday evening, she had been a happily engaged young woman, living in New York, depressed by the cold wave the city was enduring but excited to bundle up against the sweeping winds and surprise her fiancé at his apartment. Even though he had insisted that he would just stay home since the weather that night was not conducive for social plans, Beth was willing to brave the elements so they could be together. She had already prepared a special meal for Richard, in honor of their year anniversary of dating and four months since his proposal. With her roommate out of town visiting her own boyfriend, Beth had envisioned a candlelit dinner at her beautifully set table. So now, she decided she would just transfer the already cooked roast beef, potatoes, and green bean almandine casserole to his place. Even in the worst weather, her doorman was always a master at securing a cab.

Although Beth was proud when Richard revealed he was viewed as a rising star in his law firm, she was unhappy that their time together was becoming more and more compromised. This was to have been her fairytale engagement year, enjoying intimate moments with her handsome young man, making the social rounds with him by her side, shopping and preparing for a grand summer wedding.

"You have to understand. This is what to expect when you are with an associate at one of the biggest practices in the city," he had almost scolded Beth when she had complained the first time soon after the engagement. "They work you day and night." But then he softened his tone. "You know I only want to be with you, honey. But I want to secure our future. You'll see. This will all be worth it." She knew that was true, of course. But it was increasingly becoming a worry to her. She understood the disintegration of her own parents' marriage had been for that very reason. And now, ironically, it was through her father's connections that Richard had been able to land a job in a top law office, creating the same scenario. Well, at least his work ethic was proof to her ever-critical, ever-cynical mother that he was not the "slacker playboy" she had identified. Her mother had been skeptical from the beginning that Richard had only found a good position through dating Beth. She felt he was too full of himself, too slick a talker and a dresser.

When Beth arrived at Richard's Greenwich Village garden apartment, she carefully walked down the three steps to his door. She placed the impossibly still-warm meal, momentarily, on the snowy stoop. The taxi driver, in a quick attempt to pick up his next fare, had splattered dirty clumps of blackened street snow at her, and she was trying her hardest to shake herself off before she went inside. She began to search in her purse for the key Richard had given her, unaware that the warm pot had compromised the hardened snow surrounding the area and created an ice patch at her feet. In an instant, she slipped, fell against the door which had not been securely closed, and landed face down on the wooden floor of his small foyer. And then the surprise was on her.

"What the?" she heard Richard exclaim before she lifted her head and their eyes met. And then his next line was "Oh, shit!"

Beth had to blink several times before her eyes could focus, and then she had no words for what she saw. Richard and a very pretty woman, who was vaguely familiar to her as someone on his office staff, were sitting at the small table that divided the kitchen from the living room. They were each wearing coats, but from the two pairs of bare legs that were at her eye level, Beth assumed they had nothing else on underneath. They were caught, wine glasses in hand, with the contents from Chinese takeout containers on paper plates before them.

"God . . . Beth, I . . ." Richard started to say, but she knew there was no explanation that would follow. Even the best lawyer could not talk his way out of this.

Her humiliation, there, on the floor, a pathetic mess, witnessing the betrayal of her tongue-tied fiancé, while his "date" stared at her with an apologetically gloating look, could never be measured. All Beth wanted to do was break down and cry. But somehow, she found the strength to hold it in. She needed to extricate herself from this situation immediately. When Richard stood and began to move toward her to help, his coat opened just enough to confirm her assessment that he was naked underneath.

"Do not take one step closer to me," she said, emphasizing each word as if there were a period following it, although later that night she would wonder how she even had the ability to calmly and coldly speak to him. She would let the tramp know that she was a lady, although at this moment she hardly felt or looked like one. She had to regain some modicum of self-respect, as she maneuvered herself to balance on high heeled boots and stand up.

Richard sat back down, covering his eyes with his open palms and shaking his head. "Beth, I . . . I'm sorry you had to see this," he stuttered out.

Now Beth was incredulous, her humiliation melding into righteous anger. "That's what you're sorry for?" she challenged, "not that you are a cheater, but that you were caught?" Beth took in a deep breath. "You know what, you're disgusting. I need you to call a taxi for me right now," she said. "And then just go into the bedroom until I've left. Oh, and by the way," she added, "if you wondered why your place was so cold that you needed to wear coats inside, leaving a door slightly ajar creates a terrible draft."

Beth wanted to leave it at that, but then she reconsidered. Quickly, before he went to make the call, she took off her left glove and contemplatively examined her diamond engagement ring. Then she twisted it off her finger and held it in her right hand. She paused an extra moment for the drama of it, and then she threw the ring . . . into her purse.

• • •

"Thank God," the society matron, Kathryn Morgan, soundly pronounced when her daughter Beth appeared on her doorstep on Saturday morning, sobbing so deeply that she was barely able to deliver her news. "Thank God it happened before the invitations were out." Beth's mother always spoke as if she were channeling the Gilded Age matriarch who had been the first owner of her impressive Manhattan brownstone. Even when she saw the destroyed look on her daughter's face, she still could not alter her imperious tone.

Mrs. Morgan motioned for Beth to come fully into the home so the housekeeper, Marie, who had been standing discreetly to the side witnessing the ordeal but trying not to intrude, could more securely close the door against the winter elements.

"It would have come, darling. I am just being honest – and then the timing would have been worse," Beth's mother insisted, shaking her head forcefully, as if wresting away even the thought of the social embarrassment of it all. "You could have been married, maybe even with a child to raise on your own."

Beth could not help but be taken aback by that comment. Was her mother referring to her own plight years ago – to being sad and disgusted that she was burdened with *her*?

Kathryn, predictably now with her first cigarette of the morning between her fingers, gave a half-hearted pat to her daughter's shoulder. "He was a gold digger – I had him pegged from the beginning," she said, gesturing with the lighted tip of her cigarette, as if it were dotting every 'i' in the statement. And then she softened for a moment. "Darling, I am being tough, I know."

That was what Beth had known would be waiting for her. The "I told you so" implication she had heard on many other occasions. "You've always been tough, mother," she said. "But this is the bitterest 'salt on the wound' that you have ever delivered." Beth struggled to hold back tears. She was beginning to feel as knocked down and flattened as she had the night before. "Don't you have faith in me?" she asked in a cracking voice. "Is it impossible for you to believe that someone could just find me attractive and special enough to love?"

Marie helped Beth to remove her winter coat. She loosened the cable knit cream-colored scarf that kept Beth's hair protected from the winter day, and then, row by row, the thick waves of her auburn locks were released from their nest under her hood.

"Beautiful," Marie could not help but say, as she maneuvered Beth so she could catch a glimpse of herself in the mirror. The maid was willing to risk her employer's ire in an effort to bolster the young woman's confidence. While Kathryn stepped away to find an ash tray, Marie smiled at Beth. "What man would not be attracted to your beauty . . . and your sweetness?"

"Please," Kathryn said, stretching the word to twice its length, as she reentered the room. She flicked a mound of ashes into the silver dish she was carrying. "Please," she repeated, taking her seat in the grand foyer. "Do not tell me that you prostrated yourself and cried in front of Richard."

Beth lowered her head and breathed out slowly. And when she looked back up, she had a slight smile. "Funny that you should say that." She had regained her composure and spoke with a newly acquired empowerment. She described to her mother the entire encounter, not even sparing any of the humiliating details. As she finished, they were both laughing at the movie-like comic timing of it all. When she understood how Beth had told off Richard and kept the ring from their broken engagement, Kathryn stood up and maneuvered the cigarette to the tip of her fingers so that she could applaud, her elbows locked, her hands outstretched toward her daughter. "Bravo," she said. "I am proud of you."

Her mother could not have imagined what those five words meant to Beth. But after she reached out to give her a hug, Kathryn quickly returned to her usual persona, stepping back to address her daughter. "Beth, dear, I need to speak to you seriously about another matter. I was going to talk to you about this later today." She paused for a minute, until a few more puffs of her cigarette seemed to power her ahead. "I need you to accompany me for something important. Now, at least, I know you will not give me excuses." She lowered her head, as if the next words would be hard ones to deliver. "I need your help." Surprisingly, in all her life, Beth never remembered hearing those words. Kathryn Morgan was not a "helpless" person — but now she was reaching out to Beth.

And so, two days later, without any explanation why, Beth was transported from heartbreak and frost in New York City to the heat of eighty-degree, sunny Florida weather.

Chapter 3

PALM BEACH 1975

By Monday morning, as she accompanied her mother on an unexplained plane trip to Palm Beach, Florida, Beth's emotions were running the entire spectrum from sadness to anger, from embarrassment to outrage, and from shock to depression. Her hours of being able to laugh at herself and her situation had vanished, and she was acting like a sullen seventh grader being led to the principal's office, instead of the confident, young career woman that she was. When the limousine driver leaned back slightly to maneuver the privacy panel open and announce that they were approaching their hotel, Beth arched up slightly from her slouch and looked out the window. And then she sat up even straighter. "Goodness," she said aloud, reacting to the tropical landscape she had not seen since trips to Florida when she was younger. And Kathryn, who had uncharacteristically but thoughtfully given Beth some time and distance to sort through her feelings on the flight, patted her hand and agreed.

"Yes, goodness, indeed," she echoed, as she leaned closer to Beth's side and motioned toward the electronic panel on her armrest. "Press the window button down. Let's allow some fresh air to come in."

Beth had not yet understood that the dark tinted car windows, common in Florida, had done their job to obscure what awaited them. "Oh my God. Sunshine, heat – what more could anyone want?"

"Oh, look again as we approach, there's one thing more, I'm sure, that will attract you," Kathryn added, knowing her daughter quite well. "Oh yes, that is for certain. It is something rather special."

Beth stretched her neck out the window to look ahead. And then the incredibly impressive façade of a magnificent hotel came into view. "And spectacular architecture," she said, nodding. "Mother, this is the most beautiful place. Just like the Villa Medici, but perhaps even bigger."

The chauffer could not help himself. "Built in the Italian Renaissance style – you have an eye for this, miss. Sorry to chime in, but I also do tours of the area."

"Well, yes, my daughter has the eye – she is an interior designer."

Once again, Beth was surprised. Was that pride that her mother was voicing? "You know, mother, the few times we've come to Florida, it's been to Miami Beach. Lots of Art Deco and modern styles. Why didn't we ever come here? Have you ever been here before?"

Kathryn looked out her own window. There was a long pause. "Oh, I do hope our room is ready," she answered only, her privileged tone returning.

A perfect row of stately Palm trees, standing like guardian soldiers, lined either side of the long, private road leading to The Breakers Hotel. And as the driveway finally melded into a circle, it encompassed an ornately tiered fountain that would be at home in any of the grandest Italian city plazas.

As Beth emerged from the car, her mood could not help but be elevated by the lush and colorful scenery that greeted her. And then there was a flurry of activity. Bellmen were managing their baggage and escorting them to the impressive lobby while Kathryn directed, "Careful with that one, young man," as each piece was handled.

"I see we are welcoming you back, Mrs. Morgan," the front desk receptionist said, looking at the reservation notes. The hotel prided itself in meticulous record-keeping, to properly acknowledge returning guests. "It has been a long time," she added with a warm smile. But Kathryn gave no response as she signed the register. Beth, off to the side yet just within earshot, offered her mother a querulous look but chose to remain silent.

"Let me see," the woman continued, shuffling through index cards. "Yes. We have a beautiful suite for you. You arrived a
bit early for check-in time, but I promise we will have the room
ready as soon as possible. May I direct you and Miss Morgan
to the dining room to relax, perhaps with a cool beverage and
a bite to eat?"

"Well, yes, thank you, dear," Kathryn said, with her signature patronizing smile. Beth knew her mother would want
nothing more right now than to be sitting with a drink in one
hand and a cigarette in the other. And maybe this would be
the time that she would explain just what was going on and
why they had come here. When they turned from the desk area
though, Beth's thoughts took a different direction, and she was
now only interested in the grandeur of the interior. Certainly,
she was not a stranger to elegance. In the past few months
alone, she had attended business luncheons or met friends for
dinner at three of the finest hotels in her own backyard, the
Carlyle, the Plaza, and the Waldorf Astoria. But as large as
those iconic buildings may have been, the isle of Manhattan,
with its density of real estate and soaring values, could never
produce a hotel on this scale, something that included outside
acreage. Already in the short time she had been there, Beth was
able to recognize the quality of the resort. She was impressed by
how its *porte-cochere* structure welcomed vehicles so their occu-
pants could emerge to a comfortably shaded area, how the high
loggia arches that greeted the guests, drawing them inside for
the registration process, were a continuing theme wherever she
looked. And then, just beyond the tastefully decorated lobby,
was an immediate inner courtyard, open to the sky, drawing
the visitor out again into the Florida sunlight and reaffirming

the grandeur of the property at every turn. Although their coats had been hung on the luggage carts by the bellmen, they were still in their New York winter clothing. Beth and her mother found the heat of the day too intense for anything but a brief look outside, and the pair quickly retreated indoors, continuing their route to lunch. Already they could see, through the rear exit doors, the sandy beach and ocean view. For Beth, with her new American Society of Interior Design, ASID, credentials, this spot in Palm Beach was more enticing than the newly opened Orlando Disneyland, called DisneyWorld, would be to a six-year-old child. But before they could reach the restaurant, they encountered a sizable group partially blocking their path down the wide corridor.

A tall and handsome young man was leading the crowd, speaking with a booming, enthusiastic voice. He was walking backwards while directing his entourage. "As I have already mentioned to you at our introduction," he said, "Our founder, the Gilded Age magnate, Henry Morrison Flagler, proved to be a brilliant businessman in many fields. As you look around, you will no doubt recognize that The Breakers of Palm Beach is considered one of the most luxurious resort properties in America. But let's continue into this special area for a moment, and I will reveal to you some of the fascinating history of the man and the building."

Beth and Kathryn exchanged a 'why not?' look and decided to join the pack. The walls of the room were covered with museum-quality pictures and explanatory boards. As the crowd gathered closer to one large collage of black-and-white photographs dating back to the end of the nineteenth century, the docent continued. "Flagler was the consummate visionary. After securing a fortune in the grain business in Cleveland, he became interested in the emerging oil market and befriended another successful businessman, whose name will undoubtedly be familiar to you. Flagler soon became a partner of the great John D. Rockefeller. Together, with an Englishman, Samuel Andrews, they created the Standard Oil Company, building it into one of the most prominent businesses in America for the age.

"But in retirement, circumstances took Flagler's interests in a new direction. His wife, the former Mary Harkness, suffered from chronic illnesses, and he was advised to move her to the state of Florida, where the climate would be more conducive to her recovery." The guide pointed to a map of the state, with insets of buildings. "Settling initially in St. Augustine, he built his own mansion and his first hotel. He foresaw Florida as a premier vacation destination. In 1893, he came to Palm Beach and knew he had found his American Riviera. Flagler not only continued constructing hotels, but by purchasing and integrating various railroad lines, he developed the means to bring people to the remote locations of his properties at the southeast tip of the United States."

The guide now pointed to a photograph of an enormous building, fronted by an extensive veranda and populated by guests in vintage clothing. "The Royal Poinciana was the first hotel Flagler constructed in our area and it was the largest wooden structure in the world," he said, and then he paused to confirm he had everyone's attention . . . "until it was destroyed by fire in 1903.The rebuilt complex was the predecessor of The Breakers you see now."

The guide directed the group to another cluster of portraits. "After his first wife died and a second brief marriage, Flagler wed Mary Lily Kenan. When Mary Lily died, the bulk of the estate went to her Kenan family relatives. With a second devastating fire in 1925, the Kenan family kept their promise that a fireproof Breakers would be rebuilt in all its glory within a year's time. Flagler's heirs have continued his legacy in all of his ventures, and even today are the owners of our property.

"This hotel has been the site of both celebrations and disasters – and has had more than one face-lift, as any grande dame might. And when World War II came to our shore in America, she did her patriotic duty and accepted her enlistment to help."

More than one person in the crowd was voicing confusion. A pretty co-ed, surrounded by her friends for a "girl's-only" getaway weekend, was the one to pose the question. "I don't know if I heard you correctly. World War II on the Palm Beach coast?"

The docent pointed to a collection of headline stories of the era. "Yes. German U2 boats – Nazi submarines – worked to destroy Allied merchant ships right here – well . . . ," and he motioned for the group to look toward the rear entrance with a clear view of the ocean, ". . . right along this Atlantic corridor, with extremely busy shipping lanes – and along the Florida Gulf coast, as well. In total, during this period, twenty-four ships were sunk. And the area residents, from the owners and staffs of the mansions to those living in the most humble cottages, each did their share as collectors of the metals and other materials that washed ashore, or as submarine spotters with binoculars." He paused again to heighten the effect of his next words. "And too often, as spotters of bodies and body parts."

The guide left time for the reactions of the group. Almost every person wore an incredulous look and echoed "Really," or "I never heard that," or the like.

"In 1942," the man began again after clearing his throat and scanning the crowd to make sure everyone had entered the new room. "In 1942," he continued, "we were emptied of guests, and for two years, the hotel served as an army hospital for injured servicemen and women." And – oh, I don't have the exact count – but over a dozen babies were actually born at The Breakers during the time."

His audience liked that concept and repetitions of the phrase "born at The Breakers," could be heard. "Imagine, born at The Breakers Hotel."

With those words, Kathryn took in an audible raspy breath that turned her daughter's attention her way. "Did you know that, Mom?" Beth asked. And then seeing the color on her mother's face almost blanche, she persisted, "Are you okay?"

But she was shushed. Kathryn, who rarely had the patience for long lectures unless she was the speaker, had been listening quite intently. "One second dear," she finally said, tempering her tone as the group was ushered on to the next area. Kathryn reached into her purse and removed something. Then, abruptly, she took hold of Beth's hand and led her to a position at the front of the throng, closer to the guide. "Young man," she said, extending her calling card to him. "I wonder if you might be able to spare me some time for further questions?" He accepted the card and turned it over. It detailed her New York address and telephone number. He looked up at her, quizzically, and then could not contain a double take reaction when he noticed the beautiful young woman by her side, her flowing auburn hair with an almost magical glow reflecting the rays of sun streaming through the windows. He tried his best not to focus on the pools of her luscious dark chocolate eyes.

Making himself look away, he flipped the card over once again and read the name aloud: "Mrs. Kathryn S. Morgan." He looked up at the pair and smiled. And then the young lady worked to catch his attention. She returned the slightest grin to him, shaking her head and rolling her eyes in the universal sign of parental embarrassment. He forced himself to direct his comments to the older woman, most likely her mother. "Mrs. Morgan, I can be reached here through the hotel. Please just ask for Bear," he said. "I would be happy to tell you the tour times." And then looking intently at Beth, he added, "or assist you in any way."

But the ever-confident Kathryn turned the tables once more. Kathryn did not go to people; people came to her. "We are just checking in and have not yet been assigned a room. Please find my number and reach me there," she insisted.

Chapter 4

PALM BEACH 1942

As early as 1940, the United States military had identified the value of Palm Beach for its purposes, when the federal government negotiated a twenty-year lease on the county airport. And so, Morrison Field, which would one day be known as Palm Beach International Airport, became an army air base. Further south on the Florida coastline, the army acquired property in Boca Raton. "The best and the brightest" technical minds from around the country would be coming to the new training center for the emerging technology called "radar." First, hundreds, and eventually, thousands of enlisted men and women would be coming to southeast Florida. Monitoring the international war activity, America was preparing for what might come. And then on December 7, 1941, the American debate over whether to remain neutral or enter the war to support their European allies was settled. Among the first group of eager volunteers to register for the armed forces following Pearl Harbor had been Nate's brothers, the two older Bernstein boys, twenty-three-year-old Benjamin and twenty-one-year-old Frederick. Nate's father was already in an engineering advisory role in Washington, DC.

Early in 1942, the first aggressive acts of Germany in US territorial waters began, with their submarines targeting Allied merchant ships along the busy Atlantic shipping corridor. Towns on the Florida coasts were quickly mobilizing their residents to take an active role in the country's defense efforts. Nate, previously frustrated to be at home while his brothers had been old enough to serve, was now able to feel he was contributing to the cause. He, Addie, and Natalie, along with hundreds of other citizens, volunteered to help. Many property owners reconfigured their homes to be residences for single women, or for young officers and their families. Other locals chose from a wide array of opportunities. Although they all understood the serious nature of war, for those eager to help in any way, there was still a sense of adventure that was undeniable. Welcoming, hosting, entertaining, and feeding the soldiers was a fascinating diversion from life in the still sleepy towns on the Florida coast. Now, they were also monitoring that lights were turned off at night to make it harder for the enemy to discern the population centers on the coast, salvaging materials along the shore, and searching for enemy ships in the ocean and enemy planes overhead. The collective contribution of the area residents was tremendous, but the most invaluable service was that of the civilian pilots forming the Civil Air Corps. Working alongside the military in search and rescue operations, many of their small planes were even equipped with bomb apparatus. Those civilian pilots were credited with destroying numbers of the prowling submarines, saving countless lives.

• • •

On a quiet afternoon in early March, Nate's mother, Eleanor Bernstein, just finishing her household cleaning, wiped her hands on the kitchen towel hanging from the belt of her pastel shirtwaist dress and answered the knock on the door. Before her stood a pair of military men, accompanied by the neighborhood mailman, who ducked his head in apology as he asked if anyone was home with her. "Well, any minute now my son will be back from school," she said cautiously. The men accepted her invitation to come inside. Postman Mitchell Drake held, but had not extended, the dreaded telegram in Eleanor's direction. She was trembling so violently that he escorted her to the front room sofa and sat down next to her, with the soldiers standing silently nearby. Mr. Drake moved the sheer drapery slightly aside and looked out the window. Comporting himself in his postal uniform as if he wore the outfit of a decorated army officer, with his back arched and his chin held high, he rose quickly when he saw the youngest boy, Nate, just coming up the walk. The postman returned to the door to gain Nate's attention.

Eventually, as if blindsided by a sucker punch, Nate understood the postman's intent in accompanying him inside. And so, Nate wrapped his arms around his mother and sat with her on the couch. Eleanor cautiously opened the telegram, and then Nate struggled to read the contents aloud through a chorus of their combined sobs. "We regret to inform you . . ." It was the worst news imaginable. Nate's oldest brother, the handsome Bennie Bernstein, who had been the valedictorian of his high school class and the celebrated captain of many of his teams from debate to baseball, was dead. He had not even made it to a battlefield. He died at the training base where he was stationed in Norfolk, Virginia, when two twenty-three-year-old recruits, a novice navigator and a new pilot, returning from a training run, had miscalculated the plane's altitude and therefore the distance to the ground. Undoubtedly, they should not yet have qualified for a flight unaccompanied by an instructor. They were too inexperienced to avoid the catastrophe to come. Their B-17 exploded immediately upon impact with the tarmac, tragically ending four young lives, theirs and the two men in the plane that had landed just before them, the plane that Bennie had successfully piloted.

For a period of time, Nate and his mother did not move and just openly moaned and wept. The army duo, newly trained in handling the dissemination of tragic news, informed them that Nate's father and his other brother Freddie had been located and told what had happened. The postman, with experience as the harbinger of bad news knew to give the family time to display their grief, and he motioned to the others that they all leave.

When Eleanor could finally break from her son's arms, she took in a deep breath to compose herself, and she watched Nate emulate her moves. Without verbalizing the words, they both knew they would need to be strong to get through this day and the weeks ahead. And Eleanor knew for certain who she would want at her side to offer that strength until her husband could return home.

"Nate, honey, I need you to go quickly to The Breakers," Eleanor said, as calmly as possible. "Locate Addie and her mother and tell them what has happened." Turning him to face her fully, she put her hands on each of his shoulders. She sensed that the completion of the task itself could empower him to feel he was doing something proactive and important in this darkest hour. They both understood that control over their lives had just been ripped from their hands. "If anyone can help me now, it will be Rebecca," Eleanor explained to her son. "I am not sure you have any idea of this, but Addie's mother is a woman who has herself experienced great sadness and upheaval in her life. I just know I need her now." Forty-two-year-old Eleanor, who had done so much to acclimate Rebecca Abelman to Palm Beach when she came to the area in 1926, still felt she learned more life lessons from her friend who was younger by four years. "I need her clear head and her loving compassion to help me, to help us get through this," she told her son.

Within forty-five minutes, Addie and Rebecca, with tear-streamed faces, arrived at the Bernstein house. Immediately, Rebecca gathered her bereaved friend in her arms. Looking fashionable, as always, Rebecca had been coordinating a special event at the hotel when she was contacted. But still, she insisted that Eleanor find comfort with her face nuzzled into Rebecca's shoulder, with no care that Eleanor's makeup could be staining or her hugs wrinkling the fabric of her beautiful dress. She led her friend to take a seat at her own kitchen table.

Addie was amazed at her mother's composure in this situation, while she felt paralyzed and could only awkwardly approach her friend Nate and his mother to self-consciously whisper "I'm so sorry." Soon, though, she thought to ask Nate where the cups were, and together they prepared a pot of hot tea. Rebecca mouthed a "proud of you," in her daughter's direction. Within another hour, Addie's father joined them in the kitchen. After informing the hotel staff that he was needed off the property, he personally had gone to summon Rabbi Shulkin, from Temple Israel. Both of the men stayed for hours to help the Bernsteins navigate the course of arrangements.

Addie and Rebecca tried their best to comfort and distract Eleanor and Nate, encouraging them to bring out photo albums and relive some of the best memories of Benjamin growing up with his brothers. Later, they began working together to compile a list of things that would be needed for the *Shiva*, the period of mourning that would bring visitors with plates of food to the family's home for a week following the funeral. For preceding generations, the Bernstein family, like the families of Addie's parents, had lived in predominantly Jewish areas, where friends and neighbors understood the Jewish traditions. But now, in the gentile world of Palm Beach, many of those offering condolences at the home would be surprised at some of the customs. The rabbi would make slight tears in the collars of the mourners as a symbolic physical sign of their grief. There would be the covering of mirrors with black cloths and the daily assembly of at least ten male congregants, creating what was called a minyan, to go through the recitation of prayers, including the *Kaddish*. But mainly it would be a time when they would most value the support groups they had formed over the years.

Chapter 5

PALM BEACH 1942 AND
ST. PETERSBURG,
RUSSIA, 1920

As Rebecca and Addie left Nate's house and began the walk back toward their resident suite at the hotel, Addie felt her heart racing and a nervous churning in her stomach. At the end of the Bernsteins' front lawn, she turned around for a last wave to Nate. Suddenly, she understood just how close she felt to him. In the past month, she had not been annoyed when sometimes he happened by her classroom at the end of the school day, casually going out of his way to walk her home. Sometimes, at lunch, she sat at his table for a short time, asking for help with a science assignment or a math problem, and she admitted to herself that she liked the way he leaned in closely and was so patient her. Emotions were surfacing that she had never identified before. So now, as she said goodbye, she saw such sadness in his eyes that she raced back to the door. He opened it fully and accepted her light embrace with gratitude. She kissed his cheek self-consciously, and he softly whispered, "Thank you, Addie" into her ear. And then she turned away, not wanting to leave him, but not wanting to further upset him by witnessing his tears.

"I'll be back tomorrow, but I'll come sooner if you need me," she assured him. Then she turned away, crying herself.

Quickly, she was back beside her mother, and she reached for her hand. "I don't understand it. Why are all these bad things happening? I was stupid to think there was excitement in the war coming near us; now I only feel sick. I don't want to know about these things. I don't want tragedies to touch people I know and care about."

Rebecca stopped walking. She wrapped Addie in her arms, lifted her chin up so that their eyes met, and then she arranged her daughter's stray strands of hair to hold behind her ears. "My sweetheart. What you are feeling . . . it is a loss of innocence. This is what happens as people pass from a protected childhood. But this . . . yes, this is too hard to take."

"But you made it through your childhood without tragedies, right, Mama? You had a wonderful life in Russia and then you came to America and to all of this." She spread her arms wide, gesturing to include the beautiful landscape that was their environment.

Addie's thoughts stunned Rebecca. What had she done? This was her fault. She had only wanted to protect her daughter from the harsh realities of life. But now she understood; her protection had made Addie ignorant and emotionally crippled to handle the adversities that would come. She had only the best of intentions. Children should feel loved and safe and secure in their world. Well, perhaps, that was the key. Addie was no longer a child. She hadn't been for some years. Rebecca was wishing now that she had told Addie of her heritage without the sugar-plum coating, perhaps when she was eleven or twelve. She knew she could not undo her mistake, but she could correct it going forward. She pulled her daughter closer to her and gave her one very long hug. And then she led her a quarter block down the palm-lined path, targeting a beautifully carved bench where they could sit and talk.

"You are right in one way, honey. I did have many memories of a beautiful childhood." Rebecca shook her head and looked to the sky, as if her stories were embedded in the few clouds of the day. "But it was not one that lasted even until your age. And I am sorry that I never told you my whole story. But it is time now. It is past time. I can't make up for not telling you earlier. But I am ready to open up to you now." Addie gently squeezed her mother's hand and offered up a very slight smile, understanding that she might hear some things that were not easy for her mother to share.

"When I was young," Rebecca began, as she continued walking her daughter toward their residence at The Breakers. "When I was young, I felt I was like any happy child, enjoying my family, my friends, and our motherland of Russia. Of course, I realized only later how sheltered I was. I was sheltered from the politics of our nation, which were dramatically changing, as well as sheltered from our ever-precarious life as Jewish people." She paused as two guests of the hotel wandered by, enjoying the warmth of the early evening, unaware, as vacationers always are, that the ups and downs of life continue no matter where you travel. And then Rebecca spoke again. "You know that I was born in St. Petersburg, Russia. But I have told you very little else." Rebecca felt she was talking too quickly, so she waited for a response from her daughter.

"Yes, I do know that you came from St. Petersburg. You showed me on the globe, although the name was changed. I remember wondering why they would do that."

"Darling, you are a good listener. And you are a questioner. That is good. And now you are mature enough to understand so much that I will say." She took Addie's hand again, moving her to the bench on the opposite side of the walking path, positioned fully under the reach of a street lamp. And then she continued.

"We were not wealthy people, but we were part of a large and vibrant Jewish community. My father, Abraham Rushman, was a very respected man. His profession was in the civil service. But he loved learning, and, for a time, he even attended university. He had an aptitude for mathematics and hoped one day to be a professor. But the Russian economy could not sustain a man like my father with the means to continue in school.

So he secured a government post as an accountant. Although he was not in the elite circle of the Jewish advisors to the tsar, he was often used as an assistant. And, of course, he used his knowledge to keep books for his organizations.

"My last years of living in St. Petersburg were in the early 1920s. The preceding years brought a time of so many changes for our country and for our family. Each evening, before I would go to sleep, I would go over to my Mama's bedside and sit in a chair next to her. That was how I really had my first inkling that she was not well. Surprisingly, she began to go to bed right after dinner, much earlier than she used to." Rebecca paused to smile at her daughter and then posed a question. "Have I told you anything about my mother before?"

Addie thought about it for a while. "I remember one time when you told me about her. You were crying in your room and then that just made me cry looking at you. I was around eleven years old, wasn't I?"

"Yes, dear. I remember." She brought Addie's hand to her lips for a sentimental kiss. "I took you onto my lap and told you not to be upset. I told you that they were happy memory tears. And then I wiped both of our eyes with the same handkerchief. It had been my mother's *yahrtzeit*, the anniversary of her death. I had just returned from the synagogue. We always say a prayer of remembrance for our loved ones on that day, although I really do love thinking of her on her birthday instead."

Suddenly, Addie's attitude and posture elevated. "I was named after her, right? She was Adele and I am Addie. You told me that she was a sweet woman and that she was beautiful and loving and supportive. You told me that you hoped that you would be that same kind of mother, and I told you that you were." Addie gave a broad smile to her mother, but then her smile faded as she asked, "How come she was sick?"

Rebecca shook her head, with a look of longing in her eyes. "I'm not sure that is something I can answer. How come there is war? I can't answer that either. But, as I said, things were changing. Before your grandmother would leave the table to go to her room, she would ask if I minded that she did not help with the dishes. She was starting to say that every night. Papa would always get up and move to help me, but I would make sure that he settled back in his comfortable chair to read. Every night, I would say to him that there is not much to do, and he has worked hard all day. And then he would always place a kiss on my forehead. It was a wet kiss, but I would never wipe it off. It was as if I already knew that I would cherish the feeling of it." Rebecca smiled to herself at the memory. "When I was done with my work, I would go to sit at my mother's bedside.

"'Pull up the chair,' she would say. And I would laugh. 'I *am* beside you, Mama. I am sitting in the chair.'"

"'*Shana madelah*,' beautiful girl, she would say to me, although rarely would she allow the use of Yiddish phrases outside of our home. My parents had always loved the cosmopolitan life in St. Petersburg. They knew it was not just rumors they had heard of what was happening to Jews elsewhere. They knew that so many Jewish families in Russia and surrounding countries had been sent to small towns in the Pale of Settlement that was Poland and the Ukraine. They were made to live concentrated in Jewish areas, called *shtetls*. During the period of the Great War, many of the worst battles were in that region. But even before that, decades of pogroms, massacres of ethnic groups like the Jews, had ravaged these villages. But we were allowed to retain

our thriving community and even venture into a cultural assimilation with the city. We, the Jews of St. Petersburg, even spoke
Russian as our main language.

"Our nighttime talk was almost always the same dialogue
during my mother's illness. 'Did you wear your hair today with
combs and curls?' she would ask. 'I am sorry I could not fix it
myself. It seems my hands have lost their agility.' Each step
along the way that year provided me with one more hint that
my wonderful mother was declining. Was it her eyesight now?
Could she not see that I had taken the time to brush and curl
my hair as she always liked? Or worse – was her eyesight fine,
but her mind was deteriorating? I was only sixteen years old
when I realized that my mother was failing, both physically
and mentally. She was trying to hold on to the past, but she
would often confuse the times. Sometimes the past was when
she was a healthy young mother and I was a little girl. But
sometimes the past was when she herself was a little girl and
she only channeled the words her own mother would say to her.
'Remember the most glorious of the days – the day that we all
went to the dedication of the Grand Choral Synagogue? Never
had we seen such a thing – seats for over a thousand people.
And you kept saying to me, we are the first people to ever sit
in these seats.'

"But I would say to her, 'No, Mama – I was not born yet. It
was your mother who took you that day with your papa and with
your sisters. You have told me the story, many times, and I have
seen the dedication plaque on the building – 1895. You would
not meet my papa for a few years still, and I was not even born
until 1904.' It was not my intention to further confuse my mother. At that point, I did not know that she was losing her memory,

that she had a condition. I just thought she was a little mixed up. You will see. Life happens, parents age, people get ill." Rebecca scratched the back of her neck and shook her head slowly, side to side. "I was too innocent, too naïve to want to face that."

Addie's expression changed immediately. Rebecca knew Addie had seemed fascinated by the story of her grandmother, but now her face showed only concern, and possibly fear. "Addie, dear," Rebecca said, taking her daughter's chin in her grasp. "Look at me, honey. Don't be afraid. I am fine. Your father is fine. We need only pray for all the soldiers in the war. But I will tell you more of my life back then."

Once again, they were interrupted by a group of tourists happily strolling along on a most lovely evening, until they saw this beautiful pair, a mother and her daughter, sitting and wiping away tears. The group understood that they should quietly move on out of respect for their privacy.

"And so," Rebecca continued, "although my mother was not well, or maybe because of it, she wanted to make sure she told me so many things that were on her mind. So many nights, she went over the same stories. 'Remember, my darling, you will always stand upright. You will never have the stoop of an older woman. Are you standing upright, shoulders back? Are you holding your head as high as our empress?'

"My mother's words were still so confusing to me. She seemed to be living in a fairy tale world, a world where we had beloved rulers. You see, my mother had forgotten even that – she had forgotten that we no longer had an emperor and an empress. Tsar Nicholas, his wife, Alexandra, and all of their children had been ruthlessly murdered during the Bolshevik Revolution. But I didn't correct her.

"I think my mother was retreating into a fantasy, one fueled by an amazing reality that had begun some years earlier. Mama had been a highly sought-after dressmaker. Word of her talents was far reaching. She had designed for members of the Ginzburg family, the wealthiest, most philanthropic and influential of St. Petersburg Jewry. Perhaps it was at a ballet performance, I do not remember the event, but the tsarina was in attendance and sent a representative from her group to inquire about Mrs. Ginzburg's dress. It must have been the color or maybe the lacework that had caught the eye of the empress. And so, for a period of years, my mother would be summoned to the Winter Palace or to the Peterhof Summer Palace to display her drawings or have fittings or to deliver the finished garments.

"Sometimes I would accompany my mother. Of course, I could not have been expected to know the politics. So, yes, I was awed by everything I saw. I wanted to be one of the lovely princesses. I wanted to wear the beautiful dresses that my mother had designed for them, as well. At the time, I knew my mother went with a skeptical air. She and my papa would caution me not be caught up by all of this. And yet, they would call me little princess, when I was allowed to model some of the clothes. It is understandable that I would be captured by the lure of the royal family, and I realize now that, although they cautioned me, they were reluctant to say the words – 're-member, these are bad people.' They would not want their little girl unknowingly repeating phrases that could get the family in trouble. So, I thought, as any innocent child would, that this was a fairy king and queen family that we were dressing. But this wasn't the truth. The tsar and his wife had kept them-selves in an insular world and were not doing anything for the

Russian people. Of course, as Jewish people, we were used to governments with their sanctions against us. But even among the general population there was a dissatisfaction and unrest that was brewing and soon would explode."

Addie could not hold back her thoughts. "I can't believe it, Mama," she said. "I never imagined how much you had lived through by the time you were sixteen."

Rebecca was proud of her daughter's maturity. What she was hoping for was exactly the empathetic reaction that Addie had offered. And so she took her hand once more and walked with her along the palm-lined path. "Understanding my mother's condition, I was learning how to handle her memories. I grew up so much in that year. I was starting to be the one in charge of the household – of cooking meals for a mother who should no longer light a stove, of cleaning a house for a mother who had returned a glass jar of pickled beets to my father's cherished bookshelf. I was starting to understand that this condition was keeping Mama in a safe place. We were Jews, but we were Russians. We were proud of the buildings of our beautiful St. Petersburg, of the Hermitage Museum with its collections of art and culture, and of the glorious palaces. And we had been able to do some amazing things. We had witnessed the best dancers in the world at ballet performances, with seats given to us through the royal patronage. And we had walked together through the halls of the Hermitage. So many times, I had to be pulled back when I reached out to touch an exquisite piece, a porcelain figurine, or a tea set from the tsar's collection. We even loved the look of the enormous church with the high orbed spires. We did not go in, of course; the name itself kept us away – the Church of the Savior on Spilled Blood. We were always told that we must stay away when the gentiles talk of spilled blood, because the next words might be accusations of ritual murders. They can turn on us in an instant and blame us for anything."

"And my mama would tell me," Rebecca smiled as she remembered her mother's words, "'When you have a daughter and maybe a son too, you will tell them the stories of where we came from, the stories of the soaring towers of our beautiful city.'"

As Addie listened, fascinated by all of her mother's memories, she understood why she had finally decided to share them on this sad day. They were the stories of her people, her ancestors. She wanted to hear them all. They were stories of challenges and of hope and they elevated the spirit.

"And my mother always said this," Rebecca continued. 'Promise me that you will marry a boy who will work hard. And yet, you will not settle to be with someone who is not a dreamer. You will be with someone who treasures the palaces.'"

But Rebecca did not do all she had promised. When her own daughter, Addie, was born, they were living in a peaceful time, in a beautiful place. Rebecca did not even tell all of this to her husband, so busy as the assistant manager of the ever-bustling Breakers Hotel, until so many years later. She waited to tell him the story of how she had fulfilled her mother's vision by marrying him, a man of dreams, and she lived in a palace with soaring towers like the ones of her St. Petersburg days. Perhaps they did not have the oval orbs, but she knew what The Breakers towers symbolized, a building of prominence and prestige. She was careful to make sure that Addie stood straight and held her chin up, but to have insisted on the regal comportment her mother had demanded of her would have been ridiculous. She did not want Addie boastful of her circumstances. Although they were surrounded by the amenities of the wealthy and powerful, they were truly working-class people. Rebecca was aware that there were some who whispered that perhaps she was from a line of Russian royalty. But those people knew no history. The Russians were no friends to the Jews. But still, Rebecca clung with pride to the beautiful aspects of her Russian heritage.

"This much I knew of the politics in the time of my mother's illness," Rebecca said, trying to continue with the timeline. "A succession of events both on the world's stage and personally had been my reality during those years. My country of Russia had been embroiled in the world war that would ultimately stretch across continents from 1914 to 1918. It was when Germany declared war on our country that the German-sounding name of our city, St. Petersburg, was changed to Petrograd. But Russia would undergo its own civil unrest in the middle of it all. What was called the February Revolution in 1917 focused on overthrowing the monarchy, the Romanov leaders from the dynasty that had ruled for centuries. Tsar Nicholas II was forced to abdicate, which means to give up his throne. The intent was to establish a democratic-parliamentary style government set to move Russia in a new direction for the future.

"Initially, even Russian Jews embraced this regime. But later that same year, with the ever-changing political environment, the provisional government, which had briefly accepted minority groups, disintegrated. The Bolsheviks were victorious in an October 1917 revolution and had created a Soviet Communist society. Their exiled leader, Vladimir Lenin, returned and initiated a surge of crackdowns on dissidents that made many people long for the monarchy once more. Although most Russians supported the first revolution that had sent Nicholas and his family into a state confinement, a house arrest, really, the country was shocked at their mass execution at the hands of the Bolsheviks in July of 1918.

"Under Lenin, the Soviet Communist age was beginning, and my mother was dying. My father and his group of friends followed every dramatic event as best they could, but I could only be absorbed by my mother's rapidly declining situation."

"With the Soviets in charge now, my father was having more evenings of 'meetings' with our neighbors. At our apartment home, a group of men would gather for tense, animated discussions, but speaking as quietly as they possibly could. They were fueled by rounds of vodka and strong ideals. And there would always be chess sets out, as if they were hosting a small tournament. But unless there was a knock on the door, there was no mention of 'check' and 'checkmate.'"

As her mother spoke, Addie had remained silent – mesmerized by the story, feeling that she was being handed gift boxes, as if she were opening at once all the packages for the eight days of Hanukkah. For the first time, Addie was invited to enter her mother's childhood world and be introduced to her grandmother and grandfather. Already she was understanding that the image of her classically beautiful Russian mother was not one chiseled from the ivory tower she had envisioned.

Chapter 6

PALM BEACH 1975

After their first night at The Breakers Hotel, while Beth Morgan was still hugging the most comfortable pillow she had ever possessed, the generous waves of her auburn hair splayed across the pillowcase, her mother awoke with her usual cough and complained of a bad headache. She had no energy to go down to the breakfast buffet. And so, Beth followed her mother's directive and ordered room service. By the time the tray came, although she considered waking her mother so she might enjoy her first cup of coffee while it was still hot, Beth saw she had drifted back to sleep and just let her be.

Beth emerged from a long shower as the phone rang. She grabbed the hotel's luscious bathrobe and put it on.

"Hello. Is Mrs. Morgan available?"

"Who is calling?" Beth asked, thinking there was a familiarity to the voice.

"Yes, sorry, sorry for no introduction," the male caller said, with seemingly flustered hesitations to his speech. Beth had no idea that just the sound of her voice had unnerved him. But then he calmed down.

"Sorry," he repeated. "My name is Bear." He paused, hoping she would remember him, but she voiced no recognition. "I was the hotel docent you met yesterday during my midmorning tour. Mrs. Morgan had given me her card and asked me to call her room."

Beth pulled on the belt of her robe to fix her appearance, as if she could actually be seen by the caller.

"Oh yes, Bear, I do remember. We met yesterday. I'm her daughter. I'm sorry, but she's still sleeping. She had just asked me to order room service and the tray arrived, but she fell back asleep." Beth self-consciously adjusted her robe again, as the belt loosened. "But I do think she wanted to talk to you." She paused for a moment, deciding if she would share something with him, and then she proceeded. "Seriously, though, I don't know what it is about. I was actually having my own crisis back in New York, but she kind of swept that away, dismissively, and arranged for a quick flight here." Beth stopped herself from talking. She couldn't believe she was sharing these details with a stranger who happened to call.

She covered her eyes with her hand and sat on the vanity chair, just shaking her head.

Some moments later, she heard the man's voice on the receiver. "Miss Morgan," he said. There was a slight pause, "Miss Morgan, are you still there?"

"Oh my God. I am so sorry. I can't believe I'm even telling you all this. I'm so embarrassed."

"Well, maybe you just need someone to talk to." He waited for her answer, but when she didn't respond, he just continued. "So, let it be me, since I am conveniently on the other end of the phone line."

She thought about it for a minute. There was something about his voice that put her at ease. "Well . . . 'Bear,' is it?"

"Yes, Bear."

"Okay, well, thanks. This is crazy." She paused for a deep breath. "Honestly, although I am delighted to be in this beautiful hotel, I am not sure why we're here. It's kind of hard for me to explain. Something is really bothering my mother. I don't know if it's physical or emotional or a combination of the two. It's just that it seemed like it was more than my mother's spur of the moment decision to come here. It's like something has drawn her here. And she wanted to make sure I accompanied her. And, well, she's . . . well, rather – shall we just say – convincing."

"Rather hard to say 'no' to," Bear agreed. "I think I experienced that yesterday." She heard him give a slight chuckle and wondered if he found her too annoying. But he continued, good-naturedly, "And thus, this call to her, as directed."

"There you go, Bear. Welcome to my world of directives."

"Miss Morgan . . ."

"Please, Bear. Call me Beth."

"Well, Beth," he said. "If your mother is still sleeping, perhaps you would like to join me at our most beautiful breakfast buffet. And then you can tell me a little more about your world."

"Well, I'm not quite dressed yet – I just don't know."

"Then let me answer for you . . . 'Bear, thanks so much for the invite. I'd be delighted to join you, but I need fifteen minutes.'" She did not reply to him immediately. He was already regretting being too forward, but he could not help himself. "Twenty minutes then. I will knock on your door and escort you to the dining room. How does that sound?"

At breakfast, Beth was overwhelmed by the incredible food display. She chose the top buffet plate from the stack, took a quick look at the array of foods, and selected two pieces of toast. Immediately, Bear grabbed the pair of tongs she had just set down, and he proceeded to place her two pieces of toast to the side of the pile. He then motioned for her to follow him further down the buffet line and he used those tongs to lift two buttery chocolate croissants from their display and he set them on her plate. "Are you kidding? Beth, really, you would choose toast over these?"

"A gal's got to watch her figure, you know." She offered him a cute smile, and he felt he was gradually breaking her guarded posture.

"I'll tell you what, Beth, you just eat whatever you want, and I'll make it a point to watch your figure."

"You're not flirting with me, are you?" she said, giving him a most curious look.

"Well, that was certainly my intention. How's it going so far?"

"Have to say, it is somewhat impressive for first thing in the morning." Now her look turned endearing. "I need to tell you, though. I am so embarrassed that you are drawn into my world at this point in my life. Personally, my advice to you is this – run. You have no idea what happened to me just last week. I am an emotional wreck." She put her head down and shook it side to side. "This is your opportunity. I'd run now if I were you. What do you possibly find interesting enough about me to spend time with me, a total stranger – who you already recognize has a mother with her own personality issues? Could be genetic, you know; so beware."

"Maybe that's it," Bear said, keeping a serious face, and then he took both of their now full plates and motioned for her to follow him back to sit at their table. "It's not like I want to be with you because you're pretty, beautiful even, soft and sweet – although I know you will turn into a bossy older woman." He set the plates down in front of their seats and loved the opportunity to finally continue the conversation while looking at her. "Oh, I'm just kidding. It's that, despite all that, you care so much about your mother."

"I'm glad you think I'm a wimp, cowering to an abrasive woman."

"No, not quite – it's that I can tell you love your mother, and you care about her. And I'm the same. My mother is my northern star. Well, at least at this point in my life." Bear looked down at his plate, wondering if he should be embarrassed by his honesty, but then he just stared at Beth, with a sweet concern. "Give yourself a break. If you're not sure what's bothering your mother, why don't you just tell me what's bothering you?"

"Wait, are you a psychiatrist, psychologist, a therapist of some kind? You seem rather intuitive for a tour guide."

"No, not a doctor of psychology, but I've recently received my PhD in history. My dissertation was on Henry Flagler and his development of Florida. In season, when I'm in town, The Breakers employs me as their historian and guide. I like to help out at the hotel. I love her, you understand."

"Wait, I'm sorry. Did I miss something? You love her? What, your girlfriend works here, too?"

"No, Beth, seriously . . . nothing like that. No – no girl-friend, I promise."

"Okay, so who is she – who do you love?"

"Well," he took in a deep breath, as his slight smirk grew into a big smile. "It's this wonderful hotel – I love her. He looked around the room, with great pride at being a part of the establishment. "This grand lady – The Breakers. Like my mother, she has given me life." Now he focused back on Beth. "So, for me, no girlfriend. Now it's your turn. I can hardly imagine there is no boyfriend. You are from New York, right? Manhattan? I read your mother's card. Of course, that wouldn't necessarily mean you live there, at her house, but you are in the real capital city of America, with lots of handsome, successful men there, I imagine."

"Are you always like this?" Beth questioned, playfully.

"Do you mean am I continuously striving to engage people with my rhetoric? Well, yes, certainly. That's why I'm a good docent." He said this with all seriousness, looked intently at her, and continued. "And blabbing uncontrollably when out with a beautiful, mesmerizing young woman? Yes, again to that. And that's why I am still on the dating circuit."

"Wait, is this a date?" she challenged.

"Well, I did call you on the phone, pick you up at your place and take you for a meal."

"Oh my God, you cannot mean this a real date," she mocked, sarcastically.

"And I do have all intentions of picking up the tab." Soon, he had a fretful look on his face. "You still haven't answered about the boyfriend." He took a few gulps of water. "But I don't see a ring on your finger."

She gave him an exasperated look. "Hand me my purse," she answered only. He looked on the floor by her feet and picked up a large black designer bag, its contents making it a heavier load than he would have imagined. With an exaggerated pretense of strain, he brought it to the table. "Will you answer me, finally?"

"There is a zipper compartment at the top," she said. "You can open it up."

"Okay."

"Reach inside."

He did as she has asked. He felt around, then he pulled out an incredibly impressive ring with a square shaped diamond, flanked by two smaller stones. His heart sank. "Wow. so you are. You are engaged, or maybe even married. My apologies, well, that apology is for my forwardness. Congratulations would be more appropriate. So, which is it?"

"Can we move the clock back about three days?" she asked.

He waited for her explanation. "Because?"

"Because three days ago, I would have said easily, happily, 'yes' to the question posed. "Yes, engaged."

"You mean I missed my chance for happiness by just days.

Now, you are married? This was to have been your honeymoon trip, and you are taking it instead with your mother?"

She laughed at him. "Are you a fiction writer? You're not a good one. That's even more pathetic than the pathetic truth." She stayed silent for a short time. "No, not married," she finally answered. "The wedding would have been six months from now." She shook her head. "And now, I am unengaged."

His heart leaped. He felt he could breathe again and tried to summarize what he had heard. "Not married then, and there will be no wedding. Unengaged, hence the ring in the purse, instead of on the finger."

"Yes, exactly right."

"I want to say I am sorry."

"You want to say it, but you are not saying it. Is that what you are saying?"

He felt he needed to console her in some way. He needed to end the comic banter. He knew he should be listening, instead of talking. He wanted to show he could be serious, understanding, empathetic. Certainly, she is wounded by this. Maybe she feels broken. "Do you want to tell me about it? Are you okay?"

She thought for a moment. "Yes, I am okay. Angry and embarrassed. But more than okay," she said with some force, although there was still a sadness in her tone. "I found out he was cheating on me." She paused, her head down. "A classic scenario. I caught him at his apartment with another woman, someone from his office. I started to throw the ring back at him, and then thought better, and threw it in my purse instead."

"Clever move. I like a girl who can think on her feet."

Beth emitted a slight laugh. "Well, not quite on my feet," she said.

She considered telling him the whole story but shivered herself silent from the humiliating memory of it. Then Bear repositioned himself from the chair he was in across the table to sit in the one next to Beth. He inched that seat closer to her and took her hand.

She smiled at the move. She understood he didn't mean it to be aggressively forward. His eyes had such a caring look. He was a big man, as one would expect with a nickname of "Bear." She guessed he was about five years older than she was, maybe thirty-four or thirty-five. For some reason, she felt comfortable sharing the story with him, although she barely knew him. She began with a freezing, snowy night in New York City and ended when she found herself whisked away to the surprise of a warm and beautiful Florida paradise. And somewhere in the middle of her telling of the story, she noticed that Bear had dreamy, blue eyes.

He tried to be cool, but it was hard for him. He was so attracted to her vulnerability and to her strength.

Beth had only one more part of the story to tell. "You can imagine the 'I told you so' that my mother offered me, when I needed only love and support." She shrugged her shoulders, as if denying the power of her mother's words. But I'm used to that. Maybe it has made me tough," she added, resignedly.

"No, Beth," Bear said, "It's something less than tough. But it is a survival quality that gets people through tough times."

"You're being sweet, I know, Bear," Beth said. "But I just can't think about it anymore," she sighed out, shaking her head. "Can we please change the subject? I know you're a wealth of information."

Suddenly, that prompted Bear to remember the reason for his morning call to the Morgan suite. "You know, by the way, your mother did seem to want more information from me or maybe a private tour of the historical journey of the hotel. And there is so much more I want to tell you, especially about our founder, Henry Flagler, an incredible man."

Beth was an interested audience. She was happy to shift the attention from her problem and enter another world, the world of the past. Bear opened the briefcase on the floor by his side and took out a notebook of cellophane-covered pages featuring black-and-white photographs and newspaper clippings. When Beth gave him an astonished look as she started flipping through the first pages, he answered her unasked question. "Yes, like a Boy Scout, always prepared," he laughed out. "I'm a traveling lecturer; I'll be speaking up in Miami this weekend." He leaned over her shoulder to point out certain pictures. He tried to be subtle but knew she must be aware that he was breathing in the fresh shampoo scent of her hair. When he quickly moved back to give a more acceptable space between them, she smiled to herself at his nervousness and thought how she had liked the feel of his hand on hers. He pointed to a picture of an impressive white building. "This is a picture of Flagler's mansion, Whitehall. It was built as a wedding present for his wife, Mary Lily. In 1902, The *New York Herald* toasted the estate as "more magnificent than any other dwelling in the world." You can see the Beaux Arts building at the end of our Pine Walk, just down the road from here. I'd be happy to – "

Beth couldn't even process his last sentences, as suddenly she went into a frenzied state, reaching for her purse, getting ready to run from the table. "Oh my God, what time is it? My mother . . . when she wakes, she won't know where I've gone. And I'm not sure if she is totally well. How long have we been talking? Maybe I should be worried. Sorry, do you mind if I go back up to my room? Just sign my room number," she said, as she collected her things.

"Beth, I'm taking care of the check. I told you. My treat. I'll be up soon to make sure everything is okay." Beth headed for her suite before he could even point her in the right direction. He motioned for the waitress and signed the bill to his account. Knowing his way around the hotel better than Beth, he caught her at the elevator before the door had closed completely and he rode with her.

Outside the door to her room, Beth became frantic. Her mother did not answer to a barrage of knocks and Beth could not find her key.

"It's okay, Beth. We'll have you in there in a second," Bear assured her. He returned to the elevator vestibule, where a house phone sat on the mirrored table. "Addie, hi it's Bear . . . Yes, I'm on the premises today, trying to assist a guest. I need someone to open the door to room 507. I don't know for sure, but there may be a medical situation . . . Yes, thanks, please locate Nate as soon as possible. If it turns out to be nothing, then we'll apologize to him." There was a pause as he listened to the voice on the other end, and then he nodded with a look of relief. "We're in luck, the doctor just walked into the building," he said to Beth. A maid, pushing her rolling cart, looked at Bear and asked if she could help. She used her master key to open the door.

Once inside the room, Beth cried out "Mother" twice in rapid succession and it seemed to startle Kathryn awake. Beth moved quickly to sit on the bed, and she massaged her mother's hand and cheek to keep her alert. Then Bear brought the cup of water from the breakfast tray to Kathryn's lips and she took small sips. Beth and Bear exchanged a look of concern over her labored breathing, as she seemed to want to drift back to sleep. Bear whispered that he would run down to the lobby to escort the doctor upstairs when he came. Beth shook her mother awake once more, but she appeared disoriented, as the morning coughing continued.

Chapter 7

PALM BEACH 1942

By December of 1942, even the elegant lady, The Breakers Hotel, toasted by *Fortune Magazine* in 1936 as "the finest resort hotel in the world," opened her doors for the war effort. The US Army leased her and renamed her Ream General Hospital. It was the wide corridors and oversized elevators that made for an easy transition from a luxury resort to a facility providing room for patients being transported in bulky rolling hospital beds. For a two-year period, servicemen and women were sent there to recuperate from the fighting theaters, not only from physical wounds, but also psychological traumas. At Ream, area residents were essential in supplementing work done by trained doctors and nurses.

With his recent experiences, Nate was understandably drawn to a volunteer position at the hospital. While he had been quietly proud that he had helped to save one stranger's life, he was heartbroken by the tragic loss of his older brother, his personal hero. After school and on weekends, Nate would run to the hospital, eager to be of assistance. Soon, he became a trained phlebotomist, perfecting his technique of drawing blood as painlessly as possible. He was energetic and empathetic. "These guys have suffered enough, don't you think?" he had voiced, as politely as possible, to an experienced but unsympathetic older nurse, who was jabbing at her already wounded patient. Dr. Morris Friedman, hearing the exchange, gave a thumbs-up to Nate and took him aside later. "I've been watching you this last month," he said. "What's your name, young man?"

"Nate, sir. Nate Bernstein."

"Well, Nate, maybe you should consider a career in medicine."

The doctor put his hand on Nate's shoulder. "I'm saying this not just because I have seen how you handle the patients, but I'm impressed that you can already handle the toughest of the nurses." Another physician, who was standing nearby, came closer and the two doctors laughed together. "Nate. How'd you like to see an operation sometime soon?" Dr. Friedman said. "Do you think you could stomach it?"

"Yes sir," Nate said with the respect of an enlisted soldier to his officer. "Thank you, Dr. Friedman. That's an opportunity

I was only hoping for one day. I guess I have always been thinking of a career in medicine, and, well, many events recently
have strengthened that resolve." He bowed his head slightly,
hen he perked up quickly. "I will be applying for college soon,"
he said. Not wanting to appear presumptuous, he looked down,
shook his head and added, "I know it's a long road ahead, but
I'll be hoping to continue on to medical school."

"That's good to hear," Dr. Friedman replied. "I went to
Columbia University College of Physicians and Surgeons, myself. It's in New York. Keep it in mind for the future."

Nate felt like he was bursting. He wanted, he needed, to
share his news with someone, this validation of his dreams by
a respected physician.

As the day progressed, Nate continued with his responsibilities, some of which were typical duties of a hospital orderly. He
restocked supply shelves and sterilized equipment. He was just
setting out a medicine tray in a patient's room when the supposedly sleeping Matt Richter, a handsome, well-built young
man, recuperating from a shoulder injury in his once-glorious
football throwing arm, startlingly opened his eyes. "Hey Nate,"
he said, reading Nate's nametag and motioning for him to bend
down to his level. "Nate, you got a girl?' Matt asked him, with
what Nate was now easily identifying as a New York Bronx
type accent.

"You mean, do I have a girlfriend?" Nate questioned, and
then he thought about it for a moment and shook his head,
shyly. "Well, can't say that I do quite yet . . . or maybe only in
my mind. But I don't know if it's in her mind as well."

"I'd like to show you a picture of my girl," Matt said proudly, opening his bedside drawer. It was a phrase that Nate had

heard again and again, as the soldiers, most just three to five years older than he was, seemed to like confiding in him. It was something that kept these wounded young men positive and optimistic. "Having a girl" was a great pill for recovery.

"Lucky you. She is surely a beauty," Nate said to Matt, and would always say, no matter what picture was presented to him.

"That she is, thanks. Can't wait to tell her I may make it home soon," Matt continued. "I won't be perfect, but I'm still in one piece, thinking my bad luck may be my good luck." With the hand of his better arm, he grabbed Nate's hospital jacket to bring him closer again. "It was hell out there. But I'm not stupid, and I never would have tried to make this injury happen." When Nate gave Matt a baffled look, he added, "Don't be shocked; some soldiers do wound themselves on purpose. They'll do anything to be shipped home. You got a psych ward upstairs. Take a turn on those floors and hear their stories. You don't know until you're under fire just what you might be capable of doing." Matt leaned back on his pillow for a moment and then shook his head and sat up again. "Maybe I was a hero on my high school home field, but I just wanted to blend in as one of the boys on a real battlefield." This scenario was something that Nate had never considered when dealing with his injured patients, and it was disturbing. It was one more sad piece of evidence of the toll this war was taking on America's youth.

Later, on a break outside, Nate could not stop thinking about his day. He knew he wanted to tell someone about his uplifting conversation with Dr. Friedman and then his unsettling one with Matt. Even though he was not even finished with high school and would not be volunteering to serve anytime in the near future, Nate could not help but think whose picture he'd like to hold on to and display as "my girl."

The next day, Nate asked for an assignment to Matt Richter's room once more. He was learning enough about the psychology of recovery that he was sure his visit would help Matt's spirits, to know he was sought out for almost brotherly advice from a young hospital aide. But Nate truly had an ulterior motive. After taking Matt's vital signs, Nate got up the courage to ask him something. "I need your help, buddy," he said to his patient, and, already he could see a broad smile on his face.

"I don't know how I can help you, but I'd sure like to try," Matt returned, eagerly.

"Well," Nate said, lowering his head with a suddenly shy demeanor. "It's the girl thing. Can I ask you something? I have a girl in mind, a girl I have known forever, but I have no idea how to make her see me as more than a friend."

Matt nodded his head, with a slight smile and a look of true understanding.

"You like this girl a lot? You want to move this relationship to another level?"

"Well, yeah," Nate agreed quietly. Matt sat up taller in the bed, bolstered not just by the pillows but by the realization that he could actually do something to help someone who had been helping him.

"So, I have the answer for you, Nate. It's a simple three-step maneuver. Take a chance on romance with a dance. Give her a gift, a lift, and a kiss."

"Whoa, Matt. You are quite the Renaissance man, a poet and an athlete! I'm wondering if you have a playbook in your head. You came up with that awful quickly. Impressive."

"Well, let's just say, I got about four years' experience on you."

"Okay, so it sounds like great advice, but I'm too naïve, I guess, to really know what you mean."

"It's like a game plan from my football days. I'm hiking you the ball to take you from this girl's friend to her boyfriend," Matt said with a sly smile. "First, buy her a gift, but something simple. You don't want to start with too much, because then the future will only disappoint. First time, flowers will do, even though you will want to be giving her a necklace. Then take her to a dance, swing her on the floor, leading up to a big lift as the song ends. Then hold her close, as you give her a memorable, and I mean memorable, kiss on the lips when you set her down." Finished with his tutorial, Matt closed his eyes and simply said, "You're welcome," with a satisfactory smirk on his face. Quietly, Nate left the room, giving Matt the opportunity to sleep.

Walking down the hall, Nate processed the instructions, thinking how he could implement the plan. Nate was hoping that with luck and good timing, Addie would be around the building when his shift ended. Although the hotel had become a hospital under the auspices of the federal government, Addie's family, and some of the essential staff, had remained in their places. Their roles were not quite the same as they had been months before, but they hoped their looming presence might be enough to help keep the rough and tumble army men in check, to assure that the facility would maintain its integrity until the grand lady was theirs once more. Addie, who had been training as a part-time front desk receptionist before the transition, now became one of the hospitality volunteers to keep up the spirits of the injured troops.

Exposure to the fresh air and Florida sunshine was the best prescription for recuperation of the body, if not the soul, and a resort recreation favorite from the turn of the century was called into use again. In the early 1900s, porters would pedal hotel guests, seated in what were called wicker wheel chairs, with a rear bicycle rig. They would parade along the ocean front or the pine walk. Now Addie and other area volunteers, mainly young women, built up their pedaling muscles pushing the chairs for the hospital patients.

Nate was so anxious to see Addie that he felt like his heart was beating outside of his body. The feeling was so intense that he actually took his own pulse, with his newly acquired skills. And then he spotted her. Just as he was leaving through the rear sea door, Addie was wheeling her patient back inside. Nate's spirits rose. There was something about the midday sun throwing blond highlights into her beautiful, rich dark brown curls, something about the crimson kisses of the rays illuminated on her cheeks, something about the way her thick hair was pinned up to give her relief from the heat and weight of it on her shoulders, that he found irresistible. In the last weeks, whenever Nate saw Addie, he became cognizant of new emotions that were surfacing. Perhaps he had always had a boy's crush on his friend, but this was a sensation way beyond that.

Nate moved quickly to Addie's side to assist in navigating the chair with its occupant down the hall. As Nate helped her, although he could barely take his eyes away from Addie, he introduced himself to the wounded young man and asked his name. And something about the way Nate spoke to Lenny, something about how he inquired about his hometown and his favorite sports, made Addie feel that Nate had some of the most endearing qualities.

"Wait, Addie," Nate said, stopping the roll of the chair before it reached the elevator they were targeting. "Before we take Lenny to his room, we've got to show him the picture.

Addie looked at Nate, impatiently. "Well, of course," she said. "That was exactly my plan, before I was distracted."

Wrinkling his brow and making eye movements, indicating he was mulling over her words in his mind, Nate gave a questioning response. "Wait, are you saying you found me distracting? That could be the nicest thing you've ever said to me." He walked around to face Lenny in the chair, bending to his level and putting his hands on either side of the arm rests. "Now, Lenny, can you be my witness? She said I was 'distracting.' I find that a step up from her usual assessment of me . . . 'annoying,' 'immature,' things like that." Lenny could not help but smile and enjoy the fact that he was included in this dialogue. "You know, Lenny, I've known Addie since she was in pigtails," Nate told him.

"I never wore pigtails," Addie said.

"Oh yes, you did," Nate insisted. "I remember you did, because I pulled them when I was seated behind your desk in Sunday school." He looked directly at Lenny as he spoke. "I'm not making this up. We were seated in alphabetical order . . . Abelman, Bernstein."

"Oh, that *was* you!" Addie said, dramatically, validating the memory. "Yes, you were annoying."

"Wait a minute," Lenny, interjected, waving his hand, like a schoolboy trying to gain the attention of the teacher. He was eager to join the joke. "Think about it. It could have been me. Last name is Bateman. I could have come between you two all those years ago." They all laughed. "I could have saved you years of doing the avoidance dance," he insisted, as they looked at him and each other with acute embarrassment and denial. Lenny ignored their reactions. "As for me, when the war's over, I'm planning on marrying my own high school sweetheart."

"Oh, no, no, you have it wrong," Addie stuttered back.

"Right, like she said, just friends," Nate concurred, though somewhat reluctantly.

But Lenny just shook his head with a knowing smirk and a surreptitious wink to Nate. And a flustered Addie redirected the conversation, as she wheeled Lenny to one of the rooms off the lobby. "Isn't this the most amazing vintage picture? It's from a 1907 news article." In the photograph, a group of well dressed, prestigious looking young adults are seated in, and gathered around, a wicker chariot, quite similar to the one they were using right now. Addie read aloud the headline and then the caption.

Twenty-nine-year-old William K. Vanderbilt, Jr., and his thirty-two-year-old wife Virginia "Birdie" went on vacation at the most luxurious hotel in Florida, The Breakers in Palm Beach.

The fun-loving personality of Willie K. (far left, holding the stuffed alligator) was captured in this photo courtesy of The Breakers Collection. Mrs. Vanderbilt can be seen in the chair of the boardwalk bicycle with Lawrence Waterbury, a cousin of President Teddy Roosevelt, in the driver's seat.

"Quite an impressive group did this same activity years ago, don't you think?" Addie said.

As they continued with Lenny to the elevator and then back to his room, he was very appreciative. "Addie, Nate, Thanks for that. I mean that bit of history that I am now a part of, and just for your being nice and caring." He paused for a minute. "Sorry if I made assumptions, but I have a feeling I am not so off the mark."

When they were alone, Nate turned to Addie nervously. "I have to ask you something," he stammered, as they walked together to the front doors. "Do you have a few minutes to talk?"

"Sure, I'm off my shift now, too," she answered, looking back up at him with her generous dark brown eyes. And then everything he had planned to say left his consciousness.

When they were back outside, he escorted her to a shady bench on the pine walk and she waited for him to speak. The pounding had started again. He meant to tell her about his day. He meant to tell her how one of the doctors had validated, had encouraged, his dream of being a physician, had even invited him to watch a surgery sometime soon. He meant to say something cute or clever or complimentary. But he had lost control of his brain. The V-neck style of her nurse's aide uniform that was two sizes too big for her had been low enough to accidentally reveal just a hint at the soft contours of her breasts. And so, he said the one thing he did not mean to say too soon. "Addie, I really think I love you." The minute he said it, he thought he wanted to kill himself. He closed his eyes, too embarrassed to look at her. He opened them only when he felt the sweet kiss of her lips on his.

He couldn't believe it. He felt an amazing relief. And then, with his eyes fully open, savoring each moment of the experience, Nate put his arms around Addie, pulled her close, and was the one to initiate the next kiss. "I'm so nervous. I am messing this whole thing up. That wasn't what I wanted to say."

Addie had a look of total confusion. "So, you don't love me? Are you taking it back?"

After inhaling deeply to calm himself down, Nate answered her with determination, "I am definitely not taking it back. But I am taking you to a dance tonight. We don't qualify for the USO social halls, but I saw a poster that there's a great band from Miami playing at one of them. I've been staking it out. The location has a big outside area and we can just happen along and kind of crash the party from the patio. What do you think?"

"I think you're a genius. I've been dying to do something like that. If we're old enough to help, why should we be left out?"

"Great, I'll knock on your family's door at eight. Do you think your parents will say okay?"

"They'd better, 'cause I'm already thinking about what I'll be wearing."

Although he tried to be calm and collected, Nate couldn't help being at her door by 7:45, a small bouquet of three red roses in his hand. By the end of the night, after following each of the dance sets from outside the hall, he kept repeating in his mind, "a gift, a lift and a kiss." Matt would be proud of him, swinging the night away with his girl, certainly a lift and a kiss for each rose. As Nate walked Addie back to The Breakers, they were holding hands, laughing, feeling like they had just attended a wedding uninvited, especially as they had sneaked in a few times for the refreshments, grabbing some little cupcakes and

Coca-Colas.

Before they returned to the building, with its new Ream General Hospital sign, Addie started shaking her head and made them slow their pace as they reached her family's floor. "Aren't you worried though, Nate?" Addie asked as they approached her door. "We've become such close friends now. Aren't you worried that this will change things between us?"

He answered her without hesitation, no longer a flustered schoolboy, but a young man with determination. He brought her hand to his face and felt its soft skin against his cheek before he kissed it. "No, Addie, not worried at all," he said. "Just positive and happy that this will certainly change things between us . . . forever."

Addie opened the door to her suite and went inside, peeking back out before it was fully closed, and, with the sweetest smile, silently mouthed, "See you tomorrow, Nate." Once inside, she kept touching her fingertips to her mouth to relive the wonderful feeling of his lips on hers, something, she admitted to herself, she had been dreaming about for some time.

Chapter 8

PALM BEACH 1942

Addie felt lucky that between school and her volunteer position at Ream, she was often crossing paths with Nate. But it seemed like such a long time since she had last seen Natalie, and she really missed her companionship. Addie recognized that she must have appeared starstruck whenever she was around her older friend, who was always so sweet, so kind to her, so eager to listen to her concerns and offer opinions. Now, suddenly, Addie was wondering if she had come across as too needy. That must be it, she understood. Maybe Natalie had tired of hearing her childish ramblings. When she thought about it, she really knew so little about Natalie's life. She would have loved to have heard more stories of her world, maybe about living in the big house or her experiences with guys. She was thinking about the last time they were together, shopping in town with Addie's mother. She remembered that at the boutiques, Natalie more often turned to Rebecca to ask her opinion of the dresses she was trying on. Later, when the trio walked home after stopping at a café for cool drinks, Addie had lagged a bit behind the others, and she watched her mother pat Natalie's hand in the same comforting way that she did when helping Addie with a problem. Addie knew not to be jealous. She was proud, always, to be Rebecca's daughter. This was her mother's effect on people. She was an irresistible light that others were drawn to. She wondered how her mother had developed this intuitiveness, this capacity to win people's confidences. Could this ever be a quality she would inherit?

Addie realized that it was self-centered to feel insulted by Natalie's absence now. In this new reality, with their world changing daily as their quiet town became a center of war activity, Natalie was most likely consumed by greater callings than those of a sixteen-year-old friend. Addie had an idea which community volunteer assignment Natalie would try for. She would most likely want to be an aircraft observer because the stations were along the beach, her favorite place to be. But Addie had not seen Natalie anywhere near the resort.

• • •

Just like her two younger friends, Natalie Evington's view of life had been dramatically altered, first on that day by the ocean when they heard the explosion and discovered the beached merchant seaman, and then again, a few months later, with the death of Nate's brother. These events triggered in Natalie a strong desire to serve her country in some capacity. She wanted a volunteer position where she could be an active participant in aiding the war effort, not just a hostess passing out coffee at USO functions or helping injured servicemen to write letters home. She pictured herself at the newly constructed watch towers, scouting the sky with binoculars, searching for enemy planes.

At a well-attended community event held at the army cafeteria, where Palm Beach County residents could be matched to their area of interest or expertise, she quickly passed by desk after desk until she reached the sign for "Observers." She perused the sheets scattered on the table, as the soldier manning the booth sat with his head down, concentrating intently on collating stacks of the materials. "We would need to know that you are okay with long stints on the beach, in the hot sun." he finally said, his low voice in a most serious tone. It was a routine remark, part of his script. He had not even raised his head when he said it.

"To be honest, this is exactly how I envisioned contributing," Natalie answered.

Her sweet-sounding but determined voice captured the young man's attention. When he finally looked up at her and saw her golden tan and her beach-streaked blond hair, he felt ridiculous having posed the question. He eagerly handed her one of the folders he had prepared and placed the sign-up sheet before her. "If you could just give us your name and phone number, we will contact you regarding the orientation meeting." She teasingly gave him a quizzical look, as if responding to a pickup line she had heard many times before. But then she regretted having done it when the obviously shy soldier turned beet red and started to stutter, "Oh, no, no, no."

With her information packet in hand, Natalie walked briskly down the road to her ocean front estate. She was pleased, relieved in truth, to find her father alone at his desk in the study. It was a magnificent room with rows of beautifully bound books lining shelves of the richest hues of wood, classically striped with gold inlays. He was seated at his massive mahogany desk. Behind him, like an open photograph album, were framed pictures revealing his biography of attending elite schools, participating in polo matches and sailing regattas and meeting with dignitaries. With his head down in deep concentration, he had not even sensed Natalie approaching until she reached into his sightline and made a random move with one of the chess pieces that were his focus. Startled, he looked up at her. He quickly offered the broadest smile. She was a tonic to him, boosting his spirits whenever she was near. But so often now, when she returned to the residence, she immediately retreated to her coach house apartment.

For Natalie, the estate was just not the same home she had eagerly run to after school when she was a young girl, the place she had brought her friends for endless games of hide and seek in the grand rooms and dress-up in her mother's closet. Despite having a household staff, her mother would often be waiting for her in the afternoon with a freshly baked cookie in hand, a puff of flour on her face, and streaks of chocolate on her apron. Natalie remembered how, as her teen years loomed, her mother would greet her at the door always with the same question. "How was the day for my beautiful girl?" At just fourteen years old, Natalie was already approaching eye level with her mother, who would then wrap her arms around her daughter. And the warmth of that hug could melt away the insecurities that had plagued Natalie's day. Her anxiety that she was too tall, too skinny and gangly, that she would never be accepted like the cute, petite girls, would disappear. Even now, at twenty years old, when that scrawny girl had grown into a recognized beauty, she could not set aside a longing for those days.

"Dad, I have something to show you," Natalie said, pulling a chair next to her father. Now fifty years old, Edward Evington II was a veteran of what had been called the Great War and was now being referred to as World War I. "I'm hoping to get this assignment," she said. She placed the army literature in front of him. Turning to a page she had marked, she began reading aloud:

"Form No. 5 Instructions for Observers. The following is a detailed list of operations for each Observer going on duty."

She paused and then scanned the sheet, choosing a section to share.

Speed in reporting an observed flight is of extreme importance. It is assumed that you have

started to telephone your report within fifteen seconds of making the observation. It is of extreme importance that as little time as possible be lost in your observation of aircraft, getting to the telephone, and being ready to send your message. The telephone personnel are trained especially to handle your reports and have also established a minimum time by special telephone procedure. If you can do your part in fifteen seconds or less, we can depend on a very short overall time from Observation to the Army Plotting Board.

"Honey, I'm so proud of you," her father said, placing a kiss on Natalie's forehead. "You will do an amazing job." He lifted her chin and looked into her intensely blue eyes. "You are a good person, a beautiful person inside and out, a reflection of your mother." Then he shook his head. "I wanted to offer our residence for some purpose; I thought perhaps we could house a few officers in the out-building." Natalie looked at him warmly, having an idea of what he would say next. "But Connie wouldn't hear of it," he moaned out. "'Strangers in our house,' she said." Her father just looked down, resignedly, as Natalie gave him an understanding back pat. And then, they each knew what the other was thinking but would not say aloud – *But there are already strangers in our house.* Natalie's stepmother was too young and immature a wife for her formidable father, and she had brought with her a little girl that she virtually ignored. Connie made no effort to hide the fact that she was more interested in Edward's money and social position than she was in Edward. She made no effort to hide her disappointment that Natalie had not stayed away at school in Pennsylvania. And Edward, a sweet soul of a man who had somehow lost his strength and his compass with the death of Natalie's mother, could not summon the courage to rectify his mistake in judgment. "Thanks, honey, for sharing this with me today," he said. In the past three years since he had remarried, he had been sadly aware that Natalie had used any excuse to spend as much time as possible away from her home. He understood how much this new responsibility would mean to her.

Unlike with some of the other volunteer positions, there was a rigorous training period for those wishing to work as observers. Not only was there a written exam to make sure candidates fully understood the gravity of the responsibility and the protocols involved, but they had to prove themselves physically capable of the task. Natalie and the others were given timed tests where they demonstrated how quickly they could negotiate the path of sandy beach to the observation tower and then rapidly climb the steep stairs and assume their positions. Additionally, they had to demonstrate a visual acuity while using sets of binoculars.

Two enlisted soldiers, a man and a woman, clipboards in their hands, closely proctored the group in tests indoors and monitored their activity outdoors, timing with stopwatches and recording with sharp pencils wedged in place behind their ears. In the end, Natalie excelled in all areas.

Over the last five days of training on the beach, Natalie had been cognizant of the presence of a man who often passed by as they went through their routines. He seemed to be the age of many of the soldiers, maybe four or five years older than she was, possibly twenty-four or twenty-five. But he was not dressed in a uniform. His attire was more of a tailored suit, with an open collar and a loosened tie. Covertly, Natalie had followed what he was doing, quickly averting her eyes when he raised his head. He was intently jotting notes on his clipboard while he gathered items from the sand or the thick brush and placed them in a large sack. But in between each maneuver, she sensed he was watching her, glaring at her really, until one day, when he started smiling at her, waiting for a reaction. She found it annoying. He was purposely distracting her when she needed to remain on task, to demonstrate she was serious about her training. He was jeopardizing her chances for this assignment.

Finally, she could not ignore him any longer, as he seemed to be walking directly toward her. "Is there something you wanted?" she asked, nicely. She would have been outright rude, but she held back. She wondered if he could possibly be one of the officials, so she tried not to be overtly disrespectful. But still, on this day, there was nothing about his dress that signified he was attached to the army. Even his hat was not an army cap. So, when he tipped it at her and said, "Just waiting around to see if there will be a swimsuit competition," she was fuming. Now she recognized him for what he was, nothing more than a common flirt. When he moved his fedora completely from his head and placed it over his heart, she was further annoyed and sent a brutal scowl his way. "I only meant it was one more contest you would win," he said with an apologetic shrug and a mischievous grin.

Natalie did not find any of that funny. There she was, working hard to impress the instructors, and then some passing jerk inferred she was only to be viewed as a sex object. Another girl in her group, training by her side, tapped Natalie on the shoulder. "Why be so hard on him?" she asked. She smiled at the man and gave a heavy sigh in his direction. "Wish he had said that to me, honey. That guy is an absolute dreamboat."

For weeks, Natalie proudly served as an observer, assigned to a tower about a mile north of the training area. She loved her role. She felt she was doing something important. After her shift, she was too exhausted to do anything but fall into bed with a good book. This was just what she needed in her life right now, something with a greater purpose to keep her busy and not preoccupied with her own smaller problems at home.

Admittedly, there were times when she used her binoculars to scan the beach, instead of the horizon. She worked hard at convincing herself that she was just making sure that the stranger was not in the area. But there was a part of her, she knew, that hoped he would come into sight. Although Natalie had acted like she wanted nothing to do with the man, she knew that girl had not been wrong. There was something about his looks, about his smile, that she could not get out of her mind. So occasionally, she was not scouting the skies for silhouettes of the airplanes they had memorized. Her goal had always been to be the first to identify the model of the craft and call the information to the control center. And yet, occasionally, she was searching for the silhouette of a man dressed in a suit instead of a uniform.

For the past few years, Natalie had been drifting through each day of her life. She had recurring dreams that would shake her awake and leave her sleepless. These dreams that melded into nightmares began with her comfortable routine. She is running along the beach with friends beside her. She is waving at neighbors familiar to her for years. She gazes into the glaring sun and then back again to the water. She becomes mesmerized by the ebb and flow of the ocean waves. Suddenly, she is pacing along the beach by herself. Everyone familiar to her has disappeared and she is alone. She continues along, thinking that the glare from the sun has disoriented her, and she will regain her bearings soon. She thinks someone will call to her from ahead and say she has not kept up with the group or will approach her from behind with an arm around her shoulder to tell her that she has run too fast ahead. But this does not happen. No one is there for her. No one is looking for her. Everywhere she looks around, people are paired up. But none of these people are people she knows. She is drawn toward the water where a small, solitary sailboat rocks with the motions of the tide. At first, she thinks its captain is fishing off the far side. But then she realizes there is no one on the skiff. It is drifting alone and unmanned. In her dream, she is the boat. She is alone on the sea. When she awakens abruptly and composes herself, she believes she can interpret her own nightmare. This is what her home life has become. Her mother is gone; her father has a new family. No one is there for her.

Early into Natalie's third week, the officer in charge of coordinating the volunteers called her down from her station to come to his office. While she was anxious about the reason, afraid that she had been reported as negligent of her duties, she was also relieved to have a break. Although there was always an hourly rotation of teams on and off the towers, to keep minds and eyes alert, on this especially hot day, she was grateful to be headed to a room that she anticipated might have a refreshing fan.

"Take a seat, Natalie," Captain May said, gesturing to the opposite side of his desk.

"Yes, sir," she responded, as if she were an enlisted soldier. "Is everything okay?"

"Oh, for sure, didn't mean to make you nervous. My apologies. Everything is going well. I'll just be brief with this. We saw your potential even during the training and exam week. We were quite impressed with your scores on both the written tests and physical challenges."

"Thank you, sir."

"And you have a leadership quality. In sessions, it was obvious the other volunteers looked to you for guidance."

"Sir, it's just that even though the others are from the area, the beach is my home, my backyard." She did not want to say "literally" but wondered, perhaps, if he knew that already. Her address would have given him the idea – South Ocean Boulevard.

"So, what I'm leading up to is this. We've decided to pull you off the scouting patrol and put you as an observation instructor. We've got new volunteer crews joining weekly and we think you could help us in that capacity. Monday you'll report to the building where you were trained, and you'll find your room assignment."

Initially, Natalie was flattered that she was valued, but as the days went on, she was not at all happy to have been removed from the volunteer frontline. This was not how she planned to serve. She had approached her responsibility with the focus of the fighter pilot who would be alerted to take action from the information she would supply. During her time at the tower, she had already reported many aircraft sightings. But now, trapped in a hot classroom most of the day, instead of enjoying the fresh air and the feeling of the salt water ocean breezes during her time on duty, she was like any schoolgirl, only looking forward to lunch breaks and the final dismissal.

A week after Natalie began teaching, when she dismissed her classroom of adults, she was in no hurry to go home. Natalie sought out a shaded area of dense palms at street level and was ready to sit down with an apple. Suddenly, the man who had insulted her on the beach with his beauty contest remark was moving too closely in her direction. Without the safety of a group, she felt almost threatened. In the past week, she had seen him now and again, hovering around when she escorted her group to the towers, but she had ignored him and he never sought her out when she was alone. So now, she was assertive. "Quite honestly, I don't have any idea what you are doing lurking around here, around me, constantly."

Well, not constantly; I'd have to correct you," he said with a slowly emerging smile. "I would say it is more around lunchtime and then again around four in the afternoon. The time may well vary depending on the day."

Natalie had met this type of guy before. Cocky and self-assured. She did not need this . . . certainly not at this time in this place, where she was highly regarded for what she did, not what she looked like. She placed her palm against her forehead and just shook her head in exasperation. "Whenever it was, it was too often . . . Mister . . . ?"

"Stanton . . . Theodore Stanton," he asserted, and extended his hand for a shake. Instead of offering hers, she retreated a few steps until her back was against the tree. "But you can call me Theo," he added.

Standing closer to him now, closer than she had ever been, as he once again removed his hat, she could not help but look at him, instead of looking away as she had previously done. She could see just how tall he was, taller than she was, something that she had always valued in a guy. From far away, she had thought he looked very mature. He had the chiseled qualities of a man, a square jaw and broad shoulders. But close to him now, his face showed softer features, the curious large eyes and dimpled cheeks of the boy he had been.

Even though she felt an invigorating, unfamiliar racing beat of her heart with him so near, she could only think of words to say that would distance him. "Mr. Stanton," she huffed out, "it makes me uncomfortable to have a stranger staring at me, shadowing me."

Theo had tried to be careful, tried not to fawn over her. But he had never felt quite like this before. He certainly was not inexperienced with women. Since he had been a teenager, he had often had a girl by his side. He was not proud of his reputation as a heartbreaker, but there was never anyone who held his interest for very long. He tried to name the emotion he was feeling because it was new to him. And then he admitted it to himself. He was seriously lovestruck. This exquisite being before him was the sun, a gift of light. And he was the moon who always follows in rotation. But he had not kept his distance like the nighttime orb. He feared he was acting like the mythological boy Icarus, who flew too close to the sun on waxen wings that melted and sent him falling back to the earth. And so, Theo tried to control himself. He lowered his head like a scolded schoolboy. "Then my apologies, Miss," he said and backed up a few feet. "That was never my intention."

Natalie averted her eyes from his face. On the sidewalk, she finally saw a group of soldiers passing by and that somewhat settled her down. "I'm wondering what you are doing around here," she questioned. "At your age, and with no obvious disability, not even glasses, why are you just hanging around the beach? Why aren't you in a military uniform?" She looked him up and down. "You are in a business suit, collecting things in the sand. What are you . . . some sort of sophisticated beachboy?"

Suddenly, Theo was incapable of speech. Up close, she was even more beautiful than the image of her he had been carrying in his mind, the girl who had haunted his dreams ever since the first day he saw her. He knew he had never seen eyes so intensely blue or hair with quite so many shades of blonde radiating throughout. No matter what she was wearing, the material shifted with her movements and outlined the curves of her perfect body. He thought that she was the embodiment of the ocean and the sky. He was paralyzed. But he knew that he could not share these thoughts with her. They would only drive her further away. He already understood this. She did not like to be defined by her physical appearance.

This was a whole new experience for Theo. He had never had to work hard to attract a woman before. His experience had more often been girls, then women, flaunting themselves before him. But this one was different. Even that drew him to her. It testified to her depth of character – she was strong, and she was unassuming. He was falling more and more in love with her by the minute. He tried to remember what she had just said to him . . . something about a sophisticated beachboy. He needed to start a conversation with her. He would start there.

"So, you *have* noticed me," he teased. "And you think I am sophisticated."

"It seems you have chosen to remember only one part of the phrase and consequently misinterpreted the remark," Natalie said, wincing her eyes to his arrogance. "In this serious time of war, for a man to be called a 'beachboy' is hardly a compliment. My guess is that you are used to people being charmed by your actions, by everything you do or say."

She turned her head away from him, dismissively. As she did so, she ran her fingers through her hair and secured a large swatch of it behind an ear, revealing her long, entrancing, ballerina neck. She had unwittingly reeled him further in under her spell.

Theo understood that he was caught in an entanglement of words. "Wait a minute," he protested. "You'll be embarrassed when you learn the truth. You'll be apologizing to me."

"And why would that happen?"

"Because you don't understand. I have a reason to be on the beach. I do have an assignment, an important position related to the war effort. I am monitoring the materials that are appearing on shore from the damaged ships," he said. "But then, of course, that's just one part of my job and, admittedly, I have been spending a little too much time on it." He said this almost shyly and then he boldly asserted, "But that's your fault. Without question, you are the most valuable object I have encountered on the beach."

This guy was adorably incorrigible, Natalie thought. She covered her eyes with her hands and shook her head in disbelief. "How do you possibly come up with lines like that?" When she removed her hands and looked at him, she could not help but smile as she once more witnessed his playful grin.

Theo's spirits were lifted. For the first time, he was encouraged that he could win her over. He pointed to a nearby bench and gestured that they take a seat. He was prepared for her to back away, once again. When she followed him, he was elated. "So, you already know – I am Theo . . . and you are?"

"Natalie . . . Natalie Evington," she said slowly, in a soft, breathy tone, not because she wanted to appear sensual, but because she could not help feeling shy.

"Natalie," he repeated. Now his angel had a name. He angled towards her and put his arm over the top of the bench. He was careful not to touch her back, although it took great will power to resist the desire to do so. "The army brought me here from New York over a month ago to help coordinate the collection and salvaging of scrap materials in Palm Beach County," he began to explain. "It's an adjunct position, a civilian assignment. You are only seeing me when I'm taking a break from my duties." He laughed, slightly, at himself. "And yes, you are corrupting me, might even get me fired."

"Is that true?" Natalie questioned, almost fearfully. She could no longer keep up her charade of indifference. And when Theo shook his head "no," again with that innocent look, she was embarrassed by her gullibility. She put her head down and leaned into his chest as she laughed. Theo was amazed how easy and natural the next move was. He was able to bring the hand of his outstretched arm to cover her opposite shoulder.

Suddenly, and in unison, as if they each were afraid the other might think their moves too intimate, they stood up.

"Natalie, want to go on a walk with me? Maybe we could just talk and finally get to know each other."

As the days progressed, Natalie could not wait for time with this young man, as she finally admitted to herself, this incredibly handsome man. Here was this person, often seeking her out, wanting to be by her side. And she was truly not afraid or uncomfortable, although for weeks she had tried her best to give him the opposite impression. Suddenly, each time she saw him, emotions she thought had abandoned her began to define her days. She became hopeful. She felt wanted. At night, she began to sleep in a pleasant, dreamy state, devoid of nightmares. She knew that someone was there for her.

Chapter 9

ST. PETERSBURG 1923

During the last year of her mother's infirmity, Rebecca became immersed in meeting with customers and completing the seamstress orders, so when clients were told that Adele had passed away, they naturally accepted the transition to her daughter's design, measurement, and deliveries. The demands of this undertaking helped to keep Rebecca strong during a difficult period. She felt a purpose in honoring her mother's legacy.

Surprisingly, Rebecca's father, who had been saddened and weakened as he watched his wife's decline, was slowly gaining a new vitality. He became more alive and less melancholy, as if he were comforted that Adele was finally at peace. He had never been a very religious man, but he seemed to gather solace from joining the daily minyan prayers at the synagogue. He gained strength through the fellowship of his comrades. After work and then the evening recitation of the kaddish, he would attend political meetings almost nightly with his group. In a surprisingly healthy way, the sadness of their loss never left, but there was a renewed energy for each of them. Where there was only acceptance of the inevitable for Adele, they now had an eye to the future.

With the liberal attitude of the provisional government in Russia following the February revolution which deposed the tsar, Jews, many of them from the ultra-religious sects residing in the Pale of Settlement, for a window of time, were being allowed to make a home in St. Petersburg. And so, only a few months after Rebecca lost her cherished mother, her first love, Jacob Schaevitz, entered her life.

It was a beautiful St. Petersburg morning when Rebecca strolled through the large outdoor market in the neighborhood. She was thinking she was lucky that her mother did not pass away in the dark days of a Russian winter, when any depression could not hope to be lifted for months. But she had died in late April. The May days, which had still been hazy ones, shrouded in a sadness that would not leave, had now given way to a pleasant June. Prior to this time, she could not bear the market activity, because its vitality was something she had shared with her mother. Together they would peruse the colorful array of fruits and vegetables, appearing so succulent and inviting. They were drawn to the stalls of the loudest hawkers, who would slice off small tastes for their customers, and to those vendors they would give their business.

Even when Adele was well into her illness, Rebecca would peek into her room and see if she might be up to taking the walk to the market with her. But following her passing, whenever Rebecca needed to go to the market, it was incredibly difficult. She simply chose food from the merchants at the ends of the aisles, so she could complete the process quickly and not be saddened by memories of spending time there with her mother. Together with her, they had been envious of so many of the patrons carting large, strong shopping bags that would fill to overflowing within a short period of time, as they would be preparing meals for families of six or seven or more. But lately, it was almost unbearable for Rebecca. Once part of a small but happy trio, she was now one of a simple duet. With the June sun, she was determined to bring light into her home once more. It was important for her father's well-being and for hers.

Of all the stalls in the market, Rebecca found one the most intriguing. It held an assortment of household necessities, kitchen cutlery, knives polished and sharpened, and spoons and forks reflecting the glint of the midday sun so majestically that she felt herself compelled to lean over an array of gently used pots and pans to grab one. With her action, the strap of her shopping bag caught the handle of one of the pots, setting in motion a catastrophic chain reaction of one mixing bowl after another tumbling from their very orderly arrangement on the table and set spinning in random patterns on the uneven surface of the ground. As she bent over to gather and replace the objects on their stand, she was stunned. She felt a hard yank on the long, thick single plait of hair that made its way down her back and ended at the slight curve just below her hips. She expected that one of the schoolboys whom she had spotted earlier trying to distract a vendor and steal an apple was the culprit, and she was ready to call him out or slap his hand. But the boys lingered still at the apple seller's cart. She saw only one young man, possibly her own age, standing near her. With his long, curled earlocks, called *payas*, he was quite obviously one of the religious Jews who had recently settled in the older tenement flats that lined the streets of the district nearby. Her own father did wear a *tallit*, a prayer shawl, over his street suit when he was at the synagogue. But Rebecca could see that this boy was wearing the *tallit katan,* the little *tallit* that the most observant, the Orthodox Hasidic Jews, wore as undergarments. The fringes, the *tzitzit,* were purposely recognizable under his jacket. They were a group of knots and ties made from string, hanging from each of the four corners of a large square cloth. For the highly observant Jews, wearing this holy garment at all times was a *mitzvah*, a commandment.

"Excuse me, sir," she said in shock, turning to the young man, "Did you actually just yank on my braid?"

"I did," he said boldly, the expression on his face showing no guilt but rather the mischievous grin of a schoolboy. "I did as you have accused."

Rebecca looked at him harshly and haughtily, as if she were an elderly matron. "Is that allowed?" she questioned. "Perhaps I am not familiar with the rules of the religious community, but I thought that such touching was not permitted."

"But you are Jewish, are you not?" he shot back at her.

"I am – but I question that you are allowed this sort of behavior with Jewish women who are not relatives – I have been educated enough in our culture to doubt this."

"Oh, but in this case, it would be more acceptable than any alternative. And I would say that it is your fault, and I will wait for an apology. You did, after all, ruin my entire display, which will certainly be reflected in lower profits for the day."

Rebecca was astonished by his audacity. "Well, certainly, it was an accident. I just leaned over to gather something to make a purchase," she threw back.

"And therein lies the fault," the young man insisted. "This leaning over I found intoxicating, and pulling your hair was the lesser of the two evils, my stronger desire being to place my hands around your beautifully curved waist and pull you back from creating more extensive damage to my livelihood. Further, you might have accidentally fallen back from the surprise of that move and landed on top of me on the ground, certainly causing more of an embarrassing scene than either of us might be able to endure."

Rebecca could think of no verbal response but felt an unfamiliar, physical one that sent a titillating wave through her body from the described scenario. She felt herself blushing into her hands that were cupping her cheeks. She started to walk away. And yet, she could not help but turn back to him to catch, once again, the sparkle of his eyes, not hidden beneath the wide brim of his religious hat.

"Wait, don't go," he called after her. "I must know your name first, and then your address."

"You must be joking. Why would I tell you that?"

"You need to tell me so I can come to meet your father," he said, sending her further into an embarrassed state of confusion.

"To meet my father? You must be kidding," Rebecca said, rolling her eyes and shrugging her shoulders in frustration.

"Oh yes," he insisted, "to present him with a bill for my damaged inventory."

She laughed at him. "You are a crazy man. There is nothing damaged here; just a little soap and water is needed. It is not like you had a display of delicate dishes that were broken, or rows of intricately stitched linens that would be attractive for a *Shabbas* table."

He liked her words – even though he knew she was trying to be snobby and separate herself from his world. He was aware that new arrivals to St. Petersburg from the shtetl, like himself, were looked down upon. "I have been in the city only a few weeks and my inventory is low, but I would love to add some tablecloths and napkins to my little booth. Do you know where I would be able to secure such objects?"

"Perhaps I do," Rebecca answered cautiously, after moments of deliberation.

"Then if no street name and number, may I at least know your name and the name of a seamstress you can recommend?" he continued.

She turned quickly and began walking away, and then, abruptly, she turned back and walked halfway toward him. "Rebecca – the name for both," she said, surprisingly shyly, her voice so quiet that he could barely hear her.

"Then, Rebecca," he said, with a strong desire to repeat the name aloud, "You must meet me here at next week's market – promise me you will," he insisted.

Softly, she said, "Perhaps," and turned again quickly, now toward her home, with her head down, not realizing that for the first minutes, he was following her from a distance, unable to resist himself.

When Rebecca did come to meet him the next week, he had, once again, a most playfully naughty look on his face. He was hiding a beautiful yellow floral bouquet behind his back. He was as delighted to present the flowers to her as she was to receive them, although each of them tried hard not to overplay the move. And so, what began as a serendipitous meeting at a weekday market continued to flower, blossoming from a teasing confrontation to a flirtatious encounter, growing ever so slowly in the summer sunshine from a budding romance into a full-fledged blooming event.

By their third meeting, Rebecca admitted to Jacob that she was surprised at his familiarity with the Russian language, because so many of the new immigrants spoke only Yiddish. He explained that as his father's helper and apprentice, over the last few years, he had always been the one to buy merchandise in the bigger cities. He loved traveling to Minsk, especially, to barter for more inventory. He even dreamed that one day his merchant cart would not be a moveable stand but an actual store. He had been to bigger cities, unlike most of his friends and the other vendors, and he had dreams of growth and progress.

"Next you will be talking of the United States – where the streets are paved in gold," Rebecca had told him. "But keep those thoughts to yourself and don't let the Soviets hear you," she added with cautious concern.

"Then I will whisper only to you that I do dream of America," he confided.

Taking advantage of the best weeks of the St. Petersburg climate, Rebecca and Jacob spent as much time as they possibly could together. It was a period of getting to know each other better by sharing their worlds. The first time she was invited to the Schaevitz apartment for Shabbas dinner, she brought a magnificent challah cover of her own design. She had stitched an image of a bouquet of flowers into a field of gold fabric and edged it with a white lace pattern, but not one so delicate that it would be impractical for weekly use. Jacob's two sisters were thrilled with the gift. Having lost their mother two years earlier, they were not used to presents of new handmade items. When they showed Rebecca their shared room, she furtively looked into their open clothes closet and measured herself against their size. The next time she came, they were giddy and outwardly crying from the surprise of identical dresses. Rebecca had followed every modest religious requirement, while incorporating the richest colors of deep blue and purple, enhanced with some black velvet ties and trimming. The girls put them on immediately. They hugged and kissed Rebecca and jumped up and down in a circle with her, as Jacob and his teary-eyed father watched and clapped.

Afterward, Jacob walked Rebecca home, maintaining an acceptable distance between them on his community streets. But as they neared her district, he grabbed her hand, and they ran to a hidden alleyway where he could hold her in his arms. Jacob knew that he was violating the strict teachings of his heritage. Rebecca herself had never even experienced this level of innocent caresses with a boy. Yet both of them were too blinded, too intoxicated by love to give in to the guilt.

On certain days, with stolen time between his religious studies and his market work, Jacob was introduced to the cultural sights of Rebecca's secular world of St. Petersburg, where people from his community would most likely not venture, and he and Rebecca could have more freedom. For these hours, he wore only his *kepa* and not his broad-brimmed black hat. He tucked his religious garments into his pants and wove his earlocks into his hair. Together, they explored the gardens and fountains of the magnificent Peterhof Palace. At the Hermitage Museum, he was introduced to a world of art he had never seen. But always, viewing even the most beautiful works, he simply shook his head and repeated, "Nothing compared to you," until Rebecca eventually found a vacant area and would give him the quick kiss he desired. When they stood in front of the impressive Winter Palace, she pointed to the rooms where she and her mother had spent time dressing the tsarina and her family.

And so, as the months of Rebecca's courtship with Jacob progressed, her father, who loved his religion but had never been enamored with the Hasidic Jewish lifestyle, grew to respect what he knew of Jacob's character, his love of family, and his strong work ethic, and he was happy to see Rebecca's spirit elevate with his companionship. Abraham felt sad that his daughter had not even had the opportunity to cultivate friendships over the last years. Although other girls and boys her age had sought her out, she had little time for socialization. She was constantly busy continuing with her mother's responsibilities.

Despite the fact that Abraham would pledge his life for the cause of Jewish and individual freedoms for their nation, he felt he could not be irresponsible to his family obligations. After the first of his group had suddenly disappeared, Abraham realized that what he had feared might be true. The government was increasing their raids on dissidents, and he would possibly be targeted soon. He could not do this to Rebecca. She could not lose a mother and then a father in rapid succession. Abraham began thinking that if something developed between Jacob and Rebecca, perhaps this young man's dreams of America might be his daughter's salvation as well. Only the week before, the pair had told him some interesting news over dinner. Around the same time that Jacob's family had relocated from their home in the village of Motele, Poland, to live in St. Petersburg, Jacob's Uncle Moishe, his father's older brother, had moved his wife and daughters to New York City. A letter had just arrived for Jacob, offering him funds for the boat passage to emigrate there. He was invited to stay with the uncle's family and work at the cottage garment industry in their apartment. Jacob admitted that he was surprised at the invitation, as he always felt that his uncle did not care for him, thought he was not serious enough, not committed enough to *Halakha* codes, the guidelines for religious Jewish behavior. As nervous as any young man on a similar mission, Jacob came to Abraham with a question before he would answer the uncle. When he asked for permission to send for and marry Rebecca once he established himself in the United States, Abraham gave him his blessing.

And so, Jacob wrote to the uncle that he understood what would be expected of him. He would be working hard in

New York to pay his uncle back. And then he would need to earn more money to be able to send for his own family and a special person, Rebecca, who would become his bride as soon as he had the means to bring her to America. Knowing the uncle was in the garment business, he wrote about Rebecca's experience as an accomplished seamstress and a designer of dresses and table linens.

As Rebecca and her father floated in a world of bittersweet sentiments, they tried to come to terms with the reality that their lives would most likely be changing in the near future, that their paths might diverge for the first time. Together, they finally addressed a task that they knew they had put off for too long. They thought of something that could bring happiness to a treasured neighbor and give them both some closure. The pair walked slowly and silently down the steep staircase, each carrying a large pillowcase stuffed with clothes under one arm. "Papa, please be careful. One hand on the banister, always," Rebecca insisted. During her mother's long illness, she had hovered over her, tended to her, protected her, and now she was transferring that attentiveness to her father.

Three floors down, across the street, and two floors up, they were making their way to Mrs. Gorshen's apartment. Sophia, a long-time widow, no longer handy with a needle and thread for repairs on her own well-worn dresses, was excited by their offer of Adele's garments. Rebecca planned to keep some of the wardrobe to remake for herself, but she had no need for all of it. "You are too kind," Sophia had said. "The items are too beautiful, and where would I wear such things?" she said, as she clung to the gifts.

Afterward, as Rebecca lingered at the front stoop of their building, thinking that Jacob might be stopping by, Abraham returned to their apartment. Giving away these clothes was emotional for him. Rebecca knew that when she went upstairs, she would find him sitting at the kitchen table with her mother's framed photograph in hand, reliving his best memories with a toast of vodka. But Rebecca did not go upstairs. When she was just about ready to join her father, she saw Jacob approaching from the corner of her eye. She envisioned that soon they would be looking for a dark alcove to enjoy one more silent dance together before he would begin his journey.

Chapter 10

RUSSIA AND
NEW YORK 1923

As the date for Jacob's departure to America approached, his own father was skeptical. "Who knows what the future brings?" he whined with pessimism. It was the cry and the prayer of the Jewish people through generations, through so many years of suffering. *Baruch Hashem*. Blessed God, he will provide or we will pray that he does. As for Jacob, for weeks before he boarded the ship to America, his mind was reeling with thoughts he could not articulate to his family. The night before his voyage, there was a private goodbye with Rebecca, where they danced in the dark in an isolated park and they kissed and caressed and marveled that they had each found their *beshert*, the one destined for them. They were miserable at the thought of being apart soon, but excited and confident for what the future would hold.

In the morning, there were tearful goodbyes to his father and his younger sisters, as Jacob left the city to begin the first part of the trip, making his way to the port. Finally, in Hamburg, Jacob maneuvered through the crowds, presented his documents, and boarded the ship. On his way down to third class, he had great hopes as well as apprehensions. What would await him on the journey and then in the city that was his destination? Was he the only one who felt this way? He was emigrating to America. A supposedly golden opportunity had been presented to him. He was already interested in the modern Jewish way of life he had seen in St. Petersburg. In his mind, he was not going to New York to establish his same life in a safer environment. Rather, he was going to New York to, perhaps, reinvent himself. He was open to change, eager to change. What would it mean to be an American with a new vision?

As he descended the stairway to steerage, he was astonished. He was greeted by a musical barrage, a mixture of voices singing and instruments playing. There were melodies that he was familiar with from his upbringing, and there were new, lively tunes. With his suitcase in one hand and grasping the railing with the other, he opened his eyes to the New World, although the ship had not even left the port. Dozens of people, near to his age, young men and women together, were locking hands, dancing to uplifting songs. Captivated by the crowd, he tripped on the last step and fell into the outstretched arms of three of the passengers, two men and a woman. They were smiling and laughing and greeting him as if he were their lifelong friend. What he saw was what he envisioned for himself. The young men were already taking out scissors and snipping off their long, curling earlocks, the *payas* that had been growing since their toddler days. They were trimming their beards and tossing off their *tallit* prayer shawls and *tefillin* bags, their identification papers, in a sense, as religious Jews. But Jacob did not go so far as to throw the items overboard, as some of the revelers did later. Because they had so much history and meaning to him, he decided to place his *tallit* and his *tefillin* in his suitcase to be used when he visited a synagogue in America. But he removed layers of his religious clothing. Although he kept his skullcap, his *kepa,* on his head, he did toss away his high-topped Orthodox hat. Jacob was swept up by this group of like-minded people. A young man laughing near him flipped a more contemporary cap his way, saying that he had brought extras.

Through the days of the voyage, he learned that so many of the crowd were just like him, a group of observant young adults, seeking a more modern practice of Judaism. He had always been uncomfortable with the restrictions of his Hasidic upbringing, the old-fashioned style of dressing and the pro-hibitions against any premarital contact between the sexes. And then, in St. Petersburg, his eyes were opened to ways of enjoying a Jewish life without its suffocating Orthodox limit-ations. As each minute and hour was ticked off on the voyage, as the passengers moved further from their Eastern European homelands and closer to their destination across the ocean, they became more Americanized. They had no patience to wait until they saw the Statue of Liberty and set foot on American soil. They were already talking about changing their names slightly to be more in the American style.

The night before Jacob disembarked, he already imagined the America that awaited. He was eager to begin a new life that would, hopefully soon, include his family and his true love, Rebecca. He could not stop thinking about her. He dreamed of her soft, smiling face and her intriguing eyes. He thought how similar their desire was to embrace hard work along with the joys of play. He dreamed of her as his life's partner. He knew there could not be a more perfect match for him. He licked his lips and tried to taste, again, the sweetness of their farewell kiss. When he danced with the girls on the ship, he imagined how it would feel to be in public holding Rebecca in his arms, in a world where they could be uninhibited, where they could, unselfconsciously, enjoy music and each other. When he ate at the long tables with strangers who became friends, with men and women so bunched together, sharing and passing food as if they were close family at a Shabbas dinner, he thought only of a future where Rebecca would be next to him, always. Even though he knew it might be months before they would be together again, he could not wait to write her the first letter, so she would know he couldn't bear this separation from her.

When the boat docked and his celebrating shipmates disembarked, they began navigating through the Ellis Island immigration process. Shmuel Lipkovitz, who befriended Jacob on the ship, stood before him in line and he asked the agent to write down Lipko as his last name. When Jacob presented his papers and the agent said his name, he did not pronounce Schaevitz correctly, but Jacob liked what he heard and nodded in agreement. With paper in hand, he saw what the clerk had written down. Jacob Schaevitz had been reborn. Jacob Schaeffer entered America. Just leaving the medical examination area, Shmuel, shouted out to him – "Good luck, Jack."

Jacob thought about it. "Jack," he repeated. He liked the sound of it. He nodded with a broadening smile and returned his farewell: "Have a great life, Sam."

At the dock, countless friends and relatives of the new arrivals poured into the area where they could greet the immigrants when they had completed their processing at Ellis Island. With his new respectful but less religious look, Jacob already felt the old way of life was best left in the old country. He searched the crowd for his uncle. When he saw him, almost indistinguishable among the *Hasidim* who were waiting in the area, he did not let his face show it, but he knew that his own black hatted days were behind him. Jacob waved at Uncle Moishe. He was smiling enthusiastically, still appreciative of the opportunity he had been given. But the uncle did not seem to recognize him for a long time.

At first, his uncle did not think it was Jacob who was waving to him. His appearance was so different than he expected. And then he was drawn to the penetrating, large green eyes of the nephew he remembered, now beneath a modern hat. Jacob smiled again, seeing there was some recognition. But twice, the uncle squinted, and then he spat and turned away. Jacob walked quickly to catch up with him, trying not to lose him, as his uncle blended so easily into the religious crowd. When he was finally beside him, the uncle's returned hug was different than would be expected. It was as if he were loathingly embracing a sack of trash.

Suddenly, Jacob was skeptical that he had made the right decision in accepting his ticket to America, but he would show respect to his sponsor.

Although the incredible cityscape he could see would normally have been irresistible to him, Jacob was intent on following his uncle as he wound through unfamiliar streets. Finally, Uncle Moishe stopped at a tall tenement, in a row of similar buildings. Jacob gave a finger kiss to the *mezuzah* on the door and entered, although his uncle had not acknowledged him at any point along the route. Inside the apartment, there were at least twelve people living and working, cramped together. Beds seemed to be used in the daytime as seats for workers at sewing machines. Garments and materials for tailoring were in piles stacked about. Finally, the uncle turned to Jacob. He pointed to an unoccupied cot in the kitchen corner. "You may stay there," he grumbled out in Yiddish. "One night only, and then you leave." He refused to acknowledge Jacob's repetitive offer of thanks. He shunned him. "You are a great disappointment to me," the uncle scolded. "I will not have such a person, who has forsaken our religion, sleeping under my roof." He would not listen to anything Jacob had to say, how he tried to explain that he had not forsaken Judaism.

When Jacob awoke in the morning, he searched, unsuccessfully, for his satchel, so he could change into fresh clothing. Frustrated, he went down the steep steps at the end of the hallway and found that already his suitcase had been placed outside the front door.

Initially, Jacob spent days pacing the streets of this unknown city. He tried to hate the uncle, but he could not. He understood that generations of strict religious observance had molded him into the intransigent, dogmatic person he was. But Jacob had no idea of the extent of the uncle's retribution. He did not know about letters that the uncle would be sending back to Europe, letters filled with lies. Jacob did not understand why his own letters to his father and his letters to Rebecca, trying to tell them of other lodgings he had found, had gone unanswered.

He could not get Rebecca out of his mind. He was desperate to find a place to live and a place to work. He took any menial job available, while he tried to devise a plan beyond simple survival. He needed to be successful soon, so he could help his family and begin a life together in America with Rebecca.

On every street he walked down, he thought he saw a hint of Rebecca in the far distance, but each time he got closer, the truth became clearer: there was not a woman he saw who could hold a candle to her. The sweep of her hair, the shape of her body, the way she held her head high but demurely lowered her glance, these were things that he dreamed about at night, in the few hours he could finally drift to sleep.

There was so much happening at home that Jacob did not know and would not know for years to come. His father, Reuven, a softer version of his uncle, had never been comfortable with their move to the big city. As the world of his children had been expanding, Reuven Schaevitz felt his own world collapsing. He missed the shtetl life of their village of Motele in Poland. He was uncomfortable in his new religious neighborhood in St. Petersburg. Nobody knew him. Nobody asked how he was handling the girls since the death of his beloved wife. No one knew his history. He missed his small *shul* where he often had the honor of holding the holy Torah. He missed going with his friends to the public baths. Each week, he missed his town with all the households awaiting the arrival of Shabbas. He missed the flicker of candles in all the windows, the wonderful smells of the meals the women were preparing, and family invitations to dinners with neighbors.

Reuven had been disturbed that, with the move to St. Petersburg, Jacob cared more about his business than his *cheder* studies. Every day brought more steps toward assimilation. The girl Jacob was with was beautiful, and yes, sweet – he understood his son's attraction. But she was not part of the religious community. She could bring him further and further from his roots. One day, Reuven worried, Jacob will not respect the Sabbath; he will eat *treif,* non kosher food. There will be no matches for Jacob's sisters because of this.

Jacob's father became distraught when a first letter arrived from his brother in New York, informing him that Jacob had not been released from Ellis Island for medical reasons.

When a second letter followed, detailing more lies, that Jacob had abandoned his religion, disrespected the uncle, and stolen money, his father was so heartbroken and distressed that he made small tears in his clothing from the humiliation of it all, as if he were in mourning after the actual death of his son. He blamed it all on their leaving the shtetl environment that was their home and felt his honor could only be restored by returning to his town. Reuven Schaevitz packed up his belongings and those of his daughters and made the move back to Motele. He did not understand that establishing Jacob in America would not only have been to enhance economic opportunities but would have been the gateway to a safe and secure future for the family. The uncle's lies had sealed the fate of Jacob's cherished family, although Jacob would not know that for years to come. He would not know that was why his letters to them in St. Petersburg went unanswered. Jacob's father did not understand that his worst decision was heading back to his village, although the pull of his traditions was overpowering. The God whom they respected and prayed to could not protect them from the horror of the Holocaust to come. The family all needed to continue the move westward, not only before the 1924 US Immigration Act closed the borders of a xenophobic America, but they needed to leave before the Nazi marauders brutally destroyed the world they held dear.

Chapter 11

PALM BEACH 1975

Returning as quickly as was possible from The Breakers Hotel lobby, Bear saw that the door to Kathryn and Beth Morgan's suite was slightly open. He knocked gently and then entered. "The doctor will be here soon," he told them, although Kathryn had closed her eyes again.

"Thanks for sticking this out with me," Beth said to him, and when her mother seemed to be stirring, Beth took Bear aside and spoke quietly. Tears were streaming down her face.

"I don't understand what is happening. I came here knowing my life was falling apart, and now my falling apart life is falling apart. I'm so sorry you are caught up in my mess now."

"Don't even think that. I'm here and I'm going help you." He went back to the door to check in the hall and, seeing the doctor, he waved him in.

"Morning, Bear," the good-looking, spectacled, tall and thin physician said as he entered with his black leather bag.

Kathryn opened her eyes again but appeared disoriented. "Ladies, this is Dr. Nathan Bernstein, Bear said. "I'll let him take over. It seems we were lucky that he was on the property."

"Perfect timing, for sure," the doctor agreed. "I stopped at the hotel for breakfast after morning rounds." He looked at the two women. "I would just like to wash my hands, if I may use your sink." He proceeded to the bathroom and returned quickly, taking a stethoscope and a thermometer from his bag. "So, what have we got here?"

"This is Mrs. Kathryn Morgan with her daughter, Beth." Bear answered, before moving to wait in the hall. The doctor could tell that the older woman was in some level of respiratory distress. He pulled a chair next to her bed.

"Can you tell me what's been going on with you? I'd like to listen to your chest and give you a little exam. Is that okay?"

Kathryn nodded reluctantly and Beth said, "Yes, please, thank you so much."

"I'll be right outside," Bear assured Beth, as he closed the door to give them privacy.

The doctor took his time listening to Kathryn's heart and lungs, palpating her ribs, front and back. She had a slight fever. He withdrew his otoscope from his satchel to examine her eyes, ears, nose, and throat. He noticed bloodied tissues by her bedside. "Ma'am, may I ask if you are being treated for anything?"

Beth answered that her mother had a lingering cough, but Kathryn broke in, softly, shaking her index finger to make her point. "I can speak for myself," she coughed out. "We are from New York, you know. We have the best hospitals there."

The doctor was practiced in holding back rolling his eyes, having dealt often with the entitled patients who frequent the area as residents or tourists. "I couldn't agree more," he affirmed with a pleasant smile and not a hint of derision. "I received my training at Columbia College of Physicians and Surgeons in Manhattan." Beth knew this information would please her mother. "I think I'd like you to be transported to the hospital now," he continued. "And then I'll have the opportunity to see just what the story is. We can contact your doctors from there."

"No, I can't leave here," Kathryn cried, adamantly, surprising them both with the sudden power of her voice. The doctor was concerned that she would become more agitated. He left the room for a moment. Kathryn was searching right and left for Beth and patted the bed next to her so she would sit. "You have to help me. Make him understand. I cannot leave here now." Her stops to take in a new breath of air punctuated each sentence. "I had to come back. I need to find out what happened. You must understand this. I don't know how much time I have left." Now her voice grew softer, requiring less effort. Beth was concerned with her Mother's sluggish speech patterns and pleaded with her to just relax and stop talking. But she would not listen. "I need to find a way to make things right," she said, working hard at her word retrieval.

Beth tenderly took her mother's hands to hold, as she kissed her on the cheek. "Please calm down. Being so upset can't be good for you now. Let's just get you better and worry about whatever this is later."

Kathryn pulled Beth closer and whispered to her. "I may have no more time to wait."

"Mother, what are you talking about? I don't get what you're trying to say. Please calm down. You can tell me later."

Kathryn held on tightly to her daughter's upper arm and pulled herself up so she could speak directly into her ear. "You don't understand. I have to set things right. I can't live with myself any longer until I do." Beth moved to get up, thinking that would curtail her mother's rambling thoughts, but once again, Kathryn pulled at her sleeve. "Beth, listen, "I can't die with unfinished business. I can't tell you more. You're my daughter, and even you know this. I have been a cruel and selfish person. And I thought I could change." She leaned back on the pillow and closed her eyes before continuing. She did not want Beth to fear for her health and silence her once more. "But now, I think it's too late." She paused to fill her lungs again and narrowed her eyes, as if struggling to remember something. "It's the name. I can't think of the name . . . although her name haunted me for years. But now, I cannot bring the name back to me."

"Mother, the doctor knows what he is doing, and he wants you at the hospital."

"Not in an ambulance," Kathryn insisted, immediately. "I won't go in an ambulance! Call that limo driver."

"Ma'am, I've already had Bear call for an ambulance," the doctor said, as he moved to check the hall again and motioned for Bear to come in the room. Then he returned to Kathryn, exhibiting his most charming bedside manner. "They'll have a private suite available. You will be more comfortable with some oxygen on the ride there. And when you're in the hospital room, I'll be better able to evaluate you."

Kathryn turned, pleadingly, to her daughter. Her voice was at its softest volume, not out of politeness, but a necessity to conserve her energy. "Beth, how do we know that this doctor is any good? I mean, really, a *hotel* doctor?" She emphasized the word 'hotel,' as if it were lower than a prison. Beth knew there was no filter to what her mother would say.

"Please, Mom, you know he already told you he went to Columbia for medical school." She looked to Bear for help. He was being so sweet, she thought to herself . . . and so patient.

"Believe me, Mrs. Morgan, you have no idea of the reputation of Dr. Bernstein. The story is legend here. He was only in high school the first time he saved a life." He paused and a proud smile emerged for the man he felt was like an uncle. "And now, Dr. Nate is Chief of Medicine at JFK Memorial Medical Center. He'll do us favors when he can, though; he has a history in the area. And his wife, Addie, is an assistant front desk manager."

• • •

At the hospital, Kathryn's condition improved, and then, for a short period of time, she appeared to be drifting in and out of consciousness, until she determinedly sat up against the bank of pillows on the bed and followed the doctor's instructions on how to breathe calmly with the apparatus. After the nurse by his side took Kathryn's vital signs, he began asking questions. "Kathryn, do you know where you are?"

"I am in a hospital in Palm Beach, Florida," she said with a slight slurring of speech detectable. And then, turning to the assisting nurse, she added, with slow, but perfect diction, "and not happy to be here."

"Sounds like she's back to normal," her daughter said, sardonically, to the doctor.

"Kathryn, can you tell me your birthdate, your age, and today's date?" She told him her age and her birthdate. The pupils of her eyes arched toward the ceiling, as she configured the calendar in her head. She recited the day, date, and year in a staccato form. He tested her joints for her reflex function and then had her stretch out her arms and touch her nose with each index finger, first the right hand and then the left.

Beth did not want to leave her mother's side and accompanied her as she was wheeled to some of the testing floors. The X-ray did not show pneumonia, and Beth was especially relieved with that news, as she would be able to spend the night, sleeping on a window seat sofa bed in the hospital room. Even though she was dreaming of the crispy white linens on her queen-sized bed, the luscious down duvet, and the plush bathroom robe that awaited her in her luxurious room at The Breakers, she could not think of returning there yet. Before the ambulance came, she had thrown some necessities and night clothes in a bag for each of them, but now she was longing for the high-end assortment of soaps and shampoos, conditioners and body lotions that were lined up on mirrored shelves in the enormous bathroom of their suite.

Beth knew she had done the right thing by staying these first days, and even her mother had, surprisingly, acknowledged her thoughtfulness, saying she was the best daughter and she loved her. These were words that surprised Beth, like little stocking stuffer gifts on Christmas Eve. Beth happily gathered some of her mother's favorite magazines from the hospital gift shop, and together, they kept busy flipping through the pages of *Vogue* and *Town and Country* and *Architectural Digest*. When she saw her mother dozing, she slipped out to make calls at the pay phone in the visitor's lounge.

Beth's first call was to her office in New York. For the past year, since her graduation from the New York School of Interior Design, she'd held a sought-after position with a Manhattan firm. She explained the family situation to her boss and nervously requested a leave of absence. She just could not abandon her mother. When she was asked how much time each day she would need to stay with her mother, Beth thought they were challenging her, but she was wrong. "Beth," the firm manager said, "your needing to stay in that area could possibly work out extremely well, even give us a great entry into that market. One of our major clients has just purchased a Palm Beach mansion that needs a redo. We don't want to lose this commission. Truthfully, it will be a big one." There was a pause on the line, and Beth thought she could hear the repetitive clicking of the manager's pencil against his desktop, as was his habit. "Let me think things through and I'll get back to you."

Beth was already prepared to hand in her resignation. But only an hour later, the manager called Beth back in her mother's hospital room." Okay," he said, "I can send one of our very experienced consultants down for the architectural assessment and initial drawings, but we need someone local, and I have no one to spare. This is what we will do. You tell us if you anticipate you will have some time during the week to work with the client, to show her packets we will send down, even to take her to local stores to make her feel part of the process. We know she likes that. You would be our cheerleader and her hand-holder, and we'd look forward to seeing ideas that you envision. This will be a great opportunity to show what you can do."

By the third day, Kathryn was markedly more stable, and she suggested that Beth take a break and enjoy the hotel. "We're paying for it, dear. I'll be okay." But Beth was not sure. She was afraid her mother would wake up from a nap and be agitated again if she found Beth was not with her.

Bear had called the room often over the past days to talk to Beth and check up on Mrs. Morgan. But Beth had been self-conscious speaking in front of her mother, and she could only say how much she appreciated what he had done and that she would call him back when she could talk. In truth, increasingly throughout each day, she was fantasizing what it would be like to thank him in person, to be in his arms, to feel his lips on hers. Finally, Kathryn just encouraged Beth to call Bear, saying that she would be fine if Beth spent some time with "that nice, handsome, young man."

Two hours later, when Bear knocked on the door and announced himself, Beth jumped up to meet him in the hall before he entered. Seeing her, Bear's eyes opened wide and his smile lit up his face. He set something down on the linoleum tile and pushed her shoulders lightly against the door so that it would close again. Beth was startled by the move but liked the feel of his strong hands on her. When he saw her smile, Bear took her in his arms and kissed her. He could not help himself. He'd had one thing on his mind since he met her. It was a desire to hold her and taste her lips, while weaving his fingers through the bountiful mass of her auburn hair. It was what had captured him immediately when she and her mother joined his tour group. Since then, he had been reliving every moment of the conversation at their breakfast. He did not even know he was such a romantic soul.

Beth was happily electrified by the kiss, and her head was spinning. She did not understand this next turn of events in her life, but she felt like she was floating, and she knew her face would show it when they entered her mother's room together.

Bear wanted to kiss her again, but instead he went straight to Kathryn's bedside. He had brought a generous floral arrangement, which he placed on her nightstand. He scrutinized her face and then fluffed her pillow. "Mrs. Morgan, I'm so glad to see you are feeling better and, certainly, looking better. Now I can easily recognize you as the elegant lady who was audience to my undoubtedly tedious lecture the other day."

She smiled up at him, flattered by the compliment but skeptical that he had an ulterior motive. She saw him exchange a clandestine look with her daughter. "Beth dear, I think it's about time you took a break from my bedside. Go to our hotel room to freshen up. Maybe make this young man take you to dinner when you have fashioned yourself quite as elegant as I am." Kathryn winked at Bear, indicating she knew she had been played. "Go on you two, or I'll make you share my hospital meal."

Beth laughed at her mother's surprising intuition. This banter was not her usual style. She wondered if the doctor had given her some sort of pill that changed her personality. Beth gave her mother a hug and started to leave, as Kathryn called out to her, "Oh, and please bring a couple of changes of clothes for me when you come back tomorrow."

Beth could hardly believe how being with Bear again had brightened her state of mind, and she was eager to share that with him when they were out the door. "Thanks for coming. It really means a lot to me. And by the way, you don't have to take me to dinner, or at least let me treat you somewhere or maybe – "

As they walked down the corridor, he waited for her to take a breath so he could interrupt her monologue. "Or maybe you could stop talking so that we could kiss again."

She smiled up at him, making no pretense to hide her eager look. He was quite charming, handsome, and well built. He pulled her into his arms, and he lifted her up as he bent slightly to meet her lips. As they approached the elevator, her eye caught a full-length mirror. She asked him to stop for a minute. "Look Bear. Look in the mirror. That's us. That's the first picture of us together, even though it will only live in our minds."

He thought over what she had said, and he liked it. He was quick with a response because her choice of words had struck a chord in him. They really knew so little about each other at this point. "It's a picture of the beginning of our history together," he said. "And you know I'm into history."

When they were in the elevator, he became serious. "Listen, this is what I wanted to tell you. I spend a lot of time with Dr. Bernstein – well, Nate and his wife, Addie. I always see Addie around the hotel, of course. My own family is constantly traveling, so when I'm not away on campus and I'm at my Palm Beach place, I tend to hang with them. Basically, they're like family, even though we're separate religions. We just get double the holidays, Christmas and Easter for us, Hanukkah and Passover for them. They asked if I would like to join them for dinner and hinted that it would be nice if I brought 'someone' along, I think guessing who I would have in mind. So, they were more than delighted when I said I would like you to come. Let's do it. Ta-boo is the best restaurant in Palm Beach, great food and a truly historical setting. You'll love the décor."

"Wait. Did I ever say that I was a decorator – what made you say that?" she questioned him.

"No, but I'd like to know more about who you are. And I'm not surprised. I just said that because there is an unmistakable fashionable style about you." She was pleased with the compliment but doubted its sincerity since she knew she had only been in a constant state of disarray since they met.

Beth happily accepted the invitation. She was intrigued with the venue, but more important, she knew she needed to be with company. Being with her mother day and night had been more emotionally draining than she ever could have imagined. Her mother was doing well, but she sometimes drifted from sleep to an almost incomprehensible stream of conscious speech, pulling often on Beth's sleeve to make sure she was paying attention.

Dinner at Ta-boo did not disappoint; it was just what Beth needed. The conversation was comfortable and interesting. Beth asked Dr. Bernstein, who quickly insisted, "Call me Nate," to explain about his first saved life, and they all told her more about the history of the hotel during the war period and how Nate and Addie's relationship had changed from simply childhood friends to sweethearts when The Breakers became Ream General Hospital. Beth shared how she was surprised and thrilled about being able to work for her firm in the Palm Beach area while her mother recovered, and Bear was all smiles from that. But then Beth took the conversation in another direction.

"I'd like to confide something more to all of you, though," she said, becoming the raconteur, instead of the listener. "I really need you to help me unravel a mystery, unless my mom becomes more lucid and forthcoming. My mother has been acting so strangely ever since we came to Palm Beach – starting with the fact that she never explained why we came here. Something drew her here, but she wouldn't say what it was. She has never mentioned this place before, although we have traveled extensively." She directed her attention to Nate. "I think my mother will do as you advise. She seems convinced she may be dying, but I know she wants to live because she insists that she has something to resolve. She wants to be forgiven, although I don't know for what, and she won't say. I don't know how this is all connected. All she repeats is "the letter." That's one of the phrases I can easily make out. It is the repetition of this need to find someone or something or relay a message which is keeping her agitated. Yet, I think it may be bolstering her will to fight on until there is a resolution to what is troubling her. I think she is looking for someone in particular. She just says she wished she had the letter. And she repeats that she doesn't remember the name.

Then Beth turned specifically to Bear. "Remember how we latched on to your lecture tour?" He smiled but was laughing inside. How could he forget the moment his life became illuminated? "When you spoke of the babies born at The Breakers," Beth continued, "my mother almost turned white. She didn't even realize that she started grabbing my arm tightly, jabbing her nails into my skin. Beth pushed up the sleeve of her blouse to show lingering evidence of the marks. "Since then, I have run through all the scenarios I could think of to explain this." She had been contemplatively looking down at her place setting as she was speaking, but now she scanned the table, looking first at Bear and then Addie and Nate. "There is something I have always known. I have always known I was adopted. So naturally, that was my first thought. Could I be one of The Breakers babies? Initially, it was an almost exciting, certainly intriguing, idea. But I lingered to review one of the plaques and saw that Ream Hospital operated at the site only from 1942 until 1944. But I was born in 1948 – well, that is, if my mother told me the truth about that. She only told me she had trouble getting pregnant, but I know nothing of my birth parents. I know nowadays some sealed records are being released, but as difficult as my mother is, I've just always felt I owe my wonderful life to her. You have to understand. My father cheated on her and left us both when I was young. Oh, he still handled his 'obligation,' yes, his exact word. I used to repeat it as a joke to my mother in my teen years. 'Does he know my name is Beth and not Obligation?' Sure, he supported us, and my mother had her own trust. But I just couldn't do that to her – I mean, dismiss her to find my real mother, my birth mother. What makes a 'real' mother anyway?

"And then I started to wonder if she had been here, been in Palm Beach, during the war. Could she have had a baby here before I was born, a baby she gave up for adoption, something she kept even from my father? I know they weren't married until he returned from the war in 1945. And then, I thought to combine this information with one more fact. When my grandparents died within months of each other about three years ago, my mother's parents that is, I received a sizeable inheritance. But as I was handed papers to sign, my mother said such cruel things under her breath. She said it wasn't right, it shouldn't have been only for me."

Beth paused now, embarrassed that she was monopolizing the conversation. She looked around the restaurant and took a moment to reflect on the beautiful setting.

"Beth," Addie said, "Is there more to the story?" When Beth gave her a look, questioning if she was serious, Addie nodded her head. "Yes, go on. I mean it."

"Well, okay. I'm being honest now, and Bear, maybe even Nate, has certainly seen this – my mother is a difficult woman. As I said, my father left her, left us, when I was young. I have always wondered if I was part of the reason for their divorce. Maybe he felt no guilt in leaving the family for a girlfriend because my mother had never given him the real baby he wanted. Since I was adopted, I was not blood for him, for either of them. My father's parents were always snobby, with an elitist New York lineage. As I got older, my mother told me they never thought her family was good enough for their son, even though my mother's parents' Upper East side townhouse was so impressive that it had been featured in various magazines. 'Money can't buy class,' my father's mother would have no compunction saying. My father's family was in banking. My mother's family was in the scrap metal business."

Addie, who had been taking her first bites of Ta-boo's delicious, elegant apple tart dessert as she listened to Beth's story, abruptly started coughing, struggling to clear her throat, and reaching for water.

Nate came up quickly behind her, with the tenderness of a concerned husband and the instincts of a trained physician, and he started full palmed raps against her back. "Are you choking?" he asked urgently, and then when she responded "No, I'll be all right." Despite the fact she was still clearing her throat and reaching for more to drink, he looked at his wife's face and turned to the group, "If she can talk, she isn't choking. She'll be fine."

When Addie was able to calm down, she simply laughed. Looking at the concerned faces, she hoped to lighten the moment. "Mm, that was so delicious. Maybe I just took too big a mouthful." Anxious to shift the focus from herself, she continued, "Nate, honey, could you give me an idea when you think Beth's mom might be ready for another visitor? I think I would like to meet Mrs. Morgan and maybe I could talk to her. Maybe woman to woman, mother to mother, she could explain something to me that would be harder to say mother to daughter." Beth tilted her head slightly, as if ready to ask a question, but Addie anticipated what it would be. "Yes, Nate and I have three children, a son and two daughters, twins, all in colleges up north. "I just think, personally, I might have a hard time if my girls were the only ones that I felt I could confide in, if there was something troubling and personal on my mind. It's just a thought."

"Oh, Addie, Would you? Would you talk to my mom?" Beth pleaded. "I know what you are saying. I think you are right. Maybe you could help her to open up."

"Okay honey," Addie said, turning to her husband, "You just tell me when you think she is well enough."

As a physician, Nate understood there was a physical and an emotional component to any patient's illness. He knew that some medication, lots of rest, and a proper diet were essential for Kathryn at this point. But if Addie had some insight into what was agitating Kathryn, perhaps that could help speed the recovery process. He did not press Addie further for details, but he thought it was a good idea.

Chapter 12

PALM BEACH 1942

After almost six weeks without seeing Natalie around, Addie promised herself that she would walk down to the Evington Estate. She could not wait any longer to confide in her older friend, her mentor, just how right she had been about Nate. But as it turned out, just as her work shift ended that day, Natalie came to The Breakers to find her.

"Hey kid," Natalie yelled out, seeing Addie on the beach walk. "I wasn't sure if your family moved out when the hotel became Ream."

"Wow, Natalie, is that really you?" Addie said, turning to the familiar voice and then running to exchange hugs. "We're in our quarters for now. Seems the hotel wanted to maintain a skeleton staff to help out the army and keep an eye on them, too, not that we could evict them if they were rowdy." The girls laughed together, as easily as they always had, and each said to the other, "I have something to tell you." Then "Jinx, you owe me a soda" were their next words.

"You first," Natalie insisted, tousling Addie's hair, in an older sister way.

"Natalie, you won't believe it," Addie announced. "I'm in love. I'm really in love. And you won't believe who it is with."

Natalie focused intense, peering eyes on her friend and answered with a slight laugh, as if it were too obvious. "Well, I can only hope it is with Nate, because I couldn't bear seeing him continuing with a lifetime of puppy dog unrequited love looks."

"What do you mean? Addie shot back, curiously, "You knew?"

"Yes, I knew. We all knew. Me, your mother, his mother ..."

"But no one ever said."

Natalie put her arm around Addie's shoulders and leaned gently into her, so their foreheads touched. "And that's how love should work. You have to come to recognize it on your own."

Addie kept silent and critically studied her friend's face. "Natalie, you always look great. But today, it's like you've taken beauty to a new level." She stepped back and looked her over. "It's like you're glowing," she added, biting her lower lip, contemplatively. "And now, I'm thinking, were you ready to tell me the same thing? Are you in love, too?"

Initially, Natalie didn't answer and just shyly lowered her head, until a broad smile emerged, and she looked up again. "His name is Theodore Stanton, and he is so handsome and so sweet. I've known him just about a month, but I've never felt this way before. And I know he feels the same."

"Wow, I love that, especially hearing it from you, someone who has rejected every guy who showed any interest since I first met you." In the sky, a helicopter hovered just off the shore, triggering Addie's thoughts. "You've been assigned as an aircraft observer, right? I know that's what you had said you wanted. Is he one of the army staff?"

Natalie explained how Theo began as her unwanted stalker when she was energetic about her position working in the observation towers. "He just kept appearing wherever I was, watching me, trying to distract me. I was annoyed with him, almost afraid of him. I thought he was the most obnoxious, cocky flirt, even though, I will tell you, the girls around me were swooning over him. But soon he became my savior." Natalie motioned for Addie to follow her, as she eyed a pair of vacant chairs along the beach walk. "You see, after about two weeks, the officer in charge said they were impressed with my work and recruited me to be an instructor. At that point, I began spending much of the day teaching volunteers how to fill out their forms, when I just wanted to be in the field myself. I just felt so suffocated inside.

"And then, on a break about four weeks ago, like I said, my life changed. My stalker introduced himself as someone from civilian adjunct services. He explained that he came to the area to help coordinate the collection of salvage materials in Palm Beach County, and he really wanted me to be on his team. I told him I would love to do anything but stay inside a building most of the day. And then I asked him how it was he came to choose me.

"He admitted to lingering in my area, watching me, just as I had accused him. But he said it was because he knew I would be perfect for what he needed.

"Honestly, what he said made no sense to me, so I just asked him how he could even know I would meet the requirements for what the army wanted?

"His smile was adorable and mischievous and with each word he spoke, he looked right into my eyes. Although he is definitely a big guy, he has that little boy, childlike innocence about him. 'Well, the army wants me to be happy,' he said to me. Then he explained that he was brought down from New York to work here, although he had no guarantee that he wouldn't be transferred to a real war zone at some point. You see, his family has this scrap metal business. They know how to manage collection and repurposing on a large scale. He said the army wants him happy, so he can bring his expertise and his knowledge of the right contacts to successfully carry out the mission.

"I had to laugh at that. And then I tried to set him straight. 'You understand, of course, you serve the army. It's not the other way around,' I told him. 'They don't serve you.'

"Again, the boyish grin. 'Well. You never met my mother or my father,' he said. 'But when you do, do not tell them the universe does not revolve around them. Wouldn't want you getting off on the wrong foot. But they'll come to love you, anyway.'"

"Of course, I asked why I would be meeting his parents.

"Then he seemed flustered. 'Okay, I'm telling this all wrong,' he said, looking straight at me, lifting my chin up slightly. That's all he had to do so that our eyes were only inches apart, so near to the same level. He wanted to tell me how he felt, and yet my heart seemed like it was bursting and a pulse was echoing in my ears, so I could barely even hear what he was saying. I was captivated by him. I felt I had conjured him up. I felt I was in the middle of a dream, and yet I was awake and it was daytime. This man before me was like any prince I had ever imagined. He was my male match. He was probably 6' 2" to my 5' 9." His hair was a darker version of my own dishwater blond. But even that, I imagined, would be closer to my color, given the chance to lighten with time in the Florida sun. And without the required army crew cut, I guess since he was not officially a soldier, his hair flopped in the cutest way over one eye."

Finally, Natalie paused from her monologue and covered her face with her hands, giggling into them like a young schoolgirl. "It's so embarrassing, I know. Look how I am babbling on."

"I've never seen you like this," Addie said.

"It's so . . . I know. You can say it," Natalie admitted, "It's so embarrassing."

"No, Natty." Addie corrected. "It's incredibly amazing. I'm so excited for you," she said, and the girls hugged each other.

"You have to understand," Natalie continued, "I had never been with a boy who I didn't tower over, who I didn't feel like I was too broad, too large for, like I had the bigger hands and larger feet. I wanted to tell him how I felt, but he was the one who wanted to talk. He said that when he first saw me, I guess when we were having training sessions on the beach and in the towers, he tried, discreetly, to find me whenever he could be in the area. I laughed at that, told him he was certainly not discreet. I was close to reporting this stranger following me to an M.P."

"But you didn't, did you?" Addie had to ask.

"Well, he was a very handsome stranger, and he never actually threatened me." She paused and smiled at the memory of it. "When he finally coaxed me to walk and talk with him, he said how he had fallen immediately in love with me, and he knew he needed me by his side.' Now, this you will certainly find crazy. He said, 'You understand, I need you working with me because it'll be hard for me to marry you without getting to know you, and I think that getting to know you needs to start immediately.' And then, without even asking me, and yet with no protest on my part, he just took me in his arms and gave me the most luscious, unforgettable kiss, and it was to the applause of the soldiers congregated nearby. I felt on top of the world.

"The next morning, my superior, with a smug but understanding wink, gave me transfer papers to switch to Theo's team. Obviously, I had underestimated the influence either he or his family carried."

"I can't explain it. Theo has that New York confidence, but with a self-deprecating lack of arrogance. I know it doesn't sound like it when I am repeating the story to you, but he had a shyness and a neediness about him. It's like I recognized in him a kindred spirit. I know I've never really gone into it with you, but my homelife is not an easy one, although it is hard to believe that since the outward appearance of our estate might give an impression of a wonderful place. I promise I will tell you more about it at some point. But it was like Theo came to me with dreamy love eyes and a need to follow his passion for me and for his profession. Although early on I had called him out as a slacker, his work ethic is amazing."

"In the months before I met him, he helped to coordinate a massive volunteer enterprise in the collection of scrap metals and salvaged products, like nylon, rubber, paper, and other materials needed for the national war effort. He explained that just a short time before Pearl Harbor, America had naively depleted much of its inventory of steel with sales to Japan, never imagining the United States would soon have to rebuild its own decimated fleet."

Natalie took out a newspaper clipping from her purse. "He showed me this article about it all. Theo helped Palm Beach to institute school, business, and community collection competitions. The girl in this photo, a fifteen-year-old Palm Beach High School student, managed to collect over 100,000 pounds of scrap metal, which could eventually help to build small arms, tanks, or planes.

"Besides working with the volunteers, Theo also did the task of coordinating the shipping and disbursement of materials to the appropriate processing facilities." She put the article away.

"Natalie, I think you struck gold with this one," Addie finally broke in. "Now I understand the glow."

"So, he saved me from my tedious job in the classroom and I became his assistant in the field. In the last weeks, we have been inseparable, working together most days and dancing together most nights. You know, I think I saw you and Nate outside at one of the venues." Addie nodded with a shy but enthusiastic smile as Natalie went on. "Aren't the USO dances just what we needed? Remember just a short time ago when we thought all the men would be gone? And now we each have found love. I can't pretend it was love at first sight for me, but when it came, it was a powerful locomotive. I just wish I could live in his arms."

And soon Natalie's tone became serious, not dreamy. "I've even told your mom about him. You don't know this, Addie. And please don't take this the wrong way. Don't ever think that I used you so I could have a relationship with your mother. But you need to know this. From the beginning, when I met you, I felt so close to you, like I would toward a younger sister. And you welcomed me into your life as friend and family, immediately, not even knowing I didn't feel welcome in my own house, with a stepmother too close to my own age and a little stepsister who was a spoiled, entitled duplicate of her mom."

This was new information for Addie. She had no idea this was Natalie's life. Tears began welling in her eyes.

"So maybe you can understand, Natalie continued, "that when I met your mother, the exquisite Rebecca, I felt an obsession with her. She was a tall and emotionally strong woman, a beautiful woman who was not afraid to hold her head high. She was a regal princess to me. Before meeting her, I was self-conscious about my height, like I would never fit in. I always wished I was one of the adorable petite girls, the girls like you." Addie, who had always wished to be taller, made no comment but looked at Natalie like it was the most ridiculous thing she ever heard.

"Just before I was fourteen, my mother passed away," Natalie said. "I had no one to tell me to embrace my own unique qualities as positive, not negative. But when I recently came to know your mother, she recognized my need for some parental advice and support even at this age. We would have long talks together when you were at school."

Suddenly, Natalie felt guilty, like she had betrayed her friend. "Oh God, Addie, I'm so sorry. Please don't be upset with me for stealing time with Rebecca. Your mother has helped me, taught me a lot about life, just by sharing her story with me. She is an exceptional woman. Of course, you know, she also lost her own mother when she was young, but then she lost her country. She has lived life on the world's stage, not in our privileged part of the globe. I admire her so much."

Addie stood quietly for a brief time, just processing what she was told, especially how her mother had kept this all in confidence. But when she thought about it, she knew that was her mom's way, just another of the qualities that drew people to respect Rebecca. And soon, Addie wrapped Natalie in the warmest girlfriend embrace. "You don't understand. I feel even closer to you because you love my mother, too. As an only child, I am so grateful to call you more than a friend . . . like you said, like a sister."

Chapter 13

ST. PETERSBURG 1923

"Papa, Papa," Rebecca cried as she leaned over the winding bannister of her apartment house stairwell and saw that her father was just returning home from work. She raced down the steps to the landing of the floor below to meet him, and then she took hold of his arm so they could walk up the last flight together. "I need to tell you what has happened," she said. "Jacob's sisters came by while you were gone. And they brought such upsetting news."

Once in their living room, Rebecca sat on the couch with her father. She rested her tear-streamed face on his shoulder. He could barely make out what she was saying between her sobs. Finally, she fought to compose herself. "They showed me a letter. Jacob's uncle, the one who sponsored his passage to America, has written that Jacob was not yet allowed entry into the United States." She took a breath. "He did not pass the medical examination at Ellis Island, where they process the immigrants. It seems Jacob is being held in the infirmary. The uncle repeated twice in his note that he is a good man and has done a great *mitzvah* by sending for his nephew. And he said he would have looked forward to having Jacob's future wife for the business, if she was this important fashion designer, even to the revered Ginsburg family, as Jacob wrote in his letter. Then he complained that it looks like he may have lost his investment in sending for Jacob."

Abraham looked at her, curiously. "I must be honest," he said. "This uncle's words are disturbing."

"I quite agree, Papa."

"Yes, sending for family, that is a good deed, a *mitzvah*," Abraham agreed. "But there is something in his letter that makes me feel he is not as charitable and generous of spirit as he would like us to believe."

"I'm so worried for Jacob. I need to go there. Please don't say no. I need find out what is happening."

"Oh honey, let's think things through," her father said, smoothing her hair as he comforted her.

Rebecca stood up and paced back and forth as she spoke. "I don't understand, perhaps they were not even told, but he could be held in quarantine for weeks, maybe longer." Finally, she slowed her delivery and raised her eyes to meet her father's. "I have to believe that Jacob is strong and will get better. Maybe I should go to New York to make sure he is taken care of. I can continue to work here and save more money to earn the passage. Before Jacob left for America, I know he had written to the uncle about me and my background as a seamstress and dress designer. So maybe the uncle would let me stay there awhile and work in his business if Jacob is not yet released. If not, I will find a job." Her father sat just looking at her, processing all that he has just been told.

"Before you say no," Rebecca continued, "think about this. I have been working and have shown I am a resourceful person for a long time now."

"Darling, darling, slow down. I know what you say is true."

"And there was a speaker at the synagogue last week who gave out a list of settlement houses in New York that were places for immigrants."

Abraham Rushman took his daughter's hand and led her to the kitchen table. She was too agitated to sit still and began the preparations for tea. With cups in front of them, she just shook her head and could barely even look at her father. "Even if I am able to make the fare, I don't know if I should leave you, Papa. I need your guidance. Please, Papa. You have to tell me what to do."

Abraham barely hesitated before his response. He placed his firm hands on his daughter's shoulders and looked directly into her eyes. "I can tell you easily, if you answer one question for me."

"Yes, Papa," she sniffled out. "What is the question?"

"It is a simple one." Now he moved his hands to cup her cheeks. "Rebecca, do you love Jacob?"

"I do. I do love him," she answered, emphatically. And then she bowed her head, as if her courage had left her. "But I love you, too, Papa. I want to be with him, but I don't want to leave you. I don't want you to be alone."

Now Abraham held his daughter in his arms. "You answered the question I asked, with no hesitation, my darling." He nodded his head several times. "I know that Jacob loves you as well. He asked for your hand even before he left, even before he felt he was established enough to formally ask you. Our hope was that he would have established himself and then sent for you. But sometimes things don't fall into place as we would want. But, God willing, things will work out just as was planned, and you will be with him soon. My great regret is that I will not be there to witness my daughter under the wedding *chuppah*." Rebecca shook her head in protest and tried to cry out the word "no," but no sound was emitted. "Rebecca darling," her father continued, "I feel that without him, you, even more than me, are alone. You are a young couple with your whole futures ahead of you, and you should be together. I don't want you to travel life's journey alone. But know that I am not alone. You and Mama are always in my heart. I have my friends, my comrades, my missions. But these past years, you were given no opportunity to develop many lasting friendships, other than a few sweet girlfriends. That is, until Jacob and you met. And know this. I have been worrying that my activities may put you in jeopardy. Truthfully, I would feel relieved to know you were on your way to a life in a better place." He hugged her tenderly and whispered in her ear. "My sweet baby, all grown up for a long time now." Then he stepped back. "I have worked hard to save money, because I have always been cautious about what the future could bring. And now I know what the money will be for. It should be enough for your passage and so that you can have a small nest egg, something of your own while you wait for Jacob to recover. And who knows what will come to pass. Perhaps, one day, I may come to join you."

Chapter 14

PASSAGE TO AMERICA 1923

Passage to America for Rebecca was booked on the *SS Reliance*,
leaving out of Hamburg, Germany, on July 10, 1923. She said
her tearful goodbyes to her father that morning and proceeded
to travel to Hamburg. At the pier, Rebecca felt terribly alone.
It seemed that everyone standing before the vessel, no matter
their boarding class, had companionship, at least presenting as a
couple, if not part of a large entourage. Her attention was drawn
first to an elderly pair, extremely well dressed – a sophisticated

Jewish couple from a large city, she was thinking. They were clinging to each other tightly, each one's arm wrapped around the other's back, and in front of their bodies, they held hands. Waiting by herself, she wrote their story in her mind. She imagined them having created a successful business in Poland or Hungary or even Germany, and they might be in the group of people running from oppression in their countries. Perhaps they were going ahead of sons and daughters and families that would follow, or maybe the next generation was already settling down in America and was waiting for their arrival.

Although this was a voyage to America, this sailing vessel was filled with people running. Some people were running *from* something. Most often those traveling from the small towns were people running from discrimination, religious oppression, poverty, or from the constant threat of more pogroms to come and brutally vanquish their villages. And some people were running *to* something. They had been comfortable in their apartments or homes, thriving in their businesses, but always with the knowledge that things could change. They were dreaming of the word *freedom*, which they believed was synonymous with America. They did not yet understand how one day, they would look back on this journey as a voyage of survival.

Rebecca was self-conscious as a lone traveler, and to fill time on the dock before the boarding process was underway, she surveyed the crowd to invent more stories. Suddenly, there was a screeching voice emanating from a young woman who was flinging her arms wildly and throwing clothes from her suitcase everywhere. "You stupid, haughty woman," she yelled out. "You are blind and mean and self-centered." A minute later, the young woman vomited all over herself and the shoes of the older woman on the receiving end of her tirade. Rebecca was incredulous. What could be happening? The younger woman was obviously sick, and a uniformed man came forward to calm her down.

Rebecca felt so sorry for the older woman who had taken the verbal abuse, and she went to her aide. "Ma'am, can I help you in some way?" Rebecca asked. She opened her own suitcase and emptied a pillowcase of its contents, and then she used the pillowcase itself to help clean up the woman. "What can I do for you?" she asked again.

The woman, although obviously a lady of prominence, seemed unnerved with no one to turn to. Then the girl started yelling at her again. "I told you I didn't want to go with you on this voyage. I told you many times. But you only thought of yourself, your grand self."

"But I bought you so many new clothes to wear as you accompany me," the lady whined back. "Why would you give that all up? You know I need your help as my maid."

Once again, the young woman picked up the clothes from the open, battered suitcase and threw more of them in the air. "You stupid fool. Can't you even understand that I am pregnant? That's why I feel seasick, even on the land. You can keep your stupid clothes. Victor will take me home and we will enjoy your grand manor together, while you go to America."

Now, Rebecca identified Victor as a chauffeur and quite possibly the father, although even he seemed in a wide-eyed state of shock at the scenario.

"Paulina, you never told me this," he said to the maid. Then he turned to the older woman. "Madame Rabinowitz. I have no idea, myself, what this is about. I promise you that I have had no relationship with Paulina. I have honestly thought she was a bad seed since you hired her. Seriously, I am old enough to be her father. And I can assure you that I am not the father of this baby." He paused, put his head down, and moved closer to her. "The Great War was not good to me, I must confide," he said, inferring a battle injury had left him childless. "I will take Paulina away, back to her mother's house, and I will watch over your home while you are gone. Or I will do the best that I can."

The driver, controlling his urge to give the girl the slap he felt she deserved, walked Paulina back to the dock entrance and placed her in the carriage. He grabbed the boarding pass from her hand and returned to give it to Madame. Then he looked at Rebecca. "You seem nice. Perhaps, can you help Madame Rabinowitz in any way?"

Rebecca recognized this Madame as someone who was used to being catered to. She was concerned for her, as she looked so bewildered at this turn of events. "Young woman," the lady said, "who are you traveling with and where are your people from?"

"I am alone, ma'am."

"And you are going to New York alone?"

"It's a long story," Rebecca said, and she started to tear up. "I am going to meet my fiancé who has gone ahead to America to start our new life. But an uncle who sponsored his journey wrote that he was not allowed past the gates of Ellis Island, and he is quarantined in the infirmary."

"Oh my, from one drama to another." Mrs. Rabinowitz shook her head and then paused, seemingly exasperated. "What is your name, If I may ask?"

"I am Rebecca."

"And may I see your ticket, dear?" She looked it over and

said, "Alone and in second class?" She shook her head, sympathetically. "Listen, you are sweet, and I can see, perhaps with a good heart to help. Maybe I can help you, too. Have you been in service?"

"Service?" Rebecca questioned, innocently.

"Yes, dear, household service – paid help," the matron said.

But Rebecca laughed. "No, I am sorry, only household service – unpaid – to my parents. My mother has had a long illness and recently died. I am the only daughter, the only child . . . and a dressmaker."

"Where are you from?" Mrs. Rabinowitz asked. There was a quality in this lovely young woman's carriage and speech that she could identify. They were speaking Yiddish to each other, the universal language of the eastern European Jews, although just as Mrs. Rabinowitz herself interspersed German and Polish words in her speech, having traveled often to the major cities of countries that touch borders, she picked up Russian phrases from Rebecca's vocabulary.

"I am from St. Petersburg, actually. Jacob, my fiancé, is from a small town in the Pale. But he traveled often to the larger cities for trade. That's why he was eager to accept his uncle's offer. It could be the fulfillment of his dreams – an opportunity to move to another country, another life, to not be under the strictness of his upbringing in the small village where he was raised before a short time in my city."

"You are Jewish?" she inquired, and Rebecca nodded.

"I am as well. Our use of Yiddish betrays us. But tell me, his village – extremely observant Jews? The *yamakas*, even black hats, the beards, the, what do you call them, the curled earlocks?"

"The *payas*," Rebecca reminded her. "Yes, that and the prayer shawls, *tallis* over and – yes, fringe under their garments."

"Oh my," Mrs. Rabinowitz moaned out in a pathetically tolerant tone. "I understand his wanting to leave – this is the twentieth century."

Although Rebecca agreed, she felt she needed to defend Jacob. "You dismiss it all so quickly – but he was raised that way. I am not sure it is so easy to toss aside your beliefs." He came with his family to St. Petersburg for a few years. And just recently, the uncle in America sent him the funds for his ticket to New York."

"Well, let me make you a proposition. Obviously, I find myself alone and in need of a companion. You won't have to think of yourself as a maid. Yes, a companion . . . I would like that with a young Jewish woman of your character. Good riddance to that horrid girl! And your pay will be an upgraded cabin and table, and this valise of new clothes which should fit you just fine."

"I have brought my own wardrobe. Thank you, anyway."

"My dear, then I will be frank. I have the rheumatism and I will need your help. May I speak to the captain regarding this change?"

Rebecca nodded her head, shyly, and gave her a warm smile. "I would thank you for that, madame. I don't care as much about having the better accommodations, as I do about having the company. As I said, I recently lost my mother."

"Well then, I am pleased to meet you, Miss Rebecca . . ."

She paused and Rebecca added, "Rushman."

On board the ship, they were escorted to a very impressive suite. She knew that Madame envisioned that she had led an impoverished and sheltered existence and expected her to play the role of the grateful waif. Rebecca did show her gratitude, but she felt that over time and conversations, Mrs. Rabinowitz would come to understand who her parents were – her father an educated, respected man and a community leader, and her mother a couturier to the elite.

At dinner the first evening, as the steward led the two women to the entrance of the elegant dining room, Rebecca had to hide a slight giggle behind her covered mouth. Madame thought Rebecca was overwhelmed at her good luck. But that was not the case. Rebecca found it humorous because her friends would not believe this. They had playfully asked to see what she was packing for the voyage to America and had laughed at her. "You understand your ticket is only for second class," Sarah had pointed out.

And Gitel, continuing the tease, added, "It's not steerage, but I doubt you will have occasion to be dressed for a grand ball."

At the time, she laughed with them. "You know I am bringing the fashions to show the uncle the type of work I am capable of, so maybe I could be offered a job or lodging while I wait for Jacob to be released," she said. And then she wondered if she would find new friends like these, with whom to enjoy an easy camaraderie going forward. She would miss that. It was actually the first time it struck her that she would need to learn a new language if she really wanted to be comfortable in America. For the first night, however, Rebecca did not select a fancy dress. She chose a modest suit ensemble for dinner, but one she felt had flattering lines.

The following afternoon, the ship had reached its first destination, England, and their dinner table, which had five empty seats the previous evening, now welcomed new guests who had embarked at the Port of Southampton. There was a cosmopolitan-looking couple, the Grossmans, returning to New York from a business trip for the husband and a shopping holiday in Paris and London for the wife. And then there was a most elegant-looking gentleman, possibly thirty years old. Harrison Abelman politely introduced the table to his fiancée, Beatrice Arnberg, and Mrs. Florence Arnberg, her mother, who was accompanying them. It was an entire table of Jewish passengers. Harrison helped to bridge the conversation gap between languages, speaking both English and Yiddish. His fiancée and her mother, who did most likely speak both languages, seemed uncomfortable that he lowered himself to admit it. Through the dinner, Beatrice retained a snobbish, pinched look on her face and was more interested in admiring herself in her pocket mirror than engaging with the group. But her mother was too much a garrulous busybody to maintain a pretense of distance. Mrs. Rabinowitz made a spur of the moment decision to introduce Rebecca as her niece, rather than simply her companion. She felt that this beautiful young woman should be given the opportunity to be accepted as a social equal by the passengers, as she certainly was not a servant.

After Mrs. Rabinowitz said it, Rebecca hugged her and gave her a kiss on the cheek. It was a generous gesture. "Auntie, thank you for everything," she whispered to her. And Madame's instincts were right. Immediately, the future mother-in-law commented on Rebecca's beautiful dress. On this second night, she was wearing a sapphire blue choice. "My dear," Mrs. Arnberg said in English, with Harrison translating as the dialogue progressed. "I have to say what an exquisite gown you are wearing."

Rebecca lowered her head, accepting the compliment humbly. "Thank you. My mother designed this dress for the Russian Princess Tatiana. She thought it would be a one-and-only original, but we had never promised that. And so I feel no guilt in having copied it for myself, changing only the lace motif."

Too quickly, Harrison commented on the striking color. His fiancée would probably have reproached him with a glare, but she seemed to be more interested in continuing a flirtatious eye dialogue with a gentleman at an adjacent table. Auntie and Rebecca kicked each other lightly, unseen beneath the floor length tablecloth, and Auntie muttered under her breath, "And so the show continues." Rebecca felt that she had been plopped in the middle of a French farce like one she had seen at the Russian theater, and she was only waiting for the murder mystery to begin. The characters were stereotypes – the helpless matron, the fiancée flirting with the wealthy widower, and so on.

Soon, Pamela and Edward Grossman joined the table conversation, with Mrs. Grossman saying, "I am wondering, what if you would happen to see this princess at a future event?"

Rebecca looked at them all incredulously. "But surely you know, the Bolsheviks executed Princess Tatiana, along with her entire Romanov family, the family of the tsar and tsarina, Nicholas and Alexandra."

"My God," Pamela gasped, and echoes of the same sentiment circled around the table. The New York wife could not reconcile the brutality of the Russians having crossed the life of this lovely young woman before her.

As each course of the dinner was served, one after another, the guests left the table to retire to their rooms, the travel day and the sea air having tired them all out. First, Rebecca walked Auntie to their suite to get her settled for the night. And then the Grossmans, chatting with Beatrice's mother, all walked together to their rooms. When Rebecca returned to the table, only Harrison remained. When she greeted him, he said, "Call me Hershel, Hershey, if you wish." She doubted that the absent Beatrice would approve of the Yiddish nickname, but she knew she was not within earshot. Rebecca had seen her walking the hall with the man she was eying earlier.

"Hershel, are you aware your fiancée is not in the room?"

He shifted uncomfortably in his chair and lowered his gaze. "I make it a point not to be bothered by her actions, or I'd just be constantly annoyed."

He seemed a man of substance and prestige, and so Rebecca wondered why he would buy into such a relationship. At first, she thought she could not wait to share this turn of events with Auntie when she woke in the morning, but then thought better of it and decided to keep it to herself, lest she be labeled a gossip. Rebecca and Harrison sat together for some time, finishing their cups of tea and desserts.

Finally, Harrison worked up the courage to admit what he was trying to hide. "I say, Rebecca," he began. And then he hesitated. "I may call you that, may I?" She was captured by his formal manners and longed to understand his language without the translation.

"Or call me Rivka, my Yiddish name, when no one is around," she answered with a smirk. It was a joke.

"I do feel I would like to be honest with you about something, Rebecca."

"It seems I have nothing but time," she said, easily. She leaned into him slightly and laughed. "It needn't be a ship of secrets, you know. What is on your mind?"

Before he answered, he went through the same rigid habitual series of moves she had noticed every time attention was shifted in his direction. He would pull down on his coat jacket, secure the knot of his tie, and readjust the length to which his brilliantly white shirt sleeves were revealed at his wrists, so that they were exactly even. "What I will say is embarrassing for me to reveal. You will understand from this, that I have had too little experience in relationships with women."

She angled her head toward him, encouraging him to continue.

"Beatrice had asked that I present her as my fiancée, although I have barely courted her as a girlfriend. I am not unaware that she may be using me for this trip, this opportunity to go to America, to go to the premier city of New York, funded by a company eager to pay for any family transportation. And I wouldn't be surprised if she left me there as I proceeded on to my final destination. I have been offered a position in the United States, in the state of Florida."

"Hershel," Rebecca said with a surprising force. "I am looking at you. I am speaking with you. I am only identifying a man of good character, a handsomely presented, fastidious person, in dress and speech. It's hard to reconcile that with the person you are detailing."

He ignored her compliments, knowing they were buffering an understandably skeptical assessment of him as a man.

"Harrison, what is your job, your vocation?"

"I am in the hospitality business. Most currently, I worked my way up to a wonderful post at the Savoy Hotel in London. I was the front desk manager."

Rebecca, impressed with his answer, smiled and nodded her head. "And I have to say, I am not surprised to hear that. You look the part." But never one to keep all her thoughts to herself, she had a question for him. "May I ask you something? How long have you and Beatrice been together?"

Harrison shook his head and looked down, as if knowing his answer would only reinforce her poor view of him. "We first began seeing each other just three months ago. And then when this opportunity was presented to me, she proposed that we just get engaged, and she would accompany me."

"In other words, she literally was the one who proposed," Rebecca said, pressing her palm against her forehead and shaking her head, as if it was the most ridiculous thing she had heard.

Harrison was mortified. "I know. I am a fool. As I have said, I have had little experience in courtship. I have been singularly directed toward my career."

Rebecca thought about it. "I am wondering why you would leave your great job? It's not like you lived in my Russian borders, where our existence as citizens and especially as Jews is always precarious, with pogroms, wars, and revolutions our constant threat."

"You are very smart, Rebecca. I am well aware of your point. I would have to accept that I have been lucky. My grandfather settled years ago in a nation that has molded into a more civilized constitutional monarchy." He was serious in his delivery, and she enjoyed hearing how the British accent gave such a sophisticated sound to his Yiddish translation. Already, she was eager to learn his language, the language of America as well.

"May I tell you a story?" he asked.

"Of course, why not?"

"Our hotel, The Savoy, is a very prestigious and busy one. I will be honest; it is an expensive one. And so, we cater to an elite clientele, both British and international." He looked around the emptying dining room and saw Beatrice in conversation with a man at a table in the far corner. He made no comment and continued talking. "About a month ago, I noticed a man sitting in a lobby chair, hiding behind a large newspaper he was supposedly reading. I remembered him checking in earlier, under an American company name. I actually felt that he was watching me at my work, following each of the interactions of my morning. I wondered if he were from our hotel management and perhaps preparing a report on my efficacy. Every few minutes, he would move the sheet to the left or right and peer around the print, as if he were a spy in an espionage play. Truly, it was more than comical. After some time of this, he finally approached me with an explanation. He presented me with his card and that of a William R. Kenan, Jr., president of the Florida East Coast Hotel Company, whose family owns the most prestigious resort hotel in America, in Palm Beach, Florida. He had been sent to England by the company to stay at upscale accommodations in three cities. This Kenan fellow had charged him to be on the lookout for any suitable personnel for an assistant managerial position in America. He summarized my own morning for me and said he was most impressed with my handling of a litany of situations."

"And so, what was the morning like for a posh hotel front desk manager?" Rebecca wanted him to know she was engaged in his story.

"He detailed my usual dramas: a titled duke whose reservation was not on the books, in my opinion most likely because it was never made, was satisfied with a suite on the third floor. An elderly couple who were extremely annoyed that their room was not yet ready, although they had arrived hours before check-in time, was offered a complimentary breakfast as they waited. A young couple had three wild children creating havoc in the lobby, until I had a bellman escort them and their ineffectual nanny to the park across the street. The head of housekeeping was too loudly and publicly complaining to me about a maid once again not showing for her shift, so I discreetly brought her into my office to calm down from her diatribe."

Rebecca was amused. "And then he offered you the position?"

"Incredibly, he did so on the spot. We discussed details the next day. The pay was higher than I was currently receiving, and my post would be elevated. He was given the authority. He said that Mr. Kenan had come up with the idea that a capable Englishman would add the touch of class, the status, they were looking for." Again, Harrison adjusted his tie, pulled down on his formal garment so that it lay perfectly smooth and impeccably molded to his physique, and then he stood, turned around, and gave a slight bow, as if illustrating what that touch of class would be. "The gentleman knew they wanted someone around my age, who would have experience in hospitality, but be amenable to adjusting to a new environment. At that point, I knew what I needed to put forth to this hotel representative."

"And that was?"

"I wanted him to know, up front, that I was Jewish. If that would be a problem, then I would want it known before making the change of employment."

"And?"

"He thought for a moment, and said that it actually could be a plus. He said that one segment of their hotel clientele included Jewish families on winter holiday, stressing they were the most elite New Yorkers, such as the Guggenheims and the Warburgs, names who we have even had at the Savoy, as it turns out. He felt that, certainly, someone who understood their specific needs could only be an asset." Harrison smiled up at her, with a "who would believe it" grin. "So now I find myself on my way to this next adventure of my life." He said it with a buoyancy in his voice that was unmistakable.

"And yet, you are engaged to be married, but somehow I'm not sensing you are embracing that adventure with the same enthusiasm." Rebecca suddenly felt her words were too strong and she worked to soften them with a sympathetic smile. "You should be proud of yourself. I just hope you will be happy."

"You understand," Harrison answered meekly, after a long pause to work up his courage. "Beatrice barely knows me, barely likes me, barely tolerates the full-time requirements of my current twenty-four-hour-a-day job, or my work ethic to fulfill all of its demands."

"I think I would hide this information from your new employer, for the time being," Rebecca said, "as perhaps the hiring of staff will be included in your new responsibilities as an assistant manager." She stepped back and looked him over. "Now, I need to be honest with you. My mother always told me that the most important decision you could ever make is in choosing your spouse, your life's partner – this would be your most important 'hire.' You should have a strong passion for her, and she for you. And you should share passions for other interests. Forgive me if I am overstepping, but how can you succeed in 'guest relations' if you can't succeed in 'personal relations?'"

He just looked down and shook his head. He knew she was right. "And so, it is my turn to ask you something, and I ask this without knowing anything about you, except that I know you are traveling with your aunt."

"And even that one piece of information is not the truth," Rebecca readily interjected, her face a reflection of embarrassment.

"What?" he exclaimed, loudly enough that others, still finishing at dining tables, turned in their direction. The fiancée, luckily perhaps, had left the room once more.

"Oh no," Rebecca began, humiliated. "I would hate for you to think I was trying to deceive people in any way. I was ready to board the ship with my own second class ticket when I was swept into a raucous encounter near to where I was standing. A young woman was screaming at this flustered older lady, throwing the contents of her suitcase everywhere. It turned out that it was Mrs. Rabinowitz's maid, who was pregnant and did not want to go on the ship."

She told him the details of the story and he could barely believe it. "You are a very good person indeed, helping Mrs. Rabinowitz, even wiping up vomit. And you were just a by-stander? Certainly, I wonder, who would ever do that? And I will answer my own question. Only a very good person, a kind soul, would do that."

"It's just, I had no idea who these people were, but I wouldn't have wanted my own mother treated like that. Mrs. Rabinowitz said she couldn't make the crossing by her-self, and she pleaded with me to accept an exchange of my ticket for a first-class ticket and accompany and assist her. Of course, I realized it would certainly mean nicer accommoda-tions, but what I most liked was the idea of not being alone. And I have just lost my own mother. I had no idea she would introduce me as her niece instead of her maid or companion, until she said it. There was no intent of deception on my part, I promise."

Now Harrison was trying to make Rebecca feel better. "May I ask now, how did *you* come to be on this ship?"

"Well." She shook her head and took a sip of water. "It's a long story, but it starts with this. I am doing as I am preach-ing to you. I am following my passion. Literally, following my fiancé." In making her point, she did not want to appear rude, but it did strike her as funny. "Yes, that would be the man who proposed to me, not the other way around," she explained. "He had gone ahead to America to begin a new life in a safe place, sponsored by an uncle, and then he was to send for me, and his father and sisters would follow. But the uncle wrote that he has taken ill and is still being held at Ellis Island, the immigration processing center. And now I am counting the days until I see him, to be in his arms, once he is well again."

Harrison looked almost envious. "From your voice, I can hear that you must love him." From the way that Harrison said the word "love," Rebecca could tell that it was new to his vocabulary.

"Already you are learning from me, to recognize love. I don't want to hurt you, but in all honesty, from our conversations, I cannot tell that you love your intended from your voice." Once again, her words were harsh, though she was easily able to temper them with a compliment. "But I can tell you have a passion. It is a passion for your work; it is a passion for hotels."

He smiled at her insight. He was drawn to her, although he knew she was already spoken for, and he was as well. When he saw she was trying to hide a yawn from the late hour, he said, "Shall we call it a night for now, and continue the conversation tomorrow?"

The next day, Rebecca helped Mrs. Rabinowitz with her morning routines, and, at breakfast, they got to know each other better. Madame was a childless widow, and she planned to make her way to Cleveland to stay with her brother. She was not sure if she would be returning to Krakow.

By lunchtime, Rebecca spotted Harrison strolling the deck. Beatrice and her mother were by his side, but when they went to the table to eat, he did not follow. "I'll take a few more minutes of the fresh air," he said to them. He had caught sight of Rebecca at the railing, a sketchpad in her hand. Madame had wanted to go back to the room to rest.

Alone with Rebecca, Harrison resumed their conversation, as if hours had not passed. He looked at what she was drawing and asked if she was an artist. "No, not really an artist, only to the extent that I would need to do drawings for my dress and table linen designs."

He looked closer at the artwork. "Impressive," he said, "Just like you." He leafed through a few more of her pages. "I've been thinking about what you said to me yesterday, about having a passion. It reminded me so much of what I was told about Mr. Henry Flagler, the founder of the hotel group I will be working for. He had a passion for business and then for hotels and rail-roads. And this is all I know, but I am eager to become a part of the company."

"I'm excited for you." Rebecca broke in. "You remind me of my Jacob. He had dreams of an expanded business, but your dreams are on their way to fulfillment and on a grander scale."

On the last night of the voyage, Harrison made a show of asking each of the women at the table for a turn on the dance floor. Rebecca had a feeling that he wanted a few min-utes alone with her, to say goodbye. He was a nice man, and she truly hoped his future would be bright. He talked his way through a slow waltz with her, his arms appropriately high on her shoulders, never breaching a respectable gap between them. When they sat back down for dessert and coffee, he had the opportunity he seemed to be seeking. "If things don't work out for you, I will do my best to find you a position at my new hotel. And with my hotel experience already, I will give you a little advice, since you have given me so much. Possibly, you have already surmised this, as I have come to know how very bright and intuitive you are. The better positions will go to those who are most fluent in the language of the country. That will be your key to success in America. Language often defines people. You saw already how Beatrice and her mother cringe at my use of Yiddish, even though they know me quite capable of the King's English. A fluency in English will open a world of opportunities for you. He surreptitiously handed her a folded note on the ship's stationary. "I have written out in English the name and location of the hotel, and my name."

She unfolded the slip of paper and looked up at him, indicating that he should read it aloud. He pointed to each word as he said them: "The Breakers Hotel, Palm Beach, Florida, Harrison Abelman." And then he extended his hand for a farewell shake. "I hope you will find your Jacob and follow your passion. But, and I mean this, if something does not work out, please let me help you in any way I can. Do not think I have dismissed what you have said. You have already helped me so much." He had been looking into Rebecca's huge brown eyes and suddenly realized that he had not yet released her hand. He brought it to his lips for a European farewell, not even caring if the beady-eyed Beatrice was out of sight or not.

Chapter 15

PALM BEACH 1975

After a few days in the hospital, Kathryn Morgan had improved enough to complain about missing the plush decor of her suite at The Breakers Hotel. She was impatient for her daughter's visit, as she fought with the nurse over the day's first round of blood draws and temperatures and blood pressures. She knew that the doctor had asked Beth to be at her room around ten o'clock. He wanted both women present at the end of his morning rounds when he would give an assessment of her condition.

Awaiting his arrival, Beth described the beautiful dinner the night before with Bear and the Bernsteins, Addie and Nate. She told Kathryn that Bear considered them an aunt and uncle. "They were bragging about him," Beth said. "Bear had already told me he had a PhD, but they told me more." She paused, knowing the next piece of information would impress her mother. "He went to Yale," she said. "Turns out, being a docent at The Breakers is one of his part-time positions, while he is working on turning his dissertation on Henry Flagler, the founder of The Breakers, into a book." Beth laughed a little to herself. "Your new doctor is his biggest fan. He said Bear already has a couple of college teaching offers on the table."

Kathryn was obviously enjoying Beth's accounting of the evening, but then she suddenly grabbed at her arm as she had done in her most agitated state when she was admitted to the hospital. "Remember Beth, I needed to speak to Bear about what he said on the tour. You know I gave him my card."

"Yes, Mom. That's why Bear called our suite, but it was on the day you became ill. Believe me, he's been waiting for the doctor's okay to speak to you."

When Nate entered right on time, Beth smiled to herself at the power of his hospital jacket and professional clipboard. Last night at Ta-boo on Palm Beach's famous Worth Avenue, he blended in with the society group. The restaurant patrons were a homogeneous crowd – good-looking, successful people, likely ranging in status from affluent to extremely wealthy, all well dressed and impeccably mannered. But now, when he entered the room as Dr. Nathan Bernstein in his white hospital lab coat, taking a second chair from the corner and bringing it next to Beth's, she was compelled to stand. It may be true that "clothes do make the man," but this wrinkled, pen-marked jacket, with *Chief of Medicine* embroidered under his name, inspired more respect than the most elegantly tailored dinner suit seen the night before. He was a physician, a leader even among his colleagues. Nate motioned for Beth to sit down. He directed his words to her mother. "Kathryn, may I speak freely now, to keep Beth in the loop with your medical history and current condition?"

Reluctantly, almost ashamedly, she nodded and said, "Yes."

"I'll tell you what I am thinking," Nate continued. "I'm not releasing you now. We will be running some more tests. We'll be keeping you here for a while, at least for a couple weeks is my best guess." Nate had been speaking slowly and seriously. With his black glasses slipping down the bridge of his nose, he offered compassionate eye contact with Kathryn over their rims, until finally he paused and took them off completely. Dr. Bernstein believed Kathryn may have had a mild stroke. When he explained this to her and Beth, he said to consider it as a wake-up call, a lucky thing, a warning sign for medical attention before any major disabling episode would occur. Nate told them he had consulted with Kathryn's New York physician. And he revealed to Beth something she had not known. Her mother had been undergoing cancer screenings, but so far, luckily, it did not seem that she had lung cancer, which was suspected. "Nevertheless, she's going to need a recuperation and rehabilitation period here. We are going to lower that blood pressure and she will have to change some of her habits immediately, especially her smoking, which is obvious, and I suspect she will need to limit or eliminate her drinking. I have already scheduled consultations with some specialists."

Two days later, as Kathryn's condition remained encouragingly stable, there was a knock on the hospital room door. Beth opened it and introduced Addie Bernstein to her mother. Addie had confirmed to her husband what he had suspected. Something that Beth had revealed about her family history at their dinner together had been a trigger, a catalyst, for Addie's own memories. Perhaps Addie had a clue to the cause of Kathryn's emotional distress.

Addie walked to Kathryn's bedside. "Mrs. Morgan, I am so pleased to meet you," she said enthusiastically, extending her hand. Beth's mother covered that hand with her own.

"Please, call me Kathryn," she said, very sweetly. "You look familiar to me," she added, and then paused to think about it. "You work at the hotel, don't you, dear? You checked us in."

Beth became nervous. "You know, she's Addie Bernstein, your doctor's wife, and in these past days I've come to call her my friend." Beth added this quickly, afraid her snobbish mother might be dismissive of Addie as merely a hotel employee. Addie, understanding the scenario, just continued with her natural warmth.

"You know, Kathryn, I remember meeting you as well. You were such a beautifully dressed woman. I was thinking immediately that you were from New York, probably Manhattan. And now, from spending time with your lovely daughter, I know I am right."

Kathryn smiled at her, listening intently, not knowing that Beth was directing a "good work" sign at Addie that Kathryn could not see.

And then Addie continued, "I would like to talk to you a

bit, Kathryn. I hope you won't think this intrusive. But your daughter is concerned that something is bothering you and it might have to do with our hotel. I recall from the 'previous stay' notes that always accompany our reservation cards that you did visit us sometime in the mid-1940s."

Kathryn had an uncomfortable look on her face, and Beth was beginning to question if she had made the right decision encouraging the visit. But then Addie continued speaking, not releasing her eye contact with Kathryn. "I know what I'm going to tell you will seem strange, and it is something I have never confided in anyone, not even my husband. But I have this crazy feeling that what my own mother predicted at that time, so many years ago during the war years, might be proving true now." Addie placed a hand on her forehead and just shook her head. It was a clever move, as if she were transferring focus from whatever may have been Kathryn's problem, to a need to resolve her own issue. Beth had no idea where this was going, but she could see how her mother was relaxing and listening.

Addie started inching her chair toward the bedside, until Beth motioned for her to take the closer seat and they exchanged positions. "You see, Kathryn," Addie began, "my father, Harrison Rushman, was recruited from his position at the London Savoy Hotel to be an assistant manager at The Breakers. Just months later, he met my Russian mother, Rebecca, onboard the ship to America. Eventually she joined him, and they married. When I was growing up, I actually lived at The Breakers Hotel with my family, from my birth until the 1950s.

"Beth had told me how you followed part of Bear's historical tour and you learned how the war came to our shore.

Suddenly, everyone was focused on the war effort. Initially, I was so frustrated. I was not old enough to do anything or young enough to be content doing nothing. But my mother said that wasn't true. She insisted that I would be a very important person. Aside from my volunteer position when The Breakers became an army hospital, she envisioned that I would be the link between the generation that came before and those that would follow and that I should consider my job was to be a listener, to be a watcher, to understand what was going on and to make sense of it someday. She said that I would be one of many, perhaps, who would tell the story of our beautiful hotel. People need to know that The Breakers was not just a record of the rich of America, it was the story of the building of America. Our beautiful resort would affect the lives of people rich and poor, of guests and staff and community residents through many decades. There are big stories everyone will know, stories of the giant man, Henry Flagler, who had his vision for developing Florida on a grand scale. And there are little stories of human interactions, stories that no one will know, unless those who were there can unravel the truths."

"Addie," Beth said, "your mom sounds incredibly insightful. I would think most people could only verbalize that in retrospect."

Addie was silent for a while, thinking how to phrase an answer, to be prideful, not boastful. "My mother, Rebecca, is a special person who is greatly admired. She has lived a life of challenges, and yet she remains strong, optimistic, and caring."

Addie stood up and went to pour herself a drink from the ice water pitcher on the counter.

"And somehow, I have a feeling that my mother's prophesy

may be fulfilled through you," Kathryn sat up straight in the bed and brought her hand to rest above her left breast and patted her heart. She could not find the appropriate words to say but was gesturing that the story was grabbing her emotions. Addie turned momentarily with her back toward Kathryn. "Beth, would you mind if your mother and I spoke privately for a little while?" Beth nodded, and, taking a book from the table to put in her purse, she headed for the visitors' lounge. With perfect timing, as if on cue, Bear was just emerging from the elevator and joined Beth for a walk.

Addie went back to the bedside chair. She took out a decorated shoebox from a bag that she had brought. She placed it on her lap. "Now Kathryn. It's just the two of us here. No confidences will leave the room unless you choose them to." Kathryn, appearing confused, but intrigued, just nodded, as Addie continued. "If I told you that I may have some answers for you, would you give me an idea of what is bothering you?"

For a long time, Kathryn just bit her lower lip and said nothing. Addie had the feeling that she wanted to speak, but she was forcing herself to keep her thoughts private. "Then let me ask you just one question. Your daughter said you seemed to be disturbed about a letter or trying to recall a name you couldn't remember. You said it was like Nate, but not Nate." Addie spoke slowly, wanting to carefully monitor Kathryn's reactions to what she was saying, as if she were a nurse trained to read a heart monitoring machine. Still, Kathryn remained mute, although her demeanor was changing. Twice, she opened her mouth, as if she would answer, but she could not force the words to come. She seemed to be seriously contemplating whether she should confide in this person, this very lovely doctor's wife and front desk manager before her.

"Then can I ask you this, Kathryn. You don't have to answer me, but I have a feeling you will," Addie persisted. "Is the name that is on your mind perhaps the name Natalie?"

Her reaction time was like that of a movie reel in slow motion, moving forward, frame by frame. Kathryn brought her hand to her forehead, covering half an eye and shaking her head. Then her mouth gaped open, until finally she gave out a gasp and she covered it. Addie shifted quickly from her chair, moving to sit on the bed next to Kathryn. She put her arms around her and began talking softly. To an onlooker, they would have appeared as lifelong girlfriends, sharing a secret. "We're just taking steps to unravel a story here. Whatever remorse you feel you are carrying for something you may have done, I assure you, is a burden that can be lifted. Most often, situations can resolve themselves, and you may have tortured yourself for actions or inactions you have done, but they did not affect the outcome of something outside of your control."

"So, you know then. You know the guilt I bear. You know about the letter that I never delivered to my parents. You understand what I have done. How cruel I have been. How I only thought about myself. I stupidly wanted to protect my perfect little world that turned out to be not so perfect." After rattling off thoughts she had repressed for years, Kathryn had questions of her own. "But how do you know about any of this? How did you even know this name I have blocked from my mind was the name Natalie?"

"It was something that Beth said when telling us that you seemed tormented about your past, about something you had done, and you seemed very interested in the story of the babies born at The Breakers when you were on Bear's tour. She was telling us, just a little, about her grandparents, your parents, and she happened to mention that they were in the scrap metal business in New York. And then suddenly, I felt I knew about the letter and the person. Maybe I knew what was weighing heavily on your conscience.

"Kathryn, I am asking you to give me a chance, to hear me out, to listen to some correspondence I have always kept in this private box. It includes letters from my best friend in those years, a beautiful girl who became like an older sister to me." She paused to take Kathryn's hands in hers once more, and she looked directly into her eyes as she spoke. "Her name was Natalie."

"No," Kathryn said, grabbing Addie's arm to capture her attention and stop her from continuing. "I don't know if I can bear it. I never even met her, but I did a horrible thing."

"Just hear me out though, Kathryn," Addie insisted. "You can fill in the parts of the story that I don't know and maybe from what I tell you, you will find a chance to be forgiven for whatever you have done, and a chance to forgive yourself." Now Addie sat back in the chair and removed a folded note from the shoe box. She reviewed it before revealing its contents, making sure she had pulled the right correspondence, and then she began talking.

"Over thirty years ago, Natalie gave me this letter to read, and she asked me to keep it safe for her, as she didn't know what direction her life would take. She had met her first real love when he came to Palm Beach in 1942 to help coordinate the area's role in the nationwide scrapping campaign. He began in civilian attire, as adjunct personnel, until he received his draft orders and was called to serve the army in Europe. He was such a sweet and handsome dreamboat; I would have fallen in love with him, myself, if I had been older and wasn't already crazy for Nate.

"They were together here for maybe three or four months, until he shipped out. And so now I am thinking, I guess I am asking you, was that adorable young man possibly your brother? Was your brother Theo Stanton, the man who loved Natalie, and who she loved so much?"

Kathryn began with soft whimpers, and Addie tried to comfort her. But when her sobs seemed to be wracking her body, Addie made a move to press the call button. Kathryn stopped her.

"No, let's go on," Kathryn said, taking tissues from the rolling stand and wiping her eyes.

"You are right, of course. My brother, Theo Stanton, had been in Palm Beach for a short time, in 1942, before he was sent overseas. And then he was killed in the war."

"Thank you, Kathryn. Thank you for sharing that with me. We were all devastated when we received the news. You understand, we only have had you registered at the hotel as Mrs. Kathryn S. Morgan. But now that I know, I have something to show you. I think, perhaps, this is a copy of the same letter that was sent to you."

Kathryn looked over the note. She nodded her head vehemently, but with a look of total shock, confirming it was just like the one she had received, torn up, and incinerated so many years ago. She hugged it to her chest. "Such a tender, loving letter from my brother, she sniffled out, grabbing a second tissue to wipe her nose. "I hated myself for destroying it. I don't care what happens now. To resurrect this letter, to 'hear' his voice once more, this is a gift to me. I don't care what happens to me. I want to take responsibility for what I did. I wish I could be able to set things right, but it's too late for that, isn't it? I loved my brother so much. I never believed the worst would happen. He was the strongest, most handsome, most conscientious boy – and yet I let him down with his one request of me. She handed the letter back to Addie. "Please, will you read it aloud to me?"

April 3, 1942
FOR YOUR EYES ONLY
To my dearest sister Kathryn:

I miss you, my cuddly Kitty and best friend. I write to you still thinking of how beautiful you were at your engagement party, and how ecstatically happy Mother was that you would be marrying Oliver Morgan. This marriage to a cousin of an elite banking family was her dream come true. And even then, when you could have been the center of attention, you cared so much that I meet Oliver's younger sister, Meredith. And you envisioned that our sibling bond would always remain strong if I were to pursue steps toward a future with her when I return from this assignment. Everything seemed to have fallen in place, except that I understand now that I had not fallen in love. Instead, I had fallen in line, in line with expectations. Oh, I do not blame you for that. I love you so much and know you only wanted the best for me. And so now, it is difficult for me to confess to you that I know I cannot complete the circle and offer a ring to Meredith. It breaks my heart to disappoint you, because you have only looked out for me my whole life.

But in my short time in Florida, I have fallen in love, in head-over-heels passionate love, with the most enchanting girl. I am hoping those are the same feelings you have for Oliver, that you did not only try to please Mother but you were true to yourself. My love is beautiful, and bright, and resourceful, and I cannot bear the thought of spending my life without her. She will remind you of a fairytale princess, tall and blond and serene and regal, with a charitable heart. She will remind you of the movie star Ingrid Bergman. But my star is named Natalie.

I counted myself lucky to have been able to serve so far in this Florida paradise. But now, I have received papers for an overseas assignment. I know how the Morgan family ridiculously feels our family "trade" is beneath them, and so I assure you I will do nothing now to upset your relationship with them. I need you to understand, though, that I never made any promises to Meredith. But I will still wait until sometime after your wedding to let her know where my heart lies, unless you feel you can intervene earlier.

But I am writing you now requesting a big favor. This is called an "in the event of" letter, and I am sending it only to you. My love for Natalie has defined my being since the minute I met her. And that love, with its passionate intimacy, has been mutual. Being realistic, there is always the possibility that Natalie could be pregnant, although we do not know anything at this point. I cannot wait longer, though, to let you know that we have every intention to marry when I return from my assignment. But if I do not return and there is a baby, I would want the child to be embraced by our family. I am telling you her first name only, because if something really does happen to me overseas and it turns out she is not pregnant, I would not want to hurt her reputation in any way. She is the most beautiful, caring individual. She will find happiness again, I know, if I should die in combat. I trust and love you, my sister, to confide in you. You have no idea of the magnificent mansions that line the ocean and adjacent streets in Palm Beach, and one of them is her home. She is from an established Palm Beach family, perhaps of even greater financial means than ours. That is something I never knew until well into our relationship, as I always met her in our work environment. I tell you this only so that if she does present herself to our parents, you will make them understand it is not because she is after our money. In fact, and I find this funny, because she knows I have a special position here because of my connections with the scrap metal business, I think she may even envision that we have a junkyard on our own residential property.

I have great love for you, and I hope I will return from overseas and be able to tell you this wonderful love story personally, and you will never need to present this letter to our parents.

Missing you much,

Your Brother Theo

Kathryn's soft sobs continued through the entire reading of the letter. At the end, when Addie tried to comfort her by rubbing her back and smoothing her hair from the top of her head to the nape of her neck, Kathryn waved her away. "You have to understand," she insisted, "all too soon, I regretted that I tore up the letter and threw it away and never even told my parents that I had received it. At the time, I had been self-centered and selfish, afraid that Theo's change of heart about Meredith Morgan would undermine my own world. If he had gotten another girl pregnant, it would certainly destroy my own future prospect of marriage to her brother, Oliver Morgan. But I swear this to you. When my family received the news that Theo had been killed, I waited every day for a year for this person to come to our parents' home. I wanted more than anything for his girlfriend to come. I had nightmares that melded into sweet dreams, that there was a little baby of my brother's that someday I could come to know and love. But to my knowledge, this girl, whose name I had blocked out and now you have resurrected, this Natalie, never did come to our house."

Kathryn paused to collect herself, looking down, embarrassed to reveal more. "But, in all honesty, I knew without question that my mother would have dismissed her immediately. She would know that the scandal of such a revelation would certainly result in the Morgan family convincing Oliver to call off our wedding. Can you imagine that? Do you see what a heartless genetic heritage I am formed from? Can you imagine? My parents had lost their precious son, and yet I knew they would not want to acknowledge a child born out of wedlock, for fear they would be ostracized from society, even if they would be turning away a grandchild they could claim."

At this point, Addie felt she had to interrupt Kathryn. "Listen to me," Addie said, placing her hands firmly on Kathryn's shoulders to literally grab her attention. "And listen to yourself. You did not do anything nearly as cruel as you believe your mother would have done. When you received the letter, your brother only wanted you to know about the woman he loved before he went overseas. Your brother was alive. He was that strong and self-assured and optimistic sibling that you loved so much. He was only telling you the possibility that his girlfriend could be pregnant. I won't tell you that what you did was right, destroying the letter and not telling your parents about it. But your brother also did not want to hurt Natalie's reputation and did not even tell you her full name for that reason. He put in Natalie's hands, also, the means to inform his family if she was pregnant. She had their address. It would have been up to Natalie to pursue a connection with her boyfriend's family in her own way, with her own copy of Theo's words, as evidence."

Kathryn, leaning back against the elevated mattress, focused on the overhead fixture in the room, until she shaded her eyes from it, as if she felt she had been captured in an interrogation spotlight. She picked up the controls for the room's mechanisms and pressed the call button for the nurse. A plumped-up balloon of a middle-aged woman entered the room, sucking the last bite of a piece of chocolate candy, boxes of which lined the counter of the nurses' station. "What can I help you with, dear?" she asked sweetly. She reached over Kathryn's body to disable the call light.

"Linda," Kathryn said, having read the name tag which had hovered precariously close to her eye. "Linda, could you possibly dim the light and help me walk to the lounge chair? I'm not even sure if I'm attached to any tubes."

"No, dear. You're free and clear. I'll help with your slippers," she answered, compassionately escorting her to the chair and smiling at Addie as she did.

When the nurse left the room, Kathryn motioned for Addie to move her chair closer. "Addie, you have to tell me. Was there a pregnancy? Was Natalie pregnant? Was there a baby? Please, I can take it. It's time. And it's better to know than to wonder."

"Just promise me," Addie said, "that you will listen to the whole story." Eagerly, Kathryn nodded and said, "Yes, I promise."

Addie took Kathryn's hand and smiled into her eyes. "Natalie found out that she was pregnant just weeks after we learned that Theo was killed in combat."

"Oh my God. There was a baby," Kathryn cried out, but she struggled to keep her self-control. She did not want Addie to call for medical attention, and Addie, respecting that, continued.

"Natalie was distraught from losing Theo. There was so much to think about. She didn't know where she would live, but she knew she would love that baby unconditionally. Maybe that's why she asked me to hold the letter for her, for safe keeping. Yes, Natalie did have Theo's baby." Addie paused, giving Kathryn time to compose herself and then she gave the older woman a hug and a warm smile. "I knew Natalie then, and I know Natalie now. I am telling you the truth. She is happy with her life. She does not blame you for anything. In fact, I bet she would like to meet you one day."

"You really think she would want to meet me?" Kathryn broke in.

"You will understand, in another letter, why she made the choice not to contact the family. But let's take a break now," Addie proposed, seeing the nurse peek into the room for the third time, indicating that Kathryn should rest.

"It's been quite an emotional journey, Kathryn. I think the staff is ready for me to leave you alone for a while. But I promise to return after lunch."

Chapter 16

NEW YORK 1923

As the ship finally docked in New York harbor, Rebecca could not believe how much Mrs. Rabinowitz had come to mean to her in a period of a week. It was as if she had her mother back by her side once more. She and Madame shared a long and teary-eyed embrace, wishing each other well, as they proceeded separately to their next destinations. Rebecca did not know yet that her temporary Auntie had hidden the equivalent of twenty American dollars in gold coins in the folds of Rebecca's undergarments.

Exiting the ship and saying her farewells, Rebecca had feigned an excitement and confidence to continue to the city, so that her new acquaintances would feel comfortable leaving her. But of course, the lonely feeling returned. She wondered if Jacob could possibly be at the uncle's home already, or if he was still being held in quarantine at the immigration center. From her pocketbook, Rebecca pulled out two pieces of folded paper, gave them each a quick glance, and put one back. The second she held in her hand. It was the Hester Street address of Jacob's Uncle Moishe, which she hoped might be her temporary home.

Behind her was Ellis Island, but first-class passengers did not pass through its lines, as they were processed on the ship. In front of her was the spectacular skyline of New York City, which was beyond anything she could have imagined. Although the lure of the city had a magnetic pull to her, she decided to make her way to Ellis Island while she was so close.

When, finally, she was directed to the correct area, Rebecca addressed the man at the counter. There were translators at all the stations. "Excuse me, sir," she said. "I am hoping to see if someone is still being held for medical evaluation or if he has received permission to enter America."

"Port of origin and date, name of immigrant?" she was asked in a terse, officious manner.

"Hamburg, Germany, March 27, 1923. His name is Jacob Schaevitz."

The man searched his records. "Miss, we have no one by that name in quarantine here, and no record of his being detained." She let out a slight cry, and the man finally looked up at her. He softened at her pretty face and could not help but feel sorry for her.

Rebecca was confused, but the official rushed her to call the next in line. She was thinking that there was some misunderstanding, that most likely Jacob had been released and was with the uncle's family already. She became anxious to take the ferry to the mainland and proceed to the uncle's place.

Once on Manhattan Island, Rebecca chose to walk to the apartment house from the dock area, as she wanted some exercise after a week confined to the ship. From the dock, she was easily directed to Hester Street. Perhaps still with sea legs from the voyage, she felt dizzy immersed in the vitality of the block and was knocked about by the throng of shoppers, street merchants, and food vendors. With help from a policeman, she eventually arrived at Moishe Schaevitz's address and climbed the flights of stairs to the apartment number written on her paper. She knocked numerous times on the door. There was no answer, which did not surprise her. There were loud and constant whirring sounds coming from the room that reverberated into the hall. She decided to try to open the door and she entered with no invitation. A man came quickly to the front room. He had not heard the door knocks; it was the cessation of the sewing machine sounds that had brought him to the entrance with his grim-faced look. He was thinking it was not yet near the time for the brief meal break he allowed his workers, and yet they seemed to have abandoned any production at their machines.

Then he understood. They were all staring at the young woman who had entered. The female laborers stayed seated and looked at one another with questioning glances. The men, however, could not help themselves. They all stood at their stations, unable to resist a better look. Rebecca was a fresh-faced vision standing before them. Her brown hair cascaded gently to her shoulders, held back on one side with a pearl barrette. Her beautifully tailored suit loosely followed the curved outlines of her body, and although the sleeve length of the jacket and the shoe length of the skirt could not be called immodest, the gawkers were unsettled in different ways. At her neckline, a triangle of flesh was showing. They did not know how important it was to Rebecca that she always be able to touch the cherished locket that was her mother's. It had been her anchor since her mother's passing.

In minutes, a short, puffy faced, full-figured woman appeared with four girls by her side. They were her little miniatures, perhaps ranging in age from seven to twelve years old. The clothes the mother was wearing made her look as wide as she was tall, embellished by layers of ill-fitting patterns. The girls had none of the restraint that age brings, and they each ran to touch Rebecca. They would not leave her alone, and so she took the barrette from her hair and placed it in each of theirs, by turn. They were delighted by this, each girl modeling in a circle when it was her time. The men at their machines were further unnerved by Rebecca's newly released flowing waves, and as they gazed longer, they saw how beautiful her large brown eyes were.

"What is going on here?" the man at the front screamed loudly in Yiddish, when he came close to the door. "Back to work," he shouted to the group. Rebecca presumed this was the uncle. She knew not to extend her hand in greeting, as the most religious Jews will not touch women in this manner.

I am Rebecca, Rebecca Rushman, from St. Petersburg . . . Jacob Schaevitz's intended, " she said eagerly. But when he just looked at her with no answer, she continued with a humbler tone. "The family received your letter. We were all worried about him, and so I was eager to be the one to come to see that he was all right or to help him." When Moishe seemed only to scowl at her, she instinctively moved away. She would have liked to have extended warm greetings to the women of the family. But now they seemed to have been given visual orders to keep their distance. She walked a few steps back to Moishe so they could converse. "I am hoping that Jacob is here with you, and I might see him. I am praying that he is well and working for you."

The uncle ran his hand over his full graying beard and twisted it almost to a point. He looked her over, but not with any of the masculine interest of his workers. His facial expression went from anger to disgust. With a nod of his head, he directed her to follow him to a back room. He did not invite her to sit.

"You were told this, I am sure, in my letter to my brother's family. Jacob was not released to America and was held at Ellis Island." He barely looked at her as he spoke. "You may put your suitcase down, although I am not sure why you have come," he said and shook his head, "unless you plan to work here, to take his place." The wife came from the kitchen with an assortment of baked goods and would not withdraw the plate she had offered Rebecca, although her husband shoo'ed her from the room.

"That was actually my intent, to help Jacob and help you as well. I know he wrote you of my experience as a seamstress and designer. But I was just at the immigration office," Rebecca said, thinking now that she was right in finding out her information before she left the dock area. "They have no record of Jacob Shaevitz being detained for medical reasons. He was admitted to the United States on the day the boat arrived, although there is some question about the spelling of the name." She was troubled by this uncle, but she would give him the benefit of the doubt. "Perhaps there has been a mistake."

"Oh yes, a mistake," the uncle responded, now with growing anger in his voice. "The mistake was paying for Jacob to come here. I did not want to upset my brother when I sent the letter. I did not want him to know the truth. My nephew, his son, pretended not to see me at the dock. He did not know that I recognized him. He came surrounded by a group of immigrants who want to be American goyim. His beard was mostly shaven, his *payas* gone, his clothes and hat like that of any newspaper vendor on the corner. I tried to get him to come with me. But he refused. He showed no respect." The uncle, turning his head to the side, made a spitting sound, but released no phlegm on his own floors. "Although I sponsored him, he had no gratitude, no sense of family. He shunned me."

"Something is not right," Rebecca posed, now on the offensive. "That is not the Jacob that I know. He is a good man, respectful of his elders, of his religion, although I know he was interested in the more modern practice of Judaism he saw in St. Petersburg."

"There is one way only," the uncle shot back adamantly. "He came here once and took more money from me, and we have not seen him in all these months. And you are one to talk . . . appearing at my home in an immodest dress in front of my innocent daughters!"

Rebecca's body began shaking, as if receiving a physical not just verbal blow. No one had ever spoken to her in this manner.

She walked over to the aunt and thanked her for her hospitality. She told her that she would not return to a home where she was not wanted, even if she had to live on the street. "Please," she whispered to her, "when I do find a place to stay, I will inform you and hope you will somehow send me word of any news about Jacob or tell me if a letter arrives from my father, as I gave him this address."

The aunt did not answer, only giving a side glance at her husband, but Rebecca felt she would try her best. Retrieving her suitcase, Rebecca walked out the door and began descending the staircase. At the bottom, she turned back and saw the teary-eyed faces of the mother and the little girls at the upstairs landing. They were very discreetly waving goodbyes at her, lest the father see them from behind.

Now it was Rebecca who was roaming the streets of New York, trying to find where she would belong. In the first week, guided by a flyer she had been given before her voyage, she was able to secure a room with a single bed in an affordable boarding house, and she sent the address back to her father and to Jacob's father in St. Petersburg. Rebecca had wanted to find a place to stay for a possibly extended period, where she could be accessible to communications from home. Although she knew nothing of the intricacies of the city, it did not take her long to know that she wanted to distance herself from the lower east side, since Jacob had apparently abandoned it as well. She did not believe the uncle's story. She believed her heart. And so, after she secured her housing, she sought out the aunt and slipped her a note with her contact information, when she spied her leaving home on the way to the market. Rebecca hoped she would transfer the paper to Jacob if she ever saw him.

Rebecca's naturally optimistic disposition was depleting like a child's balloon with a slow leak. She did fear that Jacob would not be returning to the workshop apartment, and she cried often throughout each day, wondering if she would ever feel his embrace again. She understood that Jacob did not know she had come to America. She felt that perhaps letters from him could be waiting for her back in Russia. As she walked and searched for work, she did not even know where she was headed, but she surveyed the New York City skyline once again and followed a path toward the tallest, most glamorous buildings. She wanted a respite from this ghetto world existence that had never been her home, even back in Russia.

Rebecca thought about Harrison's advice to learn English as soon as possible. She signed up for evening classes at one of the settlement houses on her list. She knew there were always seamstress jobs available in the garment district, but from what she had heard from the other boarders, she could not bear the suffocating life it would offer. Instead, she targeted the department stores, her suitcase in hand as a portfolio. She emerged as the star pupil in her English classes and was starting to help other immigrants. Her constant advice was to study the language, to find places to mingle with English speakers in a work or social environment, and to read English newspapers as often as possible. Within a year, as her English improved enough to match her stately carriage, she had risen from a job in alterations at the beautiful Bloomingdale's Department Store on 59th Street to a position in sales. The management was impressed how soon customers began asking for Rebecca by name.

But time was passing – almost two years had gone by without word of Jacob, and no letters from her father or Jacob's father had made their way to her. Finally, she received an answer to a pleading note she had addressed to the neighbor who was enjoying her mother Adele's clothes. Returning to her boarding house after work, Rebecca found the letter from Mrs. Gorshen slipped under her door. She resisted the urge to tear it open and instead, gently slid the letter opener from her top drawer under its flap, careful not to rip a word contained inside. As she read it, she gasped at the message, and then she could not muffle her heartbreaking cries. Her father, as he himself had feared, was taken away by the police soon after she left for America. Mrs. Gorshen wrote that the same had happened to many of his anti-Soviet comrades. They were transported to work camps, and one comrade who escaped reported witnessing executions. The regime had become ruthless in their treatment of dissidents.

Hearing her sobs, a sisterhood of new friends from adjacent rooms came to her door immediately to comfort her. It was her darkest hour and yet Rebecca felt less lonely than she had felt in the past two years, burying herself in the circle of their hugs.

It had been over a month since she last stopped at the uncle's location to inquire about Jacob, but still they insisted he had never returned. Since arriving in America, when Rebecca had walked the city streets, her heart always skipped a beat if she saw anyone who remotely reminded her of Jacob. But now she knew she must face two harsh realities. She most likely would never see either her father or Jacob again.

Chapter 17

NEW YORK 1925

The following morning, on her way to her Bloomingdale's job, a cup of coffee in one hand, Rebecca exchanged her usual greeting with the corner news vendor. Abruptly, she did a double take when she saw the newspaper front page, and she had to react quickly to control her shaking hand so the coffee did not stain his stack of papers. There, before her, was a bold-faced headline. She was stunned. She reached into her purse and felt for the piece of paper she had been carrying since her last day on the ship to America. "Oh my God," she cried out.

"Are you okay?" Solomon, the paper seller, asked her. With her head still down, her eyes glued to the newsprint, she handed him some coins. She folded the paper, wedged it in her underarm, and walked to the corner café. She ordered toast and set her copy of the *New York Daily News* squarely in front of her. And then she scanned the story that had captured her attention:

$5,000,000 PALM BEACH FIRE
Fire Razes Breakers Hotel

She took out the piece of paper that Harrison Abelman, the Englishman, had written out for her, and she confirmed that this was the hotel where he had been headed for his new position. She read the first paragraphs of the article to herself and put the newspaper aside. She asked the waitress for water and started to cry softly into her cupped hands.

"Are you all right?" the server asked in a most empathetic manner, patting the top of Rebecca's hand. But Rebecca could not speak, did not even know what to say, and waved her off, mouthing out a soft "thank you." She felt sick. She was sad for Harrison. She took in deep breaths and tried to think. The article detailed that no lives were lost and that made her begin crying again, this time with relief. Now and again, she had thought of Harrison in the ensuing years. They were not romantic thoughts like those that filled her nights of missing Jacob. But she felt they had made a powerful connection as friends. He seemed to be a good man, the only man in America who might even care about her. He did tell her to contact him if things did not work out as she planned. But that may just have been an extension of his polite demeanor. She wondered how life had worked out for him. Perhaps he did not even remember her. Should she go to him? Should she go to work and give them whatever notice time was required to resign her position? No, she realized, she must contact him first. Harrison could be married for all she knew. And anyway, there was no hotel for employment. The hotel had burned to the ground. She knew in their brief acquaintance that she valued Harrison's friendship and respected his work ethic, but she did not know if either of them shared feelings beyond that. She thought about her discussions with him on the ship, how she tried to school him in the knowledge of passion, and yet, who was she to give instruction? Where was her Jacob now?

After days of meandering around her adopted city, with further updates from the newspaper, Rebecca tried to clear her head and process all she had been through. She wrote Harrison a letter addressed to the now-incinerated Breakers and hoped it would reach him somehow. In it, she detailed everything that had happened to her in the past two years, all her upsets and her accomplishments in the time since they parted at the dock in New York City. It was a cathartic exercise for her and maybe one that could give her closure. She remembered so well her conversations with Harrison on the ship, how she had been enchanted by his love for hotels and the hotel business, and how she had teased him that she recognized no such passion in his relationship with his fiancée. She thought now that it was impossible how often she had seen the power of passion

be consumed in figurative fires – apathy, death, war, abandonment. But this fire was literal.

May 21, 1925
Palm Beach, Florida

My dear Rebecca:

You cannot imagine how much your letter has meant to me.
To receive news of you after all that has happened here recently has lifted my spirits tremendously. I thank you for
sharing your experiences over the past several years with me.
It does make me feel that I have not just imagined that we
made a strong connection on our voyage to America. Please
believe, I was saddened by each of your disappointments and
lifted by each of your joys. That any person should show you
disrespect and cruelty is beyond my grasp. I am proud of you
for having the courage to leave the uncle's home. I had, early
on, identified your strength of character that has continuously shown through. I grieved for you on hearing of the possible
loss of your father and cannot reconcile that your Jacob would
abandon you willingly.

On the other hand, you will not be surprised to hear
of the turn of events in my life, as we both, in all honesty
(and I did appreciate your honesty), could have anticipated
that Beatrice would not be remaining by my side for long.
Surprisingly, she and her mother did accompany me as I
journeyed south to my Florida destination. An area which
I interpreted as beautiful and lush, they only saw as a hot
and humid wilderness. Although there is so much that the

bordering town of West Palm Beach and our island paradise of Palm Beach have already developed, they had their bags packed and were on board Mr. Flagler's northbound Florida East Coast Railroad with their first mosquito bites. My guess is that they spent some time in New York City before returning to England. I have made no attempt to keep in correspondence with my titular fiancée, for fear that a letter indicating her return would arrive.

And then, just days ago, your letter found me, and I feel I have connected with you once more. I cannot tell you how impressed I am to hear about your accomplishments in the city. And I will start first with not just your ability to learn the English language so quickly but your mastery of it, in eloquent rhetoric and even in penmanship. And to then take those achievements and secure a job at the esteemed Bloomingdale's Department Store is beyond comprehension. I am so proud of you. I am so happy for all your success. My only fear (and this is a selfish one) is that because of your establishing yourself in New York with a good position and good friends, you would not be inclined to accept my renewed invitation to join me in Florida. I am asking you this favor, though. Please give us time, at least through correspondence or hopefully through a visit, so that we may get to know each other better. Without the ties of each of us in a relationship, perhaps we could consider taking our friendship to a new level, or at least leave that door open until we meet again. Of course, there is no building to work at now, but the plan is that this will be a temporary situation. Before the last embers of The Breakers Hotel fire cooled, the owners made the decision to rebuild this amazing edifice in a year's time. Contracts have been signed with a New York firm to reconstruct and improve this masterpiece, but no longer as a wooden structure. It will be a completely fireproof building. By the end of this year, with luck, we should be looking to accept our first guests.

Yours truly,
Harrison Abelman

July 10, 1925

My Dear Harrison:

The date above has significance to me, as it was on July 10 of 1923, two years ago, that I boarded the SS Reliance out of Hamburg, and on our subsequent stop at Southampton, England, I first made your acquaintance at the dinner table. How greatly our circumstances have changed in that period of time, and yet, we both feel a bond that we may explore further. Thank you for your extremely encouraging words, and I do, humbly and eagerly, accept your invitation to visit you in Palm Beach.

Sincerely,
Rebecca Rushman

September 10, 1925
Palm Beach, Florida

My Dear Rebecca,
I am overjoyed that you are considering meeting me once more, adding another adventure to your life's road, and

perhaps we can determine if we might consider continuing that journey together. As you have agreed to a reunion, I am enclosing a voucher ticket for you on the Florida East Coast Railroad from New York to West Palm Beach, and I am hoping you will use it as soon as you can. With your approval, I will arrange for you to stay at accommodations near our hotel site, so that we can be reacquainted with no pressure on either's part. Of course, I will be busy with hotel matters, prior to and after its reopening, but I feel it would be prudent to bring you here as soon as possible to see if this life appeals to you, even if it is just to join the hotel staff. I am enclosing a mock-up of a newspaper article that will not appear until December. As I was given the opportunity to escort the Palm Beach Post reporter around the property, I played my "lonely heart" card, and I asked for a preview of what she would be writing, so as to entice you to visit. It will explain, far more eloquently than I could, just what you might expect to see, the grandeur that awaits you when you arrive for your visit.

> The new seven-million-dollar Breakers Hotel, on the site of the world-famous hostelry which burned to the ground in March, 1925, will open in December, according to W. E. Kenan, president of the Florida East Coast Hotel Company.

> The opening of this new hotel is heralded as one of the outstanding events of the Palm Beach season as it will re-establish in the resort a hotel, whose disappearance was regretted by winter visitors from all over the United States. Far

eclipsing its predecessor in grandeur, beauty, spaciousness and comfort, the new Breakers will continue the traditions which endeared the former hostelry to its thousands of patrons. It is already booking up for a two months' period. The New Breakers, nine stories in height, contains 400 master bedrooms, 300 servants' rooms, and 50 rooms for guests' servants, with a total capacity of about 500, very slightly in excess of the number at the former hotel. The flexibility characterizing the layout of the suites makes it possible to include the unexpected visitor in a private party, as upon his departure his room can be reconverted into an independent room. Many of the suites have private porches and balconies. The hotel is designed in modified Spanish style with an Italian Renaissance design.

There will be no formal opening of The Breakers, according to John W. Greene, manager of the hotel.

Reservations are still flowing in steadily, and the guest list includes some of the best-known names in America. The new Breakers is expected to be the rendezvous of hundreds of those who visited its predecessor regularly each season.

Yours truly,
Harrison

Chapter 18

PALM BEACH 1926

The day after Rebecca arrived in Palm Beach and was settled in her room at a delightfully appointed inn, Harrison was eager to bring her to the site of The Breakers's devastation, which was now an active construction area. He wanted time alone with her to tell her about the tragedy, but he hadn't anticipated the attention she would draw from his friends and colleagues, who also came, for some portion of each day, to watch the progress.

"So, this is the lovely Rebecca," said a dapper-looking man, who eagerly offered that he had been working for Mr. Henry Morrison Flagler since the year 1912, having started as his office boy. He winked at Harrison. "I have to say, you have not overstated her praises." He tipped his hat to Rebecca. "Welcome to paradise. Don't judge her quite yet. Our Breakers will be in her splendor soon enough."

"Rebecca, I'm pleased to introduce you to the charming Frank Hennessey," Harrison interrupted.

"Did you tell her yet? Did you tell her about the day?" Frank asked but did not pause for an answer. "There I was," he continued, "working right over there . . . at the Royal Poinciana." He pointed in the direction. "I grabbed my bicycle and hurried over to the blaze. Everyone came. You couldn't help but be drawn to it."

Soon, another friend came over. "You must be Rebecca. We've been waiting for you." Harrison offered an annoyed look to the man and an embarrassed expression to Rebecca, and then just admitted. "I guess it's no secret. I have spoken about your coming for some time now."

"Don't be mad at Harrison," William Widersham said. "We've all needed something positive to look forward to. We're just supportive of each other, and I'm sure you will come to understand that." Then he pointed to the burned-out footprint of the building. "The Breakers went quietly, in an orderly, dignified way . . . like a well-laid fire in a great fireplace."

"You won't believe this," another man interrupted, taking Rebecca's hand to shake, with a slight bow. "B. B. Lewis, pleased to meet you," he said. "I was at the picture show. What do you think was playing? It was *Dante's Inferno*. And then I come out to the biggest fire in South Florida history. Fire fighters responded quickly; engines came from many miles away, easily seeing the billowing dark smoke. But nothing could save her. She was a huge wooden structure, and the winds were strong and unrelenting. Our Breakers Hotel was burning."

B. B. touched Rebecca on the shoulder. With his reporter's instinct, he wanted a chance to describe the scene. "Before making their own dash to safety, the guests were throwing personal items from the windows, fur coats and steamer trunks, most containing a fair amount of jewelry and other keepsakes and valuables."

Harrison took Rebecca's hand and led her slightly away. He wanted his own chance to share his thoughts with her. "I was in the hotel, of course. The cry spread quickly: 'Fire in the south wing.' Later, they found out it began in the room of Mrs. William Hale Thompson. Her husband, it turns out, was a former mayor of Chicago, and I believe he will be running for that office again. She had a new gadget, a curling iron, that was left on, that was found to have been the accidental incendiary device."

Harrison's friends were not ready to part from the beautiful Rebecca when they still had stories to relate, and so they continued to walk with the pair. "We stayed until martial law was declared. Never saw anything like it. The National Guard was called," Frank said, and then they were all speaking in fast succession, reliving the day. "It was the day after St. Patrick's Day. She was gone in less than two hours," he said, looking at his friends for validation. "Terrible," another man added, shaking his head, with sad resignation. "Jumping flames spread to other buildings nearby, with sparks igniting fires in a broader perimeter. Our wonderful Palm Beach Inn went with her."

Another friend came by and introduced herself. "You must be Rebecca," she said, and Harrison nodded at her with a proud smile. "Rebecca, meet Carola Bibo. Her family owns an inn nearby."

Just like the others, she couldn't wait to tell her story. "We formed bucket brigades to pass pails, pots, and pans of water to neighbors seated precariously on their roofs, hoping to moisten the sun-parched shingles, so they might be better protected from the flying sparks." She paused for a moment and then added, "And it worked. Saved many of the properties."

Harrison continued escorting Rebecca toward the ocean, as Carola offered her memories. "I can still picture the elegant Mrs. Edward F. Hutton, Marjorie Merriweather Post, heir to the cereal empire. She was a guest at The Breakers while her own estate, Mar-a-Lago, was under construction. She wanted to help, offered her place for housing to some of the homeless out-of-towners."

"A great lady," Harrison added, and they all nodded in concurrence. Rebecca was already feeling part of Harrison's world with this introduction.

Eventually, Harrison had Rebecca to himself, and they used barrels holding construction materials as a bench. "I'm glad that you are seeing it now, so far along in the rebuilding, so only the newspaper articles will have the pictures of what occurred, and you can already see what it will be again.

Rebecca put her arms around Harrison. She hugged him as a sympathetic friend. With his reserved manner, he had made no overt romantic gestures since she had arrived, beyond a kiss on the hand when he had helped her descend the railway car steps.

But there was a joy in his voice and a warmth in his eyes that made her feel he was more than excited that she had come. "Tell me about the day, Harrison. Tell me what you saw, if you can," she said, cautiously, "but if it is too hard to relive, I understand."

"Actually, I do want to talk about it. You need to know what it was like, so that you will know what will remain forever in my memory," Harrison took in a deep breath and continued, "I can," he started, with an emotional stutter, "I can talk about it, because when all is said and done, no one was seriously hurt; no one died at The Breakers Hotel. And this is how I find it easier to accept what was. I imagine what could have been. I imagine the horror that could have accompanied the nightmare of a huge burning building, filled with over a thousand innocent people, all the guests and staff. I think of what nightmares the survivors of the Titanic must bear always, to have seen the drowning people, to have heard to the screams, to have drifted in lifeboats in freezing waters while others tried to board and found no room, to have lived while so many others perished." He shook his head to rid himself of his reverie. "You would not believe this, and maybe you will meet her in the future, but one guest, a Margaret Brown, survived the 1912 Titanic disaster and was in residence at The Breakers on our tragic night. What are the chances that would happen?"

He took Rebecca's hand and led her to one of the beautiful new benches that were bordering the sea walk. The brilliance of the black wrought iron was so shiny that she felt it might be newly painted and she touched a portion of it lightly to assure it was no longer wet. When they sat together for the first time since she arrived, she interpreted it as a slight move towards an acceptable intimacy that the public venue would allow. But then Harrison's thoughts returned once more to the tragic day. "It was the plumes of smoke, visible from far in the distance, that brought the community to the hotel. You can imagine, a curiosity, they were running to see what was happening. And then the spectators stood watching the fire, and then they were running to get away from the heat." Certainly, there was panic, but then there was resignation. The Grand Dame was dying, we all knew. Soon she would be only a memory.

He was choked up for a moment, as if the smoke clouds that he was describing as billowing from the building were present again. "By midnight of that night, March 18, she was gone. Only glowing ashes spotted the blackened area, as if the last night-lights were turned off." He shook his head resignedly. "Only one thing remained. It was the vault, unmoved as a stalwart sentry guarding the devastation. But it was so hot, it was five more days before it could even be opened. It had done a good job in its mission. Members of the National Guard, who had quickly imposed a curfew on the area to prevent looting, still stood around as we opened the steel tomb. Later assessments said over $300,000 in jewels and valuables were recovered. I was there, itemizing and documenting items that would be returned to grateful owners."

When The Breakers eventually reopened, the headline of the December 31, 1926, *Palm Beach Independent* eloquently stated:

FROM ITS ASHES OF TWO YEARS AGO
Greatest Winter Hotel, the New Breakers, Phoenix-Like Has Arisen, in Even Greater Excellence

Chapter 19

PALM BEACH 1975

When Addie returned to Kathryn's hospital bedside in the afternoon to resume their conversation and review more correspondence, she remarked that the patient looked bright eyed and rested. "And look at the healthy color of your face!" Addie complimented her, enthusiastically.

"Well, I should tell you that I made them hand me my makeup bag when I awoke. And then one of the nurses who had worked at a cosmetics counter took over."

Addie laughed. "Okay then, but you felt well enough to want to put on makeup. I'm excited for that. And I'm presuming you had a good nap."

"The best in years," Kathryn affirmed with a sweet smile. "Could this be my future? Is this what happens when you have some resolution to issues that have drained you?" She motioned for Addie to take her seat again. "Addie, dear, you promised the whole story. Remember, you are to fulfill your mother's prophesy." Touched by how well Kathryn had listened to her recitation, Addie gave her a kiss on her cheek.

"You were the listener, the watcher, the one to reveal what went on in the past," Kathryn added, while sitting up straighter against her generous bank of pillows. "You told me how your mother is a special person, greatly admired. I am going to guess that you have inherited your compassionate manner from her." Addie tilted her head and nodded, humbly accepting the compliment. "Let's continue, shall we?" she said, as she leaned toward Kathryn. She pulled a letter from her box and skimmed it. She nodded her head to meaningful sentences that resonated once again, as she read them to herself. Finally, she leaned back and spoke. "In this letter, I learned so much about Natalie that I never knew myself."

February, 1944
New York, New York

My dearest friend Addie –

From your letters, I know how much you have grown up in just these several years that we have been close friends. As always, I hope you are well.

I want you to believe that I am truly happy now, and the only things I miss in my time away from Palm Beach are you and Nate, your wonderful mother Rebecca, my father, and the weather. My sweet baby is a blessing to me and not a burden. Except for my time with Theo, I have never felt so connected to another human being as I do when holding our son in my arms."

Briefly, Kathryn interrupted, "Oh my God, a boy."
Addie nodded to her but continued reading.

I never was able to explain to you fully my home situation and how my privileged childhood of love and security so quickly turned into the nightmare of the Cinderella story. I know for sure something that so many others do not, others who chase financial success. Sometimes, yes, wealth can be a burden. When we lost my lovely mother, my father, the sweetest soul of a man, pledged to be both mother and father to me, to be my protector, my companion, my teacher. He was a man, as you know, from a family who helped to build America, and with it their fortunes. His father, my grandfather, a friend of Mr. Henry Flagler, chose to have his own mansion built to be nearby Whitehall, Flagler's Palm Beach home.

My father admitted to me often that he had no profession, although he carried an elite college diploma. By the time he was ready to join the family financial business, it had been sold and he could live, more than well, as a man of leisure, like his other trust fund friends. They became philanthropists and yachters, sportsmen, and game players. My mother, his one true love, had come from a similar society circle. They had been together since they were eighteen, and so he had no experience in the world of dating and courtship, which would have been so formal for his time. He was an educated man but naïve to the ways of the world. A few years after my mother passed away and a young woman, barely fifteen years older than I was, set her sights on my father, he had developed no barometer of evil to judge her by.

It wasn't until after we received word that Theo had been killed in combat that I knew I was pregnant with his child. And that was when I confided in you and your mother. It was my saving comfort that I could always count on you both. You and Rebecca were so supportive during my pregnancy, my delivery at Ream, and my first months raising my baby. You were with me when I named him. Of course, he is Theodore, but I love calling him Trey, as in the third. That is in homage to my father as well, who is Edward II and would have loved a namesake, if I had had a brother. So, my son is Theodore Edward Evington IIII. I know my father will, at some point, be a major influence on Trey's life.

You will now know the reason for my decision to move to New York to live with an aunt. As you can imagine, my stepmother would not allow me to remain at "her" estate (which had, of course, been my house, until she latched herself on to my father). She said she couldn't have her little girl exposed to such loose morals, while offering no explanation as to just who was the father of the five-year old daughter she arrived with, as one more piece of luggage. To be honest, when they first came, I tried so hard to befriend little Patsy. Who knows better than you that I craved a little sister? But her mother kept her (figuratively) on the same tight leash as the Palm Beach ladies do with their pet dogs.

My stepmother was Constance, but I called her Connie, or at least that is what I am sure she heard, when actually I said "Conning." With a thick ribbon of gray weaving its way through her raven black hair, she could have been the inspiration for any witch in a Grimm's fairy tale, if she had been a bent-over elderly matron. But she was an hourglass-figured temptress. Despite that though, my father was becoming a weaker version of his former self, with no ability to challenge how his new wife treated me.

Addie, believe me, and I think you know me well enough to understand, that I would only wish for my father to find happiness again with a lovely woman, someone of my mother's character, someone worthy of him. But that was not who he chose.

I am so glad that my father had a chance to meet Theo, taking us out to dinner twice in the time we were together. Like everyone, my father was drawn to his warmth and personality.

Although Theo and I had plans to marry after he returned from the war overseas, when he left, we were not husband and wife, and I would not qualify as his legal next of kin.

But for Theo, acceptance of responsibility was part of his character. He was more concerned about leaving me alone when he went to war than he was about what would lie ahead for him. That is how he was.

I awoke from our first night together, yawning and stretching and searching to reach for him next to me, where we had been inseparably molded together for hours. But I found him sitting at the writing desk at the inn where we had stayed. I came up behind him and put my hand on his shoulder to see what he was busy doing. Without looking up at me, he explained that he had just finished drafting a letter to his sister and he was making a copy of that same letter for me to keep.

"This is the moment," Kathryn said abruptly, startling Addie who had drifted to the world of the past memory. "This is the moment when the letter was written!" Kathryn said again, and then she calmed down. "I'm sorry. I shouldn't have interrupted," she apologized. "Please go on with Natalie's letter."

Addie gave her an understanding smile and searched for her place again, continuing with her friend's words about her first morning, waking with Theo.

He wanted me to understand how truly and deeply he loved me. When he finally turned to look at me, his head quickly rocked back, and he had the most astonished look on his face. That kind of scared me, like something was wrong. But then he just said that he forgot. He forgot how breath-taking I was. Those words can only make you want to melt into him. He abruptly lost his focus on the letter, stopped talking, and he covered my face with kisses, the kind of kisses that form air bubbles under your feet and set you floating. And so, it was easy for him to carry me back to the bed, to relive the romance of the night before.

After we fed each other from our breakfast tray, he led me back to the desk again, showing me the letter itself. He had written out a most charming and meaningful "in case of" letter for his adored sister to show his parents only if he died and it turned out I was pregnant. Of course, I started crying because he spoke of his life ending on the very night that our real love was beginning. But I know, truthfully, he never really believed he would not survive the war to come back to me. People like Theo, people who life has treated only with positive reinforcement, feel they will be one of the lucky ones, that they are invincible.

Hopefully, you understand, now, that when I did have my baby, I was very content to raise him on my own. I was not seeking to be an interloper on any family that didn't really know me and maybe wouldn't want us. It was hard enough navigating the complicated relationship with my father, step-mother, and stepsister. And so, if anyone questioned, I presented myself as a war widow. Although I did not qualify for a pension, I could easily support us with money from my own trust fund, something my father was happy to provide for me, because he was sad that he could not do more.

I have been taking some classes at New York University, enjoying courses in writing the most. Although I have made friends at school, I also am happy just spending free time with Trey by my side, feeling comfortable with my anonymity in this city. My Aunt Gracie, who never married, has been more than gracious and welcomed us eagerly to stay in her co-op apartment. She loves to babysit, and I believe she really means it when she says we have done more to illuminate her life than she is doing for us. I'm not sure that is true though, because she has been an angel. I have been enjoying this adventurous year in New York and especially love exploring all that Central Park has to offer. I find that I love the writing process, as I am hoping is evident in my letters. I even wrote a story that will soon be published in a New York magazine marketed to tourists.

My father was also crushed by Theo's death, but he finds such joy being with Trey and visits us often. He is a proud grandpa and grateful to have his little grandson as an heir to carry on our own family name.

When Addie folded this letter and placed it back in the box, Kathryn thanked her for reading it to her. "What a special woman. If what you said is true, that I could meet her one day, I only hope I can garner the courage to do so." She leaned over Addie's lap and looked in the box. "Is there any other letter you could read?" Addie rifled through the folded notes, then looked up and smiled at Kathryn.

"Well, this one, maybe you'd like it. It goes back a little to the beginning of my history together with Natalie." And then she had another thought. "Let me go see if Beth is in the lounge or cafeteria. I'll get her caught up on all that you have discovered. I know she is tortured by your being troubled. Let me tell her the basics of the story."

"No, wait, Addie," Kathryn interrupted, as suddenly her agitation returned. She grabbed hold of Addie's arm. "You have to promise me something." She paused to take in some breaths and to gather her thoughts. "Addie, you have to promise me something. And you have to make Beth promise . . . promise not to tell anyone else what I have done . . . not Dr. Nate, not Bear, at least not now," Kathryn pleaded. "I am ashamed."

Quickly, Addie took Kathryn's hands in hers. "Kathryn, I know you will be forgiven. But I know, also, that you have to forgive yourself. And that will come with time. But I'm glad that you'll let me share this with Beth now, because she is so concerned about you. I agree, at this point, Bear and Nate just need to know you have resolved your emotional issue, without any details. And, of course, Nate is on your case to resolve your physical issues until you are totally well. I will return with Beth tomorrow morning, and then we can read this next letter together with her."

Chapter 20

PALM BEACH 1975

The next day, when Beth and Addie returned to Kathryn's room, Beth ran to her mother and hugged her tightly. "Addie explained everything to me, and I saw the letters that she read to you. I'm so happy for you, Mom, to have this resolution, after all these years. It must have been so hard to keep this all to yourself while raising me on your own."

While they spoke, Addie searched for another envelope to pull from the box of correspondence. "Now that Beth has joined us," she said, looking up, "I would like you both to hear this next letter from Natalie. Again, I will let her own words tell you her story. Already, I'm sure you're not surprised that she became a professional writer."

New York, New York
April 1951

My dearest Addie:

How excited I was to hear the news that you and Nate are engaged to be married! Please extend my love and congratulations to everyone.

You know that both your families were the only Jewish people that I really knew in Palm Beach. Now that I am living in New York City, where there is an extensive and vibrant Jewish presence, I know to wish you *Mazel Tov*! I will proudly admit this to you. I am gloating, just a bit, and taking some credit for being the one who lit the spark, making you realize that day, as we spent time together on the beach, just how cute your friend Nate was and that he had a crush on you. It does not really seem that long ago, and yet I just can't believe how much has happened since then. I remember that day vividly. The sun was a brilliant orb in the sky. We cupped our hands over our eyes, but we could hardly shade our sight enough to see each other. Powerful rays reflected off the metal beach chairs and even the sand pails of the children playing along the shore. I Remember how Nate stopped to toss a ball with a group of little boys. He will make a good husband; he will be a wonderful father.

I recall details of that day like few others, our feet in sneakers, pushing against the soft sand that remolded with our every step. We walked or ran or stopped to search for "treasures," as you would say. I think of our footprints, ephemeral evidence that we were there, that we experienced that day, and yet how soon the tide would wipe the imprints away, and with it our innocence. With that first loud boom of a German torpedo setting a ship ablaze, the perfectly blue sky was marred by black plumes of smoke clouds, and nothing was the same again.

I guess if I were truthful to you and to myself, after our son was born, I chose to go to Manhattan just to savor a feeling of being where Theo had been, of walking the streets that were part of his world, before he was transplanted, so briefly, to ours.

On hearing those words read, Kathryn couldn't help herself. She had to say something. "Addie, I know exactly how she felt. You mentioned from the reservation notes when we came that this was my second time as a guest at The Breakers. You said I had been there before. I ignored your words because I did not want to explain anything to Beth. Yes, I had been there before. It was after the war, after I had been married a few years. I convinced my husband that we needed to take a little trip. I knew he'd like the idea of a golf weekend in the middle of our harsh winter in the Northeast. I knew I wanted, that I needed, to go to Palm Beach, but I didn't tell him why.

"I wanted to be where Theo had been, to view the Atlantic Ocean, not from the isle of Manhattan, but I wanted to be

where he walked in the warm sun on a sandy beach with someone he loved. I wanted to breathe in the salt air of the last happy
time of his life. But I explained none of this to my husband.
He was not an empathetic or sentimental man. That was something I was already recognizing in our brief marriage. I knew I
couldn't share my motives with him. But when he was enjoying
his rounds on the golf course, I had time to myself. I went to
the management office. I asked if there were any lists of babies
born at The Breakers when it was Ream General Hospital. But
I was told the hospital files were confidential military property
and not part of The Breakers' records."

"That was true," Addie affirmed, enthusiastically. "I remember the week the army left. A small group of The Breakers' staff
was just returning to work. Of course, I was still in high school,
but many of the employees were serving in the military themselves and wouldn't come back for some time. But those of us
available lined our long driveway, cheering and waving as tons
of Ream files, hospital equipment, and assorted paraphernalia
were carted off in army convoys and freight trucks. Three area
firms worked on the reconversion of The Breakers to our resort
facility, bringing back precious objects and carpets and artwork
that had been stored off-site during that time."

Addie shifted her chair as she left the memory world of
decades ago. "You see, Kathryn, I believe this, and you need to
believe this. Your coming back to check if there was a record
of the birth just proves it. You are a good person, with a good
conscience. I feel so sorry for you, that for all those years, you
just couldn't remove a coat of guilt that you didn't have to
wear," Addie said as she held Natalie's correspondence once
more upright in her hand and continued reading.

Just a few times, when Aunt Gracie was babysitting, I did go to visit Theo's grave, as if I needed concrete, unmistakable evidence that he was really gone. I went through public records to find the site. I ran my hand over the mound of grass that marked his body, pulling out some green blades to keep in my purse and replacing the bare patch with a bouquet of flowers I had brought. I think I just needed that closure. But I have never presented myself to his family and I have no intention of showing up on their doorstep. And so, maybe it is time for me to return to my home and be a family with my sweet father and my son.

Kathryn had been a riveted audience of one to the reading of Natalie's first letters, sitting so close to Addie that she followed each line of correspondence as it was recited aloud. But, as she and Beth heard this next letter together with each on one side of Addie, Kathryn felt she had to interrupt.

"I was there one of the times," Kathryn said.

"I'm sorry," Addie responded, not understanding her. "You were where, Kathryn?"

"At the cemetery. I was there at the cemetery one of the times that Natalie had gone to see the grave. You see, I too had a hard time accepting that Theo was gone, even though I had been there at his burial. The first year, I visited the cemetery many times. I just could not rid myself of it, of the guilt. There was always the guilt." Kathryn started to whimper between words.

"You don't have to continue now, Kathryn," Addie said.

"Really, Mom, you don't have to go on," Beth said, taking her mother's hand and kissing it. "You have to conserve your strength."

Kathryn nodded with an emerging smile, wanting to assure them she was fine, even energized by this bedside confessional. "Oh yes, and one time, when our driver parked at the cemetery road, I did not get out of the car. From a short distance, I saw a young woman bending over my brother's grave. She had a statuesque beauty, as he had described. I could see my brother falling in love with her. She was so much more a match for Theo than Meredith Morgan, who became my sister-in-law. I could not get the image out of my mind. Could this be the girl who Theo wrote about in the letter? This young woman, hovering over his grave, held no baby in her arms, although the baby could have been elsewhere. But she had never come to knock on our door. I knew nothing of this girl's story. I knew only that our paths crossed this one time and I doubted that they would ever cross again." Kathryn purposely spoke slowly, pausing for extra breaths every few sentences, monitoring her own pace so she would exhibit no signs of distress that would alert the nursing station. Addie and Beth knew how determined she was to continue her story, and so they were patient and respectful listeners.

"I should have felt relieved, possibly vindicated, like I did nothing wrong," Kathryn said. "But instead, I felt sad. And then I started to think if I had just told them all about the letter, if I had told my parents, and Meredith and her parents about the girlfriend and the letter, would that just have been better? But with Theo gone and no evidence of a baby, that would have just been cruel to Meredith.

"Years later, when my marriage was falling apart, I questioned myself again. If I had told my parents and they had acknowledged that Theo had another girlfriend, that he possibly had a baby, then my marriage would have been called off, my fiancé's family having found me unacceptable as a bride for their son. It would have validated their snubbing of the Stanton family. At a social gathering, his mother would sometimes moan in exasperation to her friends, not completely out of our hearing, 'in the trades, scrap metal of all things!' And then, maybe, I could have moved on and followed whatever path would present itself. Maybe I could have found somebody to marry who really loved me and who I really loved. But then I thought of my precious daughter, Beth, and how much I loved her, even though I knew it was often hard for me to be soft and patient and sweet with her. Perhaps I just had a flawed nature, more of a reflection of my own mother than I would ever want. I know I have always pointed out only Beth's faults and not all of her wonderful qualities."

She leaned toward Beth, kissed her on the cheek and patted her hand. "What would I have done without my daughter?" she said, and then turned fully toward Beth. "Darling, you are the best thing that has ever happened to me." She shook her head and her focus moved to the window, as if the blue sky harbored her memories of the past. And then she looked singularly at Beth. "These letters have brought me back to that time so long ago. And now I know the answer.

"I wondered about this woman standing over the grave. If it was Theo's girlfriend, was there a son or daughter, born out of wedlock? Was the baby kept or adopted away? Was the child the best thing that ever happened to her, or did she give to another family who couldn't have a baby, the chance to raise a miracle, like your real mother did when I adopted you?"

"Mom, you are my real mother," Beth shot back, crying out the words. "You are the definition of a real mother. I am the luckiest girl alive." Kathryn squeezed Beth's arms, at her generous words. "Culpable or not, you must understand, I was punished. I said nothing because I wanted to protect my marriage, and yet once my marriage took place, I knew I had made a mistake. I was never happy with my husband. Why would I think that he would be so different from his mother? It didn't take long for him to reveal the arrogant snob that he was. He wanted me to be grateful that he condescended to marry me."

As if the impact of the revelation of events had suddenly registered with her, Beth bent over, started sobbing and could not stop. She went to the washroom to compose herself. Unexpectedly, her own issue of her broken engagement, which she had set aside while she dealt with her mother's illness, came rushing back to her. But she was not upset from it. She was crying because of her mother's story. And she was grateful that it taught her something about life. She was thinking she had dodged a bullet. She felt relieved to have discovered her fiancé's true character before it was too late. She still held a wad of tissues in her hand when she returned to her mother's bedside. "I love you so much, Mom. I wish I had known my Uncle Theo, but I just love him anyway, knowing how you loved him and how he cherished you, as I do."

Kathryn wiped away tears and reached to comfort her daughter. When she leaned back on her pillow, her eyes began slowly drooping. Addie and Beth looked at each other and motioned toward the door, as Kathryn's energy dissipated, and her lids closed completely.

That night, Addie admitted to her husband Nate that she felt proud. She knew that she had played a part in helping

Kathryn to heal emotionally. And she was hopeful that Kathryn and Beth's relationship going forward might reflect the same closeness that she had always felt with her own mother, Rebecca.

Chapter 21

PALM BEACH 1926

As the first weeks of her Palm Beach stay progressed, Rebecca was introduced to, and seemingly charmed, all the people who had been a part of Harrison's world in the last few years. As the second week drew to a close, Harrison was eager to share one more group with her. "I think you'll like what is planned for tonight," he told her when he joined her for breakfast on Friday morning at the inn where he had arranged her housing.

"Harrison, every day, every evening, has been an adventure for me. A simple dinner for two would be great." She smiled up at him as she spoke, wanting to show her appreciation, while inferring that perhaps just the two of them should be alone.

"But you know how much I want you to feel comfortable here. I want you to be happy. Selfishly, I want you to choose to stay with me in Florida." All of this he had repeated before, varying only the phrases, but never including the words she wanted to hear, never mentioning a hint of loving interest. And still, those words were not there. She understood they were made of different emotional constitutions. She was loving and romantic; he was reserved and pragmatic. Did she love him? It was a question she had asked herself often since she arrived. She thought she could; she wanted to have that feeling she had had once before. Certainly, she felt a deep friendship with him as someone she admired. But a love relationship goes beyond that. She longed to be hugged, to be kissed. Once, she had been with someone who was hungry for her, and she had felt a physical desire tht had made her heart pound and her head spin.

As Harrison took her hand and led her from the dining room table to the front porch swing, her spirits were elevated by even this slight move toward intimacy. He seemed to have a burgeoning enthusiasm that she hoped would lead to an embrace and a kiss, but as he sat next to her, he only continued talking.

"Would you believe," he began, 'just a few years ago, Temple Israel, a small Jewish Reform congregation, was founded near here, in West Palm Beach. It was established by six Jewish families. And tonight, in honor of your arrival, they have organized a Shabbas dinner at the home of one of the founding members. I can't wait for you to meet the group. If you choose this town as your home, we'll be okay here. We'll be happy here. We will have a sense of being part of a Jewish community, however small, in this area of Florida. It is something I think we each value. Months ago, they were so welcoming to me, having heard there was a bachelor Jewish assistant manager at the hotel, and now they can't wait to meet you."

At five that evening, they were at the home of Eleanor and Charles Bernstein, joining the group in lighting the Sabbath candles and saying the traditional Hebrew prayers over the wine and bread, the sweet freshly baked challah that the Meyer family had brought. There were at least ten children running around the front room, three of them introduced as the Bernsteins' own young boys, Benjamin and Frederick and one-year-old Nathan. Rebecca learned that the family had moved to Palm Beach a few months after The Breakers' fire. Mr. Bernstein was one of the engineers brought down by the New York construction company contracted for the rebuilding of the hotel. Harrison was right, Rebecca thought. She was experiencing a joyous contentment that was filling a hollowness in her soul which had been there since she ran from the shtetl Hasidic environment of the uncle's place on Hester Street.

She did not want a life devoid of any faith. This group reminded her of her parents' friends in St. Petersburg. They loved their Jewish heritage, but they were cosmopolitan, young and vibrant, enjoying their Judaism in a modern way. Although there was a beautiful spirituality, the discussions were of civic and community matters, not only of biblical texts. Rebecca was eager to participate in the conversations, beginning with a few questions.

After she helped the women clear the table of the meal and they were settled back with fresh cups and plates for coffee, tea, and desserts, she addressed her hosts and the others. "I can't thank you all enough for welcoming me here tonight. I don't want to disturb a most upbeat mood, but because of my own family history, I would just like to ask this question. Has it been easy for Jews to establish themselves here? Do you find no anti-Semitism?"

Arthur Goldstone smiled at Harrison, and then looked for the attention of everyone at the table. "She's a smart girl, this one," he said, gesturing with his fork at Rebecca, before addressing her directly.

"Certainly, we all pay homage to the memory of Henry Flagler. He was a man of great vision. But, sorry to say, even the great Mr. Flagler had his prejudices. Just a few years before Flagler extended his Florida East Coast railroad tracks on to Miami in the year 1904, the first Jews had come to the area. All through history, wherever we try to set down roots, we are treated as an unwelcome minority. This time it was in Palm Beach. Of course, there were no pogroms, nothing so violent, but there was discrimination. Flagler blatantly established restrictive covenants on his land deals to exclude Jews from owning property near his resorts." He paused for breath and to see if he held the attention of the group. "And yet, our enterprising Jewish brethren, some of them our own parents, the grandparents of some of these children playing in the next room, established themselves as merchants, with their stores on Clematis Street in downtown West Palm Beach, right across the intracoastal waterway. It was a town Flagler built to house workers as he developed his railroad and resort community.

Samuel Levy was the next to speak. "For decades now, the most elite Jewish families of New York, Chicago, and Boston have been coming to our hotels, including Mr. Flagler's own Breakers, now owned by his Kenan heirs. These Jewish families host parties and enjoy the winter season activities with all the other affluent guests. Yes, there are private clubs here, too, and their charters seem to change from one season to the next, sometimes welcoming Jews, sometimes excluding them – patterns, I understand, that are similar to those seen in many of our American cities." The group nodded in agreement.

Soon, Rebecca stood at her seat and Harrison rose with her, his arm around her waist. "Thank you so much for inviting us to this special dinner," she said to their hosts, and then, looking around the room, she added, "It was such a pleasure to meet each of you. Thank you for that history and those insights."

"We haven't scared you away, I hope," Eleanor Bernstein said, almost fearfully.

But Rebecca laughed her response. "Hardly," she said, "I am not running from this paradise. I appreciate your candor, and you will understand how serious I am, if one day I tell you my story. What you have said does not scare me. I spent my teen years in a country with revolving wars and revolutions."

Rachel Levy and Eleanor Bernstein nodded at each other, smiling with the same idea. "What a wonderful, educational afternoon that could be for our sisterhood. Perhaps, one day, you would feel comfortable to tell us about your life in St. Petersburg and your journey to America," Eleanor said, as she helped Rebecca on with her light jacket. "Our con-gregants share a desire for both religious and cultural events programming."

Just a few days later, Harrison invited Rebecca out to a private dinner. This one, finally, was for just the two of them. After the meal, he led her to a secluded park bench in a beautiful area of lush trees bordering Flagler's former estate home, which had just become the Whitehall Hotel. "Rebecca," Harrison said, as he sat down close to her and took her hands in his, "I truly love you." She smiled at him with an almost astonished look. Had he really offered those words she thought him incapable of saying? He continued speaking, as if he had read her thoughts. "Yes, I know I am not good with words, but I do love you, and I hope you love me too, and I am asking this now, will you agree to marry me? I want to spend my entire life with you, and I hope you will say yes." He took out a small black box from his coat pocket. He opened it part way and handed it to her. It was a gold band with a sprinkling of diamonds laced through the center. Her hand flew to her mouth.

"Oh Harrison, it is beautiful. It's perfect," she said, and then realizing that he was holding his breath, she continued, smiling back at him. "I love you, too. And yes, yes, I will marry you." And then he pulled her tightly to him and gently kissed her on the lips.

On the walk back, he told her of one more person he would like her to meet in the coming days, someone who he knew would hold the next key to Rebecca's feeling happy in her new environment. "I want you to know that when we marry, we will live at the beautiful new Breakers, as soon as it is ready, in our own apartment suite. It is customary for the top management

DEBY EISENBERG

to stay on the premises, and it will make for a wonderful life. But I know you and your talents, and your passions, and our life should not just revolve around my pursuits. When The Breakers burned, so did all of the finery, the clothing, the linens, the scarves, the imported goods, from Madame Najla Mogabgab's exquisite hotel boutique shop. She will be reopening with the hotel in our new retail section. I have told her all about you and she is most interested in meeting you to discuss your alterations, design, and couturier experience. I need you to understand, you do not have to work. But I know what an accomplished, independent person you are, and I want you to feel fulfilled."

Days later, when Rebecca met and presented her portfolio to the famous Mme. Mogabgab, the boutique owner was thrilled. She hired Rebecca not just as an employee, but as a possible future partner.

Two months after Rebecca's arrival in Florida, she and Harrison were to be married under a canopy of flowers at Temple Israel in West Palm Beach, surrounded by dozens of friends from the congregation and the hotel. On so many occasions in the days preceding their wedding, Harrison had needed to hold Rebecca in his arms and wipe away what he identified as her bittersweet tears. She had longed for just such embraces, and she tried to stay in the moment, to savor the joy of the present and not be drawn to her memories of a past that could not be resurrected. In the past weeks, Harrison would cup her chin and bring her eyes to meet his. He would smooth his hands over the thick texture of her brown waves that continually grew in volume from the humidity of the Florida climate. In his most intimate gesture, he gathered a handful of her hair into a ponytail, sweeping it to the side so he could whisper in her ear. Although she anticipated the pleasure that a kiss in that sensitive and erotic area would deliver, he offered her only sincere and supportive words. "Rebecca, dear," he began, and then he stepped slightly away from her to readjust the knot on his tie. She could no longer feel his breathe at her ear, as once more he returned to his officious manner. "I want you to know that I do understand how hard this must be for you, how much you must have hoped that your mother could have lived to see this day, how much you must have wished that your father could have been the one to walk you down the aisle."

Poor soul, Rebecca was thinking, as she shook her head, resignedly, and gave him a sweet smile. *He tries so hard. He is a good man.* And he was correct; Rebecca was certainly struggling to cope with the sadness of missing her parents. But in a whole other dimension of feelings, she tried to fight off her true fear – that her tears included an unrelenting despair that Jacob would not be her groom, the one to greet her under the chuppah. She wondered how it could be possible that Jacob Schaevitz, the scruffily bearded and traditionally dressed Orthodox Jew, could have awakened in her a sexual awareness and insatiable desire that this handsome, well-dressed, aristocratic-looking hotelier could not. Jacob still appeared in her dreams so many nights and even in her daydreams. In her fantasy, he was not just touching her waist in the open market, but he had somehow found a vacant space in a building across town where they could be alone, and he had taken her in his arms, planting kisses on her lips, her neck, and the top of her breasts, before he broke away from her and the dream ended.

As her wedding day approached and she stood ready to walk down the aisle, Rebecca was fully in the reality of the moment. Jacob had disappeared from her life and this wonderful man, Harrison, would soon stand as an anchor by her side. She composed herself before the small orchestra began the first chords of the wedding processional. At the end of the ceremony, when Harrison soundly broke the ceremonial glass, she was his smiling and adoring wife.

The exquisite wedding gown that Rebecca had created for herself was laced with silver embellishments and threading, which had never before been envisioned and executed so meticulously. Once the photograph of Rebecca in the dress appeared as an advertisement in fashion sections of newspapers in most major American cities, orders for copies of it, or more original designs, kept Madame's Palm Beach shop extremely busy.

Chapter 22

PALM BEACH 1930S

As her time as a working resident of the hotel and as wife of the elegant Londoner, the very distinguished assistant manager, continued, Rebecca began to distance herself from the guest seamstress work. Initially, she had eagerly embraced her role, although she would often just oversee the staff at their sewing machines. But after five years, she left the magical world of the eccentric Madame Mogabgab's stores. She felt that Madame was a most charming, talented woman, but her exquisite inventory of fabrics and fashions from France and the Orient only catered to the wealthiest clientele. Quoted in a 1926 article in the *New York Sun*, she encouraged husbands to consider spending a minimum of $6,000 for their wives' spring wardrobes. But that was only if they wished to "appear smartly dressed." To follow the guidelines of the French fashion trends, that figure would be closer to $15,000.

Rebecca decided to partner at a shop where her designs could be more accessible to a woman of comfortable means and still make her look and feel like a millionaire.

With Harrison's tenure at the hotel placing him as a most valued and respected member of the management team, Rebecca's station became more and more elevated. She was often called upon as a hostess for events, as the welcoming grande dame of the hotel itself, although she maintained a young, debutante look for more years than would be expected. The other managers' wives had neither the inclination nor the personalities for the position. One of them, a sweet and demure woman, seemed more relieved by than jealous of Rebecca's prominence. Often, she appeared paralyzed to even attend many of the lavish events. She was content to be overlooked, to blend into the wallpaper as best she could, while Rebecca was at ease in the hotel environment.

Many of the men coming for business meetings or accompanied by families – wives who ranged from extravagantly bejeweled beauties to overweight matronly-looking women, breathlessly chasing their pack of children – viewed her as a princess. The men found excuses to hover around her with inconsequential questions about hotel services or directions to this or that. Rebecca was not raised to be self-absorbed, to notice this type of attention. But while Jacob was by her side, she was made aware of this truth. At the time, she accused him of making it all up when he called her exquisite and irresistible, insisting that most of the men in any room were sending approving glances her way. And through the years, she thought of Jacob when she became cognizant that many of the male guests would surreptitiously brush against her. They were cautious to do so only slightly, so as not to receive her subtly remonstrative glare. They were trying to find a way to tell her that she was beautiful, as if that would be an acceptable comment to someone who was not your own wife. And so, they searched for a way to compliment something about her without saying the words directly. "Your dress is beautiful" was what she heard the most. The most forward would ask if she could direct their wives to the salon that does her hair, although they were hoping Rebecca would say, "Oh, let me come to your room to help your wife." Their hearts palpitated at the thought that she would be in their own bedroom.

So many of the men in her life at the hotel, whether professional staff or registered guests, seemed drawn to her – that is, every man except her own husband, who had no interest in praising or even touching her. His passion was for the hotel only. He saw beauty only in the stature of its columns and the breadth of its halls, or in the fabrics of its rooms. As he made his daily rounds, he would touch, here and there, a framed painting on the wall to make sure it hung perfectly straight and was not marred by any dust or stray scrap of flotsam blown inside from the breezeway. But he would never really take the time to admire or examine her, as she dressed for an evening event. Even though she knew that a thick lock of her hair had loosened from her chignon bun, even though she was bothered by a few thin strands over her eye, he would make no move to adjust her and set her perfect. She longed for his touch and attention. She did not think that he was a homosexual, but perhaps he was just not sexual. How could it be that so many men responded to her with an overt attraction, but not Harrison? She had tried, first for months, and then for years, to just accept that and hope that love would grow, that she would teach herself ways to woo her own husband, who may have too quickly asked for her hand in marriage, without loving her first. It was true that she had had the most minimal of experiences in romance, until she met Jacob who swept her off her feet. She thought, initially, that Harrison was just being polite, being respectful of her innocence. But eventually she wondered if he had no feelings for her at all, or perhaps he was just devoid of any sexual appetite. And when she looked back, she understood that he had never presented himself otherwise. She was grateful that they did have, at least, their one beautiful daughter, Addie, conceived a month after their wedding night. She speculated later that her husband had checked off that obligation as one more item on a "to do" list.

She willed herself to be content. When she had met Harrison on the ship, he seemed so debonair and erudite. She felt honored that he was interested in her as a friend. Was she a fool or was she fooled? Did he know, even then, something she never imagined, that she would be an important asset for the advancement of his career? She had thought she clung to him for security and survival, and yet it may have been the opposite.

Images remained in her mind of her St. Petersburg days accompanying her mother to the homes or estates of those with extreme wealth, from members of the royal court to the

Russian society customers who requested new gowns each season for the opera or ballet. Husbands were not self-conscious as they entered the room to view their wives' new apparel. They thought of her and her mother as objects in the room, accouterments of their privileged world. If they noticed her at all, sitting in the corner, ready to hand pins or needles to her mother on demand, they identified her only as the young, innocent adolescent that she was. And so, when her mother had done her final gesture, a solitary clap of her hands and lowering of her head to signal her pride in the perfection of her work, and then leave the room, often the men would not notice that Rebecca had remained in her corner chair, or they noticed her and were not ashamed by what they would do. There were husbands who would immediately proceed to unbutton the perfectly fashioned dress. They wanted to touch their wives' skin beneath the fabric, beginning first with kisses at their necklines and proceeding lower as they released each button or delicate tie. This was Rebecca's first introduction to the power of sexual attraction, although she was on the brink of womanhood herself. She understood enough to know that it was time for her to leave the room, that this couple needed their privacy. At the time, however, she was not quite certain what the next moves would be.

But in her experience as a married woman, she shared a bedroom with a man who had no interest in her. When she would ask Harrison to zip up her dress as an evening began, in her imagination, she longed for a man who would zip it up, ask her to model it and then insist on zipping it back down immediately so that he could touch and smell and taste the beauty of his wife, his lover, before she was paraded to the public.

Sometimes she wondered if, perhaps, she had not met Jacob, could she be content now? Jacob opened her eyes and her heart to the secrets of the adult world. Although they were young and not married in their brief time together, she believed that he would have been a sweet lover. She remembered his simplest gestures. Jacob would try to secretly hold her hand in public even though he knew it was not something he should. But Harrison, her husband, would never reach to take her hand, even though he rightfully could. Although Jacob betrayed her by disappearing, she could not imagine how colorless her life would be now, if, on her sleepless nights, she could not conjure up memories of their moments together.

As for her husband, sometimes at night when she went to touch him, he simply turned away from her, and he slowly rolled in the opposite direction, encased in his blanket, as if it were protective armor. She felt sad and humiliated by his action. She cried so softly that no sound emerged, only a few breaths and stifled sniffles. But sometimes, she turned away herself, offering her back to him, trying to make the dream return. It was not a dream really, but a fantasy she had evoked from the slightest seeds of memory of her time with Jacob. In this fantasy, one time, she had let it slip that her father would be across town at a meeting. Jacob already knew that, like him, there was no mother. And so, Jacob tenderly tackled Rebecca in the privacy of her own bedroom, holding her down on the bed and touching her most private parts. In real life, he sat next to her and then moved away. She reached her hand to keep him there beside her. Although she had never been in her room alone with a boy, she wanted this almost man to hold her. She playfully pulled out the religious fringe under his garment and began weaving the strings together. In her dream state, Jacob began to strip his own clothes off, but then he stopped. He put his shirt layers back on and grabbed the door handle to leave the room. "I want to be with you," he said. "But you are too perfect, too lovely, too innocent, to understand what you may be agreeing to." It was the first time that Jacob said, "I love you." He said, "I love you too much to make love to you now. But I want to, soon. Think about it. I want to marry you, and I want to spend my life with you." He was ready to open the door and fly out before he would be unable to control himself. But he moved back toward her, took her in his arms and maneuvered her dress enough that she felt his hands upon her small breasts. He had done her no favor, she understood. Although he rushed out as a gentleman should, he had forever awakened in her an unsatiated desire. Even though in reality, he did not do this final act of touching her so intimately, in her mind, forever, she had taken the story to fulfillment.

After several years together with Harrison, Rebecca realized she was making every comparison of her husband to Jacob. Harrison was humorless, compared to him. Jacob, the market vendor, had a sprightly manner, a quirky attitude, an optimistic insistence that each hurdle would be successfully passed. Harrison was serious, sometimes somber and remote. But she still gave him the benefit of the doubt. He was a good man. He was her husband, the father of her precious daughter, Addie. She was grateful for that brief period when he had an interest in her body. But that time was short lived. He had tremendous responsibilities in his position at the hotel. He was her life's partner, and she wanted to be supportive of him, always.

There were evenings when Rebecca knew Harrison needed her. One night when he appeared especially contemplative, she cupped one of his cheeks with her hand as she led him to sit next to her on the divan in their suite. "You are stressed, darling," she said, sympathetically. "You massage your temples in just such a way that I know your day has been trying."

He quickly nodded in agreement. He stood up and began pacing the room, with his fingertips at his forehead, as if to illustrate her point. "I admit you're right. I am realizing this is a cultural education for me. So many people asking, demanding in the American way, for the best. I want to please them all, but it is almost impossible. The management hired me because they saw in me someone who could do it all, cater to the needs of the guests, and direct the staff. But it is nothing like in London.

"This property is equal to the quality of my hotel experience in London, although, of course, on a grander scale. But in England, there is a defined class system, and the people of means who frequent such hotels are comfortable with that. We have nobility, aristocracy, and royalty that has its own tiers – and that is accepted. But here, everyone wants the best room, the grandest view, the fastest maid service, the best table at dinner.

"I remember when I could please everyone at the Savoy Hotel." Suddenly, he stopped walking and turned a desk chair to face Rebecca on the sofa, as he smiled slightly about a memory. "It is all in perception. Guests would each feel they received the best for their station. If their room faced the street and not the courtyard, they each just presumed a person of greater prestige was in residence as well, perhaps a duke or an earl, possibly a prince, whether British or from another country, had arrived. It would be a treat to see who was at breakfast the next morning, they imagined. There were no perceived slights, or they were met with the British stiff upper lip.

"Have you noticed, Rebecca," Harrison continued, "how Americans act? They do not even queue up for services. They descend *en masse* to the reception desk or the host stand, bellowing their demands."

Rebecca stood up and tried to be supportive. She went behind his chair and began to massage his shoulders, although he tensed from her touch instead of relaxing into it, as she had hoped. She tried to brush off his reaction. She went back to her seat to face him again. "Dear, you are being surprisingly hard on them, don't you think?" she said.

And quickly, Harrison softened his rhetoric. "I don't disagree, really. I was truly leading up to something. I am just trying to explain my frustrations with these cultural differences. This is America, the land of opportunity, the great capitalist nation. But don't get me wrong. Since I have been introduced to the biography of our founder, Henry Flagler, I have nothing but admiration for the process. Passing through our doors are men who have worked to make this an affluent, powerful nation. Our guests all want the same best rooms, best views, best lounge chair locations by the beach, because they know they can flash their money around and they are validated as to their status.

"Without British titles, they can still feel like a king or a queen. And it is our obligation to respect that. Money here will buy you the prestige of that title. Ironically, back in England, some of our aristocrats have impressive lineages and great estates but depressingly little money to support them. And what has emerged over the past decades has become a symbiotic relationship that has benefitted both sides. Crossing the Atlantic Ocean, the most notable American heiresses have been seeking to marry titles. And the aristocracy needs the funding they can offer." He paused and smiled at his wife. "Certainly, you will be familiar with the name of one example. Before the turn of the century, Consuelo Vanderbilt married the Ninth Duke of Marlborough."

"You're kidding. I don't know anything about that," Rebecca answered immediately, indicating she wanted to learn more about the story. This was one of the things Rebecca loved about being married to Harrison. It didn't make up for her struggles with his emotional distancing, but it fulfilled her in another realm. She learned from him. He was knowledgeable on so many topics. He was like a student of history and psychology. From their first meeting, he would be her tutor of sorts, an educational guide to expand her world. She hoped all of Harrison's qualities would be reflected in their daughter, Addie.

"But do not worry, my dear," Harrison continued, referring to his managerial duties. "I will work it out. I will always strive for one hundred percent satisfaction, no matter the impossibility of it. The English are reserved in their demeanor, less bullish in their demands, and yet I find the Americans more effusive in their appreciation. And I am not speaking about what the almighty dollar can buy. Truly, they are more appreciative of the work others do for them. They have worked to get where they are, so there is less a sense of entitlement when they finally get what they want."

Since its beginning, the guest register of The Breakers Hotel mirrored many of the exclusive social registers of the eras, with the names of the wealthiest, most prominent, most philanthropic families filling the books. During Rebecca's first years helping to plan events at The Breakers, frequent visitors included a host of Rockefellers, Astors, Huttons, and Vanderbilts.

When Harrison was recruited for employment at the hotel, he was told they also had a nice following among the wealthiest Jewish families in America. And that proved to be true. The name Guggenheim appeared on the registry on the day The Breakers reopened after the inferno, the last day of the year in 1926.

In 1931, New Yorker Felix Warburg, of the prestigious banking dynasty originally from Germany, spent his sixtieth birthday at The Breakers, playing golf with family and friends. In New York, he was the president of the Federation of Jewish Charities. Rebecca helped the chef with meal ideas for his luncheon celebration. Of course, there was no kosher kitchen, but she made sure that nothing being served would be offensive to the traditions the Warburgs still upheld, restricting pork and shellfish from the menu. In 1933, the Jewish publisher of the *New York Times*, Adolph Ochs, and his wife celebrated their fiftieth anniversary in the beautiful, new rotunda dining room of The Breakers. They returned the following season with their whole family entourage, including Schiffs and Rothschilds.

With the progression of decades, more and more often, the most affluent families, whether Gentile or Jewish, who had spent the winter season in residence at The Breakers Hotel were buying or building their own mansions to the north and south of it on Ocean Boulevard. Although they would be able to socialize through their private clubs, they would sometimes miss the convenience of endless rounds of social events, sports, and activities that a vacation resort provided.

Chapter 23

PALM BEACH AND
NEW YORK 1947

In the past five years, Rebecca knew she had existed in a melancholy haze. The feeling had transported her back to her last years of living in Russia, with its share of fear and anxiety, love and hope. There, she had witnessed her mother's illness and subsequent death. She had suffered through the political and social upheavals that made her worry for her father and that led to her own flight to America. Often, she thought of Tchaikovsky's compositions and hummed the tunes to herself to recreate her best memories of that time. The renowned composer had been trained at the St. Petersburg Conservatory, and those in her city took a special pride in his accomplishments.

For so many of her years in America, Rebecca had been residing in the symphony of sun that was Palm Beach, her life as charmed and luxuriant as a ballet performance of Tchaikovsky's Swan Lake. Even the war years with their expectant cargo of tragedies emerged as something positive, with a rich brotherhood of people from all religions, races, occupations, and levels of society coming together for a common cause, a victorious outcome for America and the Allies. It was like a discordant era destined to be capped by the maestro's 1812 Overture, with rich and elegant musical movements leading up to a powerful, exploding crescendo.

Although she tried to appear strong and content with her life, she had been hiding behind her fashionable clothes, wearing her smile as a mask. And often, the charade was hard to maintain. Even the perks of a satisfying life could not fill the void of a marriage without love. Sometimes, the cacophonous melodies of other musicians invaded her consciousness.

And then the year 1947 became a milestone for Rebecca's family, with the engagement of Addie and Nate. Rebeca was truly grateful that her daughter was blessed with the fairytale romance that she, herself, was denied. When Ream closed and became The Breakers again in 1944, Addie and Nate were still in high school. Nate continued with his civilian volunteer duties, working as an aide with the Red Cross. And when the war ended in 1945, Nate had just turned eighteen and enrolled in a predominantly science curriculum at the

University of Miami, in Coral Gables, just ninety miles south of their homes. On many weekends, Nate made the drive from his campus north to Palm Beach, so he and Addie could be together. During his last year of college, Nate came to Addie's parents to ask for her hand. Addie, a year younger, worked part-time at The Breakers during her senior year and then became a full-time employee after graduation. Although her father, Harrison, tried to be professional with their work interactions, he beamed with pride as he watched and listened to Addie's charming manner with the guests in her position at the front desk.

Rebecca knew she should be grateful. She knew she should only be happy. But the melancholy continued to resurface. Following Addie's engagement, Rebecca was anxious to have a special lunch with her daughter, just the two of them, on Worth Avenue. But as soon as she began to leaf through her sketch book to show Addie some wedding gown concepts, her daughter stopped her. "Mother, are you serious? I don't want you to design a new dress for me," she insisted. "I want to wear the dress you wore for your wedding. I know I'm not as tall as you are, but this is what I imagined. Since you will certainly need to cut it down, anyway, how about making it tea length for me, and then maybe adding a tulle overlay."

Rebecca started to tear up. She wiped her eyes with the corner of her cloth napkin. Addie thought it was for the sentimentality of her wanting to wear the dress, but that wasn't it, at all. Rebecca held no sentimental feelings toward the dress or her wedding ceremony, even though she knew her marriage enabled her a wonderful life and a daughter who was her greatest joy. How could she tell Addie that she wished her to have her own fresh, beautiful start? She struggled to keep her complex thoughts to herself.

"Sorry, Mom. I didn't mean to make you sad. I thought my wanting to wear your dress would make you happy."

"Oh, Addie, remember when I told you about 'happy memory tears'? It's just that your enthusiasm for the designing process is reminding me of the time when I was just around your age, working with my own mother. We loved collaborating on the details for so many glorious ball gowns for St. Petersburg nobility and society, before I had to take over all of my mother's commissions."

With those sentiments, Addie quickly left her seat to move behind her mother's, placing her arms around Rebecca's shoulders. "Mom, I understand what you mean. And I know you had a rougher, more complicated life than anyone should have had by the time that you were married." She gave her mother a strong hug and continued. "But Thank God, you and Dad will be here with me for my wedding and on my journey ahead." Slowly, Addie's shining façade started to dim, and she moved back to her seat to face her mother again. "I was afraid of what you maybe wanted to say to me today. I know how you are, and I love you. And I admire you. But I know you are refined and cautious and practical and methodical. And so, I was afraid you were going to tell me I was too young to know my head and my heart." Then just as suddenly as it had disappeared, Addie's sunshine smile returned, as broad as ever. "Mom, don't worry about me. I am crazy happy, like it's a dream. I mean, isn't Nate just the best? I feel so lucky to be marrying him. Is this the way you felt when you were engaged to Dad?"

Rebecca smiled at her daughter, although in her ecstatic state, she felt that Addie most likely did not realize that no answer was given.

Addie eagerly continued sharing her thoughts with her mother. "I know people might say I've never had any other dating experience. But Mom, don't you think it can be – that your first love can be your true and only love?" This was an effortless question for Rebecca to answer. Now, she walked behind Addie's chair and wrapped her arms around her daughter, who had begun focusing on some of the enchanting drawings in Rebecca's sketch book. The oblivious Addie did not see the sadness in her mother's face as Rebecca easily said, "Yes, I do, Addie. I really do believe that."

In August of 1947, Addie and Nate were married at Temple Israel. The next week, they moved together to New York City. Nate was beginning his first year of medical school at the prestigious Columbia College of Physicians and Surgeons. Addie, who would be the breadwinner during those medical school years, was excited to find a reception desk position at The Waldorf Astoria in Midtown Manhattan. The employment office was impressed by her experience at the famous Breakers Hotel in Florida. The manager, giving Addie a tour through the glorious Waldorf lobby, walked with her into the dining room. When they saw Addie, Helen and her husband, Sidney Weinberg, a partner at Goldman Sachs, a man whom the press had titled "Mr. Wall Street," rose from their chairs. They began calling out to her. "Addie, is that you? Come on over here, dear. We are counting the weeks until we go to Palm Beach," the pair said. With that, the manager looked at Addie with a new respect. His serious face melded into a slight smile as he directed her to his office to fill out employment forms.

Although Rebecca was excited for Addie to begin her own journey to New York City, the melancholy persisted and intensified. For the first time in her life, she could not overcome a feeling of depression, fueled by a sense of sadness and abandonment. Her only child was moving away. "What is wrong with me?" Rebecca whispered sometimes to herself. Although it was not without regrets, she had left her own father and crossed an ocean to a new country, a week's trip away on a passenger liner. Addie was only off to another state, a train ride away if she were desperate to see her. The ambivalence of Rebecca's feelings should have been emotions she could share with her husband. But he was too busy, too directed in his passion for perfection at the hotel, to help fill the empty space in her heart.

Chapter 24

PALM BEACH 1948

Surprisingly, as if Rebecca had willed it to happen, Natalie Evington decided to move back to Palm Beach, just a year after Addie and Nate relocated to New York. Natalie would have loved to have stayed in that city, especially with her friends from home as new arrivals. But she knew her father needed company. His young wife, Connie, was off to her next prey, abandoning Natalie's father, Edward, and filing for divorce when she found a younger "sugar daddy" to support her and her daughter. Even over the telephone lines, Natalie had recognized her father's lone-liness. His sweet spirit lingered precariously, as a last drop of candle wax will keep a wick alive and glowing for only so long.

Natalie knew what it would take to rekindle that light. And so, she packed up their belongings and came back to live at the Palm Beach estate with her son, a spunky and smart boy, tall and husky, like his grandfather. Trey loved asking questions of everyone and was quick with answers when quizzed himself. With his lovely daughter and precious grandson now back at home with him, Edward Evington II was revitalized. Over the past several years, as his shock of hair turned from salt and pep-per to silvery gray, his visage lost its Florida glow and his face appeared whitewashed and sallow. But now, with days and then weeks back in the sun, regaining a joy of the sporting activities that he once loved, his skin was gradually earning a golden tan and his look changed from that of a sedentary, aging senior to an active, handsome, mature gentleman. As he did years ago, he looked once again like someone who had just stepped off a yacht or finished a round on the golf course. Often now, he could be seen walking the Atlantic Ocean beach front from his mansion to The Breakers' property with Trey by his side, holding his hand and calling him "Grandpops."

One of the first Saturdays after their return from New York, Natalie joined the inseparable twosome for lunch at the hotel, following her morning run.

"We'll make a sailor out of him in no time," Edward said assuredly to his daughter. "And a chess player, no doubt." She gave him a cautionary glare and he knew what was on her mind. "Don't worry, honey, he won't be an entitled trust fund gadabout like myself." And then he added, teasingly, "Well, he will have a trust fund. Don't deny him his birthright or deny me that pleasure. But he'll be a serious fellow." Edward motioned for the waiter to come by for their order, and when the man left, Edward reached out and patted Trey's hand. "He will have a profession, I promise you," Edward continued, looking at his daughter, as he spoke. "Like many in our Palm Beach society, we were lucky to come through the Depression well enough. During that time, I saw opportunities before me. As real estate values were plummeting, I started to make some purchases. As the war came to our shores, I continued really putting my money and my mind to good use. I envisioned that many of the servicemen and women who came here might just spread the word about our piece of paradise when they returned to their homes up north or on the east coast. To our assets, I've added a substantial portfolio of properties in Palm Beach, Broward, and Dade Counties."

At this point, Natalie felt compelled to break in. "Dad, I had no idea . . ."

"I know I am not a young man, but it's never too late to grow up. I knew, the first time I saw Trey, that I needed to set a good example for our little guy." He rifled his fingers through his grandson's hair and returned to his seat across the table.

Then Natalie rose from her chair and went behind her father's. She wrapped her arms around his neck. "Dad, I'm so proud of you. I had no idea you've been working at this. We never discuss money. That's always been taboo in our world." She released her hold on her father and came in front to face him. "Dad, you amaze me. I only hope I can amaze you some day."

"Are you kidding me?" he returned. "Look at our boy here – your son. You've already done an amazing job raising him, and mainly on your own." He placed a kiss on her forehead as she bent toward him, and he nodded his head with confidence. "Yep, he'll choose his own profession, or he'll work managing real estate with me – or maybe he'll just take it over and let the old man retire someday."

• • •

During the high-season Christmas weeks, when her husband's responsibilities seemed to triple, Rebecca would often join Natalie's family for meals at the hotel or at their estate. Rebecca was touched that Trey himself asked to call her Aunt Rebecca. "We were with Aunt Gracie when we lived in New York, and she was so nice, too," he had said.

Edward Evington was a gracious and welcoming host, happy that his household staff had more responsibilities to occupy their time and justify their salaries.

Through her years at The Breakers, with its heavily gentile clientele, it was a hotel in its grandest splendor at holiday time, embellished by Christmas trees, wreaths, and lights. But Rebecca had never experienced the power and magic of Christmas at a home with a child. Of course, this was no normal home and Grandpa Edward's gifts were extreme, a small battery-powered car a child could actually sit in and drive, and a colorful little sailboat – a dinghy – designed as a training vessel, with Trey's name painted in navy blue at the rear. The little boy naturally was ecstatic with each grand surprise. But he was courteous enough to appear delighted when opening Rebecca's simpler present to him, a craft store box of cardboard airplanes to assemble, and he quickly sent them soaring through the high ceilings of the estate. He ran to hug her and whispered in her ear, "Aunt Rebecca, best gift ever!"

"What a sweet boy!" Rebecca mouthed across the room to Natalie.

When Trey finished with his presents, he was eager to search back under the tree again, this time for a medium-sized box to hand to Rebecca. "Grandpops picked this out and he said I could give this to you from all of us." And then he sang out, "Happy Hanukkah," asking if he had pronounced the word correctly. Rebecca was touched by the thoughtfulness of a gift for her. It was a shiny, sterling silver menorah, a stunning candelabra, the centerpiece for a Hanukkah celebration, complete with the box of ceremonial candles that would shine bright on the eight nights of the Jewish festival of lights.

Throughout the evening, the front door had been opened countless times to welcome a parade of Christmas carolers. Trey loved joining in on singing the songs that he knew. Rebecca saw how much Edward took pride in his little grandson. When the door was at last closed, Trey turned to her. "Aunt Rebecca, do you have any songs for your Hanukkah?"

She had to think about it. It had been a while since Addie was young and they went through the songbook each night. "Well, certainly we do. Let's see. I have no musical talent, but I'll give it a try. She sang a few bars, "Oh Hanukkah, Oh Hanukkah, Come Light the Menorah," and then, "I Have a Little Dreidel." She thought for a moment. "They're cute songs, but you know, our great Jewish composer, Irving Berlin, from Russia, like me, gave you the best song."

When Edward moved to sit at the piano bench, Rebecca thought it was just because it was by the tree. He started to stretch his fingers. He stood up, lifted the top of the seat and rifled through a stack of sheet music, until he apparently found the right one. Then he began playing and singing "I'm Dreaming of a White Christmas." With the house staff also gathered around, they all applauded wildly.

"Time for bed, little man," Natalie said to Trey after Grandpops had taken his bows and they all laughed at his grandiose gestures. Before Natalie followed her son up the grand staircase, she put her hand on Rebecca's shoulder. "I did the right thing," she said, pausing briefly, "by coming back, I mean. My dad's becoming himself again. And thanks for joining us, lately."

"You know what? Tonight's been great for me, too," Rebecca insisted. "I don't know why, well actually I do. Trey's done it for me. It is the first time since Addie and Nate left that I've started thinking of the future. I've been obsessed with missing the past. But now I am thinking, God Willing, Harrison and I could have grandchildren lighting the menorah with us, some-day, maybe when Nate finishes his medical training."

That evening, Edward insisted on escorting Rebecca back to The Breakers. "Can I ask you something?" she said when they were walking. "Where did you ever find such an exquisite menorah? Certainly, I've never seen anything like that even in the nicest stores in Palm Beach. It was an extravagantly thoughtful gift. Thank you so much."

"I'm glad you like it," Edward said, humbly. "I owe you a lot. You stepped up for Natalie when I was incapable. I have never forgotten that. And as to where I found it . . . I own some retail property in Miami. One of my tenant stores carries a large inventory of things you would like."

Chapter 25

PALM BEACH AND
LONDON 1950

Over the next few years, Rebecca found her spirits lifting again. Although she had selfishly feared her loneliness would be unbearable when her daughter moved away, it turned out that she had easily filled the days with responsibilities at the hotel, work from her boutique fashion orders, her involvement in temple activities, and her time with Natalie and even Trey. She was delighted that her visits to New York and visits home by the newlyweds had occurred more often than she would have anticipated. She was bolstered knowing that her daughter was happily married. The way Addie and Nate looked at each other with love and desire in their eyes, their constant need to hold hands or touch a cheek or share a kiss, could have been embarrassing to witness. But Rebecca secretly smiled at each gesture of affection, something she had longed to exchange with her own husband, Harrison.

• • •

In the third week of March, Harrison was busy with the dining room manager, finalizing preparations for the upcoming Easter Sunday brunch. Harrison was asking him to consider a new idea, a special children's miniature-sized buffet area, when the head concierge cautiously interrupted the pair and handed Harrison a telegram. As the assistant manager of the hotel, Harrison was not even considering that it could be disturbing personal news. He treated the cable in a cavalier fashion and set it aside while he continued talking. A minute later, the bright sun streaming in through the massive windows had suddenly been covered by a black cloud, and Harrison reacted as if a dark premonition had cast a shadow in the room. He reached for the envelope, opened it carefully with a knife from the table setting, and read it to himself. He gave out an audible gasp. He covered his face with his hands. He laid the message on the table, forgoing any act of confidentiality. COME IMMEDIATELY STOP FATHER CRITICAL STOP HEART ATTACK STOP. The message was from his only sibling, his sister Victoria, whom he had not seen since their mother passed away in 1935. At that time, he had brought Rebecca and Addie to England for the funeral and to meet Victoria and their father.

He understood that what he had read was telegram wording, although truthfully, it mimicked Victoria's own harsh, judgmental voice. Harrison asked the concierge if he could please book a plane ticket for him to London, as soon as possible. The concierge saw that Harrison was extremely upset by the news and was eager to help him. He had never seen the usually reticent assistant manager in such a distraught state.

When he spotted Rebecca walking past the front desk area, he moved quickly to catch her. He told her briefly what had happened, and he escorted her to Harrison, who was now slumped at his chair in the almost empty dining area. The concierge pulled out the adjacent seat for Rebecca, and he and the other manager walked away, giving them privacy. Rebecca put her arms around her husband's shoulders, but he shook off her efforts. "Let me go to London with you, darling. You don't have to handle this alone," she pleaded with him. When he finally collected himself, clearing his throat as if he were not allowed to cry, she tried to make him understand that it is okay to be emotional. Something sad had happened. But he was not listening. His English reserve was already in full gear.

"I need to go," he insisted in a monotone. Please tell Addie what has happened." Rebecca tried hard to convince him that they should go together. She wanted to share this loss with him, and she wanted to make sure he would be okay. But Harrison kept insisting that he would go alone. Eventually, Rebecca just shook her head resignedly. She knew Addie would want to comfort her father. She encouraged Harrison to take the time to call New York and talk to Addie about her grandfather, but she knew it was something he could not even think about now.

At the London airport, Victoria met Harrison at the gate with tears and more of a handshake than an embrace, but then she broke down in sobs. Their father's decline was even quicker than anticipated, and Harrison did not make it to London in time for a final farewell. Victoria wasted no time in voicing her relentless criticism of his selfishness, his thoughtlessness, his refusing to leave his work post for the past years, valuing his American life above his responsibilities toward their father. "Do you think Father cared so much about the money you sent? Of course, it helped to supplement his pension. But as I wrote back to you every time, with any envelope that came, he only asked, 'Does it say when Hershel and the family will come to visit again?' I think you have always been missing an emotional component in your being. He sought your love; he deserved your respect. Well, don't worry yourself about it now. I held up your end for all of these years."

When they arrived at the Abelman house, Harrison walked into each room of his childhood home, trying to reconnect with his father's essence. When he walked into the room that was still Victoria's, he understood her anger and disappointment. She had devoted her life to taking care of responsibilities he had shirked. He had known this, but the impact of it slapped him in the face. Next to her bed, there were no pictures other than those of her parents, Harrison, Rebecca, and Addie. This was further evidence that Victoria had devoted her life, her colorless life as the old maid daughter, to fulfill her family responsibilities.

He could not take it. Even now, even though he had traveled thousands of miles to be there, he left the house and his sister, and she would have to start making the funeral arrangements without him. He needed a brisk walk to clear his head, although only the London gloom awaited him outside. All this weighed heavily on him. His feelings of grief and guilt were intermingled and overwhelming. He knew Victoria was not wrong in her criticism of him. Harrison hated himself for never visiting, even though Rebecca had tried often to remind him of his obligations. But now, he needed a break from his sister's tirade. He just needed to walk toward the city center and escape. He searched the skyline for the clock tower of Westminster Abbey, but he could not even remember which direction to look. Instead, he became dizzy focusing on the tops of two double decker red buses as they maneuvered a busy traffic circle with their contingencies of tourists, excitedly pointing every which way at the sites surrounding them. He had no idea where he was headed. It had been a long time since he was last in London. Overtired and overwrought, he had forgotten that he was not in his adopted country of America. He had forgotten that in England the traffic pattern is reversed. Although there were admonitions on the pavement cautioning pedestrians to look right, whereas in America you would look left, Harrison, a born and bred Londoner should have known this anyway. But now he was distracted by all his emotions. He was not processing anything and looked at the sky while crossing the street.

Soon, the iconic sound of the London police cars and ambulances filled the air. Horrified witnesses would remember turning to the sound of screeching brakes. The bus driver would insist there was no way to avoid the inevitable horror. The image

of the flying man would be what made him choose an early retirement, although the authorities and the bus company absolved
him of any blame in the death of Harrison Abelman.

Chapter 26

PALM BEACH 1952

Since the shocking death of her husband two years earlier, Rebecca had tried to act normal, had worked to maintain her usual positive outward disposition so that she would not be the focus of attention and concern. Her friends and colleagues knew what she was doing, and they gave her leave to come to terms with Harrison's death and her grief. Their greatest fear was that she, who had always been the brightest butterfly of a woman, would retreat into a cocoon. But most of them had no understanding of what Rebecca had been through in her life. There was no measurement tool that could quantify her resilience.

Ultimately, Rebecca was energized that Addie returned often from New York so they could spend time together. And when her daughter was away, Rebecca found great support from Nate's parents, especially his mother, Eleanor Bernstein. The Bernsteins were there for her at Harrison's funeral and well beyond the *shiva* week of mourning that followed. It was a bond that started when she had first come from Russia and she and Harrison joined Temple Israel. When the Bernsteins' eldest son, Benjamin, was tragically killed in the training base explosion at the start of WWII, Rebecca barely left their side for a month. And the ties continued to grow as Addie and Nate's friendship developed into a romance. With the marriage of their children, the Bernsteins and the Abelmans officially became *machatunim*, the Jewish term for the in-laws of married children. At the time of the wedding, Rebecca had no idea how important that relationship would prove. Over the years of their friendship, Rebecca had confided so much about her past to Eleanor, including stories of her youth in St. Petersburg. There were sweet images she wanted to hold onto by sharing them aloud – working with her mother, as seamstress to Russian royalty, and her pride in her bright and respected father. There were sad images she wanted to share for cathartic purposes – experiencing the decline of her mother, and her horror on learning her father's fate. She had even told Eleanor how it was her love for a religious boy, Jacob Schaevitz, that had paved her way to America. But she had never revealed to Eleanor how memories of that young man would occasionally resurface. She told her only that this young man had disappeared, leaving her alone in a strange country.

As Eleanor had listened to those stories of the past, she sensed a longing and a passion in Rebecca's voice and in her eyes. And although Rebecca had often told her she felt blessed with her life in Florida, Eleanor knew she had never recognized that same spark in her friend's exchanges with her husband.

After Harrison's death, Rebecca continued her role as a Breakers' unofficial hostess and event consultant, but now in a paid capacity. Although the Kenan family, the owners of Flagler Systems, which included The Breakers Hotel, had shown only compassion upon the loss of her husband, Rebecca knew she would soon be expected to vacate their management suite. Without having to be approached, she voluntarily ended her long-time residency at the resort and rented a lovely small home nearby. She looked forward to having a place to decorate as she wished.

With her husband's passing and her daughter now a married woman living in New York, Rebecca's continued association with a fashionable boutique in Palm Beach was a godsend. Days flew by when they could have been filled with long and lonely hours. She kept active in her design work for the store, in arranging fashion shows for charity groups, and in helping to bring music and theater events to the Palm Beach area. She served on her congregation's sisterhood board and enjoyed shared activities with Eleanor Bernstein, including bridge afternoons and cooking lessons. Until recently, she had taken most of her meals at The Breakers complex. But now, in her moderate-sized but amply equipped kitchen, she was eager to cook and bake herself.

And she continued to spend time with Natalie's family. While she would sometimes join them for meals prepared by their chef, she delighted in having them as guests at her home to try out an assortment of the new recipes.

Finally, she accepted Edward's offer to drive her to the Miami Beach store where he had purchased the menorah. At the Judaica shop, she found a beautiful Jewish Star of David and bought it as a gift for her daughter, Addie. She would give it to her on an upcoming birthday visit. She wondered why she did not think of this years ago, before they were separated by so many miles. She remembered when her own mother gave her the gold locket, her most meaningful keepsake, the one she always had worn around her neck.

When Rebecca and Edward walked Collins Avenue, the main street of Miami Beach, they saw many hotels that lined their path, with guests sitting in front, fanning themselves for relief from the heat. On certain blocks, she heard Yiddish conversations, and they resonated with her, bringing her back briefly to another place and time, as she smiled to herself. It was interesting seeing how Edward had actually entered this world through his business dealings. As they walked further, music from some of the lounges along the strip enticed them inside to sit for a while and have a cool drink.

• • •

More and more often, thirty-year old Natalie began accepting dates from her throng of Palm Beach admirers. Some were the seasonal visitors from the hotel; some were men who had built new mansions in the area along the coast. They wined and dined her, quite elegantly, at the best restaurants and private clubs, but many of the men, she sensed, were too old for her. And when they asked to take her on their yachts for trips to the Bahamas or Key West, she turned them down.

On an early evening in March, Natalie was at a newly opened upscale eatery on Clematis, and her interest in the conversation with her date was darkening like the diminishing light of the approaching sunset. She had no idea how she had put up with him past the first few drinks he consumed. She would have left, but she was waiting for the appetizer that was ordered to come. She needed a few bites of something to sober the effect of her one martini.

"Come on, Natalie," her dinner companion said with a slow and slurring speech pattern. His hand was reaching out to keep her from leaving her seat. Just then, a very handsome younger man, who she felt looked somewhat familiar to her, passed the bar counter where they were seated, and then he turned quickly for a second look. He intercepted Natalie's date's arm with his left hand and then offered his right hand for a swift and powerful handshake. "Mr. Sheridan," he said, "perhaps you were waiting for your wife. I just saw her exiting a taxi out front."

Arthur Sheridan quickly pulled a large bill from his wallet and laid it on the placemat. He moved quickly toward the door, and the newly arrived younger man seamlessly took his vacated seat. He straddled the bar chair, angling towards Natalie, one foot resting on her high-backed stool to block her exit. For a second, Natalie had an uncomfortable feeling of being trapped, as the man insistently followed each almost frantic turn of her head, until she took a moment to really look at him. His smile broadened while he waited for her recognition, and then she returned a smile of her own.

"Natalie, is that you? Natalie Evington – is that really you?" he said. "I can't believe it's really you."

"Will?" she questioned, "Will Whitney? I haven't seen you in forever."

"Whew," he emitted, letting out a puff of breath. "You do remember me. The beautiful Natalie Evington recognized me." He got off the stool and bowed to her. "I am honored. You barely said my name in all our school years together. And now, imagine that," he said, looking around as if searching for someone to witness the event. "Imagine, the enigmatic, unapproachable Natalie Evington is going to have dinner with me."

"Am I having dinner with you?"

"Oh yes, accepting my invitation is the least you can do for me, for politely dismissing your date. He held up two fingers to catch the waiter's attention. "One steak, medium, please," he told the man and then turned to Natalie, " . . . and?"

"The roasted chicken," she answered, after a pause to consider what was happening.

Will pointed to her half-finished martini. "And one more of those for each of us."

When he was done ordering, Will pulled Natalie's chair closer to his. "Now," he said and paused to scrutinize her face. "What was that about, anyway? Why were you even with that lech?"

"I don't know, and yes, thank you for saving me. I've kind of started dating again." She paused and shook her head. "Mainly it has been challenging, but I've also reconnected with some of the old group, and that's been fun." She paused to look him up and down and tilted her head to one side, with a quizzical look. "You've changed a lot, Will. You look different." When she realized he did not know how to take that, she added, "Different in a good way. I mean you were always cute, but . . . oh, will you please stuff some bread in my mouth, so I will stop talking?" He tore off a small piece of focaccia but did not let go of it until her tiny bites landed her lips at his fingertips. With him standing next to her now, she stepped off the chair herself. "That's it – you grew," she said emphatically, with a pleased, surprised look. "You grew a lot. When did that happen?"

"Actually, I think my growth spurt came my first year in college, just when I was called to the service. Imagine growing taller with only the most meager food available. I became a beanpole."

She looked at his physique, easily discernible with his perfectly tailored suit. "It looks like you've filled out just fine."

"Can I say something without being kicked?"

She was not sure what he meant.

"Can I say the same to you? You filled out more than just fine, Natalie. You filled out in all the right places." She gave him a mocking slap. "Maybe that's why you never talked to me. You'd have had to look so far down. I probably graduated high school at five feet six." He put his arms on her shoulders and spun her so they were back to back. "But now, I think I may have a couple inches on you."

"Possibly more," she said, in a tone approaching flirtatious, as they faced each other once again. "I'm wearing heels."

"God, you're gorgeous." Will said. "I always admired you from afar, but now – wow, so close to you, I'm a tongue-tied teenager again."

She remembered him better than she let on. Will was part of the crowd that had grown up together on the island. As she resurfaced in the dating world, she found, surprisingly, that she was most comfortable spending time with some of the Palm Beach school boys who had pursued her years ago. The boys she described then as juvenile, narcissistic, and spoiled had grown into serious, well-educated, and accomplished young men and joined successful family businesses. And now William Perry Whitney appeared before her as the best evidence of that. She was remembering that he was one of the brightest boys, and one of the nicest. She recalled him helping her in algebra or geometry.

She had never meant to appear aloof. But she knew often she was misread. He probably would not believe that she was the insecure one, self-conscious and embarrassed of her height.

When their drinks came, they raised them for a toast.

"To the past," they said, in unison, clinking glasses. Unable to help himself, Will gave her a quick kiss on the cheek.

"Catch me up on everything," he said, and for the first time he noticed a ring on her finger. "Wait now, maybe I'm remembering. You were married."

"It was just a short time, and then I was a war widow." She knew she was not being totally forthcoming, but she would leave it at that for now.

"You still wear your ring," he said as he brought her hand closer to his face, pretending to admire the stone, but only wanting to touch her.

"It helps to keep undesirables away," she said.

"It didn't work for me," he threw back, quickly. "So, I guess I must not be undesirable."

She laughed. "Well, then I have a second surprise that repels those who still linger."

"Okay, and what is that?"

"I have a son. I have a nine-year old son."

"Wait," he said and then thought about it. "Now I think this story is coming back to me. You had moved to New York for a while, maybe to be with your husband's family?"

"No, not exactly, just to be away a bit."

"Well, you're lucky." Will said. She looked at him oddly. "I was hoping that would be me by now, at this age. With a child of my own."

"That's a sweet thing to say. You are a surprising man, Will Whitney."

"I had a brief marriage myself, right after the war. Turns out, she didn't expect I'd be going back to complete college and business school. She knew the family I came from. She was thinking dream house, not dorm room. Well, not quite a dorm room, but Harvard married student housing wasn't much better. He paused and shook his head. "It was a quick divorce . . . no kids," he said, but with a somewhat sad shrug.

"I'm sorry if you were hurt," she offered empathetically. "But I think your story is far from written. You're still young . . . and kind of cute, like I said," she laughed out, teasing him. "You'll find the right person. And you're right; my son is my precious joy." Natalie raised her glass. "Let's toast to your future."

"To our future," he said quickly and with no filter. After he said it, he worried those words would scare her. She'd already inferred that her guard was always up. But something about the way she kept staring at him, reflecting the same way he knew he was staring back, gave him courage. Through dinner, they caught up on all the escapades and pranks of the

DEBY EISENBERG

privileged set that was the world of their youth in Palm Beach. As they reminisced, they laughed into each other, knocking foreheads more than one time. Suddenly, Will pushed her shoulders back, playfully. "I'm still mad at you about something, by the way," he shot out, looking right into her eyes.

"Now, what kind of grudge could you possibly have kept all these years?"

Without missing a beat, as if it had always been on his mind, he said, "Spin the bottle, seventh grade."

"Oh my God, you are serious. What did I do?"

"You made a face when the bottle pointed to me. You wouldn't meet me in the circle for the kiss."

"Incredible. How would you even remember something like that?" She was still laughing, but his face turned serious.

"Because I was embarrassed. And I really liked you, even then."

She was about to make a funny, dismissive comment, like "if only you had been taller already," but she thought better. She had not felt so happy, so comfortable, so drawn to a man, so physically attracted to anyone in a long time. She maneuvered off her stool and stood right in front of him. She uncrossed his legs so that she could be as close to him as possible. She wrapped her hands around his neck and brought his head closer toward her. She targeted her lips to be perfectly centered on his and gave him a moist and increasingly powerful kiss. Just as she was ready to release him, he wove his fingers through her hair and kept her close. He returned the sweet gift of a kiss, with a consuming passion that sent erotic waves through her body.

When they opened their eyes and could compose themselves, they noticed they had an audience of onlookers.

"Forgiven?" she asked.

"Definitely forgiven," he said.

Chapter 27

PALM BEACH 1952

For the past few months, Edward and Rebecca had each been aware that Natalie had been keeping company with William Perry Whitney. Natalie had told them about many of the most entertaining afternoons that they had spent together with some of the Kennedy family at their compound nearby. Edward Evington had known Joe Kennedy, Sr., for years and in November, his son, the three-term congressman from Massachusetts, John Fitzgerald Kennedy, would be challenging

Henry Cabot Lodge for his Senate seat. "You can count on a legion of press photographers wherever there are Kennedys," Edward had said. In the past month, pictures of Natalie and Will, alongside the Kennedys, had made their way into local and national newspapers and magazines. In the pictures. they were laughing and dining, playing touch football, and lounging on yachts with Bobby and Ethel Kennedy, and Jack Kennedy and his fiancée, Jacqueline Bouvier. In the photo captions, sometimes Natalie and Will were named and sometimes referred to, anonymously, as "another golden couple." They had a standing tease in the beginning weeks. "But Natty, would you still choose me if Jack Kennedy were available?"

"Sorry, I just can't commit to that. He is Jack Kennedy, after all," would always be her sarcastic answer.

"But Will, would you still choose me if Jackie were available?"

"Sorry, but that's a tough one," would always be his retort.

They had great times during those early spring days with the famous family, but soon Jack and his campaign manager, Bobby, needed to return to their homes up north, to complete a campaign plan to visit every village, town, and city in the state.

With each progressive day and night in their ensuing months together, with public outings and private evenings, Natalie and Will caught up on the intervening years. A few times, they went back to the Hut, a popular teenage hangout in West Palm Beach since 1930, and they sat at the counter, sharing chocolate milkshakes and sodas, on tiny red leather stools. Natalie talked about her time in New York and her desire to do more writing. Will told her about his experiences at school and his position with the Whitney financial firm, at its headquarters in Connecticut.

In truth, Natalie did think Will was quite as handsome and appealing as the senatorial candidate from Massachusetts. Will was tall and broad shouldered, his smile was ever present, and every person who received its greeting would think it was only meant for them. Although he complimented her blue eyes, she swore his sparkled with a greater intensity. He had a serious, successful look about him, but the natural thick blond streaks that channeled through his brown hair gave him a playful look. He looked like a lifeguard who went to an Ivy League college. Each time she met him, she almost swooned into his arms, like the ravaged heroines on the covers of drugstore paperback novels.

Little by little, they were moving closer to the edge of the cliff, until they had completely fallen in love. Will was the one to say it first. At a candlelit dinner in a quiet corner of The Breakers' most beautiful dining room area, he simply said, "Natty, I'd choose you over Jackie any day of the week. I love you."

And she answered coyly, "Jack who? Never interested in the guy." Then she turned serious and spoke into his lips. "I've loved you since our first kiss at the bar," she said, with her blue eyes illuminated by the glowing flame.

"I've loved you since the first kiss you never gave me," Will returned.

On the night that Natalie finally brought her bright, tall, and sophisticated boyfriend to the Evington home to meet her father and be introduced to Trey, she had asked Rebecca to join them as well. Watching the interactions of the young couple, both Edward and Rebecca understood that Natalie had been swept off her feet for the second time in her life. And they couldn't blame her. As Will told old stories of Natalie as a schoolgirl and recounted the boundless energy of the Kennedy clan, they both found Will to be charming and charismatic.

"It's funny," Rebecca told them, "I do remember how Joe Kennedy always required that his family play to the photographers, even as they spent the day at The Breakers, and I was often called into service to make sure their needs were accommodated. It was as if, even those many years ago, he knew their lives should be chronicled, that they were meant for great things. I remember the day a picture was taken that still hangs in one of The Breakers' historical rooms. It's a picture from 1934, in front of one of the beach cabanas. Walk in the room and you'll see a very young Robert Kennedy pushing his baby brother, Edward, in a stroller."

After the meal, Trey appeared by Will's side with a baseball in one hand and a mitt in the other, and his mother's same eyes offering up an appeal to play. Without being coaxed, Will asked if they could be excused for a while, "I always keep my own mitt in the car. If you don't mind, it looks like Trey and I have some business to do in the backyard."

Covertly peering out the window, Natalie was almost in tears. Will was bending down to Trey's level, scrutinizing the ball, showing him the correct position to place his fingers along the seams, and then watching Trey imitate Will's pitching stance and arm movements. When the pair looked back and saw her, she threw them a kiss and quickly moved from their sight line to let them continue.

Chapter 28

PALM BEACH 1952

The following day, Natalie was anxious to meet with Rebecca. Rebecca intuitively knew Natalie had asked her for lunch because she wanted her opinion of Will. And so, she decided she would make the conversation easy for her by just saying what she thought. "I can see it. You are glowing again. I haven't seen that special glow on you in a long while."

Natalie couldn't wait to break in. "He is the one. You're right. He is . . . well, he's everything I could want. I love him."

She bit her lower lip and forced the next words out, "and he loves me, too."

"Oh, Natalie, I am so happy for you. It's time, and you deserve this."

"It's crazy. He wants to marry me. She took Rebecca's hands in hers, as the waiter set down their drinks. "You know I've never had any date meet Trey before. I didn't want him confused or disappointed if there were men going in and out of his life."

"I know, honey. You've done everything right."

"Even you saw it," she said, with a burgeoning enthusiasm. "Will and Trey – they took to each other immediately." Then she paused, contemplatively. "But I'm not rushing into anything, especially for one reason."

"You're thinking you can never love anyone like you loved Theo. I understand that," Rebecca posed.

"Surprisingly, it's not that," Natalie said. "This is what is hard. I can't bear to tell my father that we'll be leaving him again." She took more sips of her iced tea. "Will has been groomed for a position in the venture capital firm of his extended Whitney family." She laughed at herself for minute. "I'm not exactly sure what that means, but it is a financial firm, an investment firm. He just returned to this area after being in their main offices in Connecticut right out of Harvard Business School. But now they want him at their new Boston offices."

Rebecca took a long sip from her wine. "Oh my. That is a big move, a big decision. Let me process this." She gave an understanding laugh. "But, of course, my opinion doesn't matter. What are you thinking? That's what's important."

"Rebecca, your opinion always matters to me. You know that. And I want to hear it when I tell you what I am considering. I want your thoughts even before I present this to my father. Rebecca nodded and remained silent.

"I think Trey and I should move to Boston. But we should have our own apartment in the city. Before I make a permanent decision on marriage, I want to have more time getting to know Will as the man he is now. Obviously, I love how I feel about him, so far, but maybe we need more time together. You probably don't know that Dad and I had been discussing private schooling for Trey. We still think he is too young for overnight boarding, although we always knew we'd want him to go a boarding academy for high school. That's something the men in our family have always done. But that's a few years down the road. I'm not sure our area here has developed a grammar school system that can adequately prepare Trey for entrance to an elite prep school, the first step to a top university.

"My impression is that he is a very smart little boy," Rebecca said.

"Will has even looked into this," Natalie continued. "His firm has connections with the best schools in the Boston area, and as you can imagine, with a large circle of business executives and university professors living there, all wanting the best education for their children, there is no shortage of choices. I know he seems smart to us, but the competition for spots can be tough. I'd like to enroll Trey at a private day school for the next four years, and not do complete boarding until high school. Coincidentally, moving to Boston, so we could be near Will, could also be the best way to get Trey the head start we want for him.

Natalie looked to Rebecca for a response.

"You've thought this out. And everything you say makes sense. But my gut feeling?"

"Yes, please, tell me." Natalie had always craved Rebecca's advice, like a child reaches for that first lick of a chocolate ice cream cone.

"My gut feeling is . . . I think you and Will won't make it that long."

When Natalie had an almost anguished look on her face, Rebecca felt she needed to clarify her words, and quickly. Rebecca cupped Natalie's chin to bring her eyes to meet her own. "I think you won't make it that long until you are walking down that aisle."

Natalie was visibly relieved. "I'm so happy, and so happy you see us that way."

"Well, it's hard not to. I could see easily how you could hardly keep your hands off each other," Rebecca teased. "And I love that – that's the way it should be."

"You're right. Each time we kiss goodnight at the door, we're back in each other's arms for one more round. Honestly, this isn't a fling. This is a 'meant for each other' type of love," Natalie said, and then turned cautious. "Do you think that you can have that kind of romance more than once in your life, Rebecca?

She thought it over. "I'll be honest with you. I never did," she answered. And then she added, "but I think I do now."

Three weeks later, as the fall school term was approaching, Edward, Natalie, and Trey came to Rebecca's door.

"Aunt Rebecca, I'm here to say goodbye to you. I will be leaving tomorrow." Rebecca winked at Natalie, indicating she knew this day was coming.

"And just where will you be going, young man, so handsomely dressed up like a miniature adult?" He had on khaki pants, a white shirt, and a navy tie. "Have you a sports jacket, as well?" She was teasing him, and his stalwart posture was a match for his well-elocuted answer. "Not as of yet, ma'am. I believe they issue the blazer with the crest when you arrive." He looked to his grandfather for confirmation. "Or maybe, there is some ceremony where they present you with the crest."

"I'm going to miss you, Trey. You won't forget about me, will you?

"You know, Aunt Rebecca, this is all so I can follow my legacy. I will just go to a day school now in Boston to finish grammar school. But when I graduate, I hope to go where my grandfather went to for high school, at Phillips Exeter Academy in New Hampshire. It's a steppingstone to the Ivy League schools." Rebecca couldn't help but give Trey a sweet kiss on his forehead. It was obvious he was echoing back adult phrases he had heard, but still, he seemed to have a grasp of their meaning. "I am hoping I will do well enough there and might be accepted to a top college, like Grandpops." To hear that last term of endearment made her smile and think of the little boy opening his Christmas gifts.

"You are right if you are thinking I'm worried about my father." Natalie said to Rebecca, as they were just finishing their meal, waiting for tea and coffee. "I'm hoping you might check on him from time to time. I mean just make sure he doesn't go back into his lonely mode."

Rebecca laughed, "I have a feeling you don't have to worry about that. Your coming back to Palm Beach brought him out of a lethargic state he will not likely be returning to. I think between monitoring his properties and meeting his group for his club and sports activities, he'll be fine. Just send him notes and pictures and don't forget to call on Sundays." As Rebecca went to hug Natalie goodbye, she added, "and call me, too, sometimes." She took a slip of paper from her purse. "And I have another idea to occupy his time." Natalie's eyes widened, but before she could overreact, Rebecca said, "I've been thinking about this, and I've already run it by my good friend. You've met her, I'm sure. I know you have been to the store. She's the owner of the boutique that sells my dress and decorating designs. Her husband passed away after a long illness about a year ago. Did you know him, Dr. Marcus McCormick? He was a much-beloved physician, making house calls, when necessary, to the most elaborate society mansions, where they paid him with large bills, insisting that he keep the change, and giving him stock market tips when they walked him to the door. And he helped at the smallest homes of those with the most modest means, who paid him with vegetables from the gardens in their yards. Mary Elizabeth McCormick is a beautiful lady, classically elegant but down to earth, an independent woman who loves the arts. I know she and her husband traveled often, and they loved to cruise the intracoastal with their motorboat. She actually thinks she may know who your father is from Bethesda-by-the-Sea Episcopal Church. I would like to talk to Edward about her, and I'll just leave this slip with her name and phone number in his possession – no pressure, no expectations. But maybe he could invite her to dinner one time and just see where it goes."

"Rebecca, like your designs, you are one of a kind," Natalie said, smiling at her mother-figure, as they walked into the front room together.

Edward and Trey had been playing chess in Rebecca's living room, with Will sitting as a sidecar, whispering a few tips in Trey's ear. For a moment, watching them in their intense competition, Rebecca had a flashback. She was in her St. Petersburg home, and it was her father and his friends, his comrades, at the table. It was one of her most vivid memories, heartwarming and disturbing at the same time. She had wondered over the years just how her father was taken away, had the Communists broken up one of their tournaments that were really their anti-Soviet meetings? Despite this memory, she refused to be drawn back to the fearful times. She looked out her window to her front yard and saw only sunshine and the perfectly sculpted bushes that exploded with newly opening buds. Life was good.

Chapter 29

PALM BEACH 1954

It was a beautiful Thursday afternoon, a light breeze swirling from the west, choreographing the palm fronds into a seductive dance. Rebecca strolled toward Flagler Street after presenting her decorating concept to a bride's family for an upcoming wedding in The Breakers' ballroom. One of the hotel transportation vehicle drivers, having just dropped off guests and making his rounds with an empty car, pushed the switch to lower the passenger window and he waved Rebecca over his way. "Come on in. Let me take you wherever you're going."

She turned towards the man's familiar voice. "Oh, that's okay, Martin. It's such a beautiful afternoon. I'm happy to walk. Thank you so much, though," she said.

Receiving her signature smile, he could not give up so easily. "But your outfit is too attractive! Your hair is, what do people say, perfectly coiffed? I cannot bear thinking of you fending off wolf whistles on your route. Come on. Where are you headed?"

He was the sweetest man, Rebecca thought, and she gave in to his persistence. "Well then, Martin, thanks. You know what? I will take you up on that offer. Just going to Temple Israel, on Flagler, you know." She had given herself plenty of time to reach her destination, but she was now thinking it would be nice to arrive at the synagogue still feeling fresh. In the car, she looked through the accessory bag she always carried in addition to her purse and checked to see that it held her nice pair of heels. At her destination, she would take off her simple flats and change into them. She was going to meet with a committee of sisterhood ladies to discuss the agenda for an upcoming cultural event.

When Rebecca entered the building, a cluster of women were standing in the foyer. Rebecca smiled at them but kept walking toward the temple library, where they would be working around a large boardroom table. The ladies seemed to want her to stop and talk before she entered the room, but she gestured to them that she needed to change her shoes. They understood. They knew their Rebecca. Always perfectly put together, she was their style icon, and they admired her.

As she walked past, though, she began picking up bits of their conversation. "Isn't he the most handsome?" "And what is that accent?"

When Rebecca opened the door to the library, only a small desk lamp was already turned on, as their meeting was not scheduled to start for a while. Immediately, she chose a chair in the right corner, sat down, and began changing into her black patent pumps. Then she looked up, startled when a moving shadow indicated someone else was in the room. Abruptly, before she replaced her second shoe, she stood and backed up against the wall. Now she saw the silhouette of a man, a *kepa* clipped to his mass of ebony hair. He was obviously nonthreatening, just a volunteer helping with the library shelving. He was reaching his arms high above his head to place books, one by one, on an upper shelf. Only his back was in her sightline, but she immediately admired the cut and the design of his suit. From her position, she had no idea who the man was or even how old he could be, although even the dim light reflected highlights here and there of silver strands in his hair. And there was, inexplicably, something familiar about him, possibly something about his hair and the thickness of its waves as it met the nape of his neck. Rebecca laughed at herself. For a minute, she felt a chill run through her body. How silly she was! This man was taller, bigger, obviously a more sophisticated, wealthier man than the boy who lived in her dreams. The lines of his suit were in the latest style with slightly padded shoulders angling toward a slimmer waistline. How foolish that images of one young man she had known so long ago and was a mess of a dresser in Hasidic garb, were surfacing now.

But as this man turned and reached for the next book from the stack to place up high, he stepped down from a stool that had been out of her view. Suddenly, he was not as tall as she thought, although certainly of a substantial height.

As the man turned again, he saw the silhouette of a woman at the back of the room, and apologized immediately. "So sorry, I didn't know anyone was here. I was asked by the ladies to help when I came in the building."

Rebecca had to stifle a gasp on hearing the man speak, and then she whispered so softly that it was audible only to her own ear. "Oh my God." It was his voice, an older version, without question, but unmistakably his English speech was resonant of a Russian, Yiddish dialect that had never left her memory.

He sensed she was uncomfortable with a stranger in the room. "Again, my apologies, I can finish later," he said and started to gather his personal items, so he could leave quickly.

"Oh my God," she cried aloud, hearing him speaking once more. She stood up quickly, but with only one shoe on, she fell back from her precarious stance. With this move, she apparently activated the switch for the broader overhead light fixture, and it illuminated the room. The man began blinking, as his eyes adjusted to the brightness. And then, suddenly, everything came into focus for him, and he looked directly at Rebecca.

"And those are his eyes," she continued still talking to herself. They were a color of green that she had seen duplicated only in her fantasies.

"My God," he yelled. He didn't care who heard. "It can't be true" he panted out, as if breathless from the simple act of stepping off the stool and walking toward her. But then he berated himself silently. "No – it's just another illusion. Don't fall for it. Every time you see that beautiful brown hair, you think it is her. Just like every time you hear the name Rebecca, you turn in the direction. But every time, it is not her. Why now? why here? when you've searched for over three decades?" But then he gave into the fantasy. So, he would make a fool of himself, as he had so many times before.

"Rebecca?" he questioned, tentatively, knowing he would only be given a curious look. How could it be her? This person before him looked too young, not appropriately aged as the one would be whom he had said goodbye to so many years ago. But still, he risked humiliation one more time. "Is that you?" He paused and rubbed his eyes. "Rebecca, is that really you?"

She backed up as he came closer and so he made sure to keep his tone soft and unthreatening, hiding his desperate edge from surfacing. "Is it my Rebecca, my love, who I've never stopped loving, who I've dreamed about and searched for every day of the last thirty years?" Quickly, without hearing any answer, he maneuvered his way around the table and chairs, oversized furniture for the room, and he made his way to Rebecca. When he was next to her, he bent down on his knees. He started to cry. He looked first at her neck and took hold of her small locket with the tips of his fingers, caressing it, as if this tactile act was the only proof that he was not imagining all of this. He was crying and he was laughing.

Having him so close, looking into his unmistakable dark emerald eyes, Rebecca was overwhelmed by emotions she could not contain. Suddenly, she felt faint, and then, like in a scene from a silent screen melodrama, she was the movie star collapsing slowly to the floor. He begged her to wake up, issuing tender slaps to her cheeks that grew in intensity. And when she finally opened her eyes, Rebecca could not believe what was happening. "Jacob?" she questioned in a soft, intimate voice. After all these years, after all this time, Rebecca was cradled in the arms of her first and only love. She was breathing the same air as Jacob. The roguish boy who disappeared from her life had returned to her as a sophisticated man.

Lifting her slightly, not caring if he had her permission, Jacob kissed every exposed area of her body – her cheeks, her forehead, her arms, her neck, until she clasped his handsomely mature face in her hands and directed his kisses to her lips. They lay in the corner against the wall, her head in his lap, her arms around his neck, like he had just saved her from drowning.

There were so many questions running through their minds that Rebecca and Jacob did not know where to begin. "Why?" Rebecca cried only this one word softly, as in "Why did you disappear?" But she did not complete the sentence. And Jacob only wanted to taste the sweet breath of any word she spoke. He kissed her lips with such intensity that her head was spinning. "Where?" she said next, quivering out the word, but again, she did not complete the question – "Where have you been all these years?" "How?" she asked, again just crying out the one word and not the completed thought, "How did you happen to be here?" There were so many more questions she could not articulate, and he could not answer.

When the ladies walked into the room for their meeting, they did not know whether to step back to give the pair privacy or to go forward to rescue their friend. But there was no need. Rebecca had already been rescued.

When Eleanor Bernstein entered the room, she was both frightened and astonished by the scene before her and did not know what to make of it. And then she understood the feverish longing in the eyes of the couple, as they gazed at each other. She knew that she was witnessing the most loving look that she had ever seen on her friend's face in all the years they had known each other. "Rebecca," she said with an ironic laugh, "I guess you've met our newest congregant, Jack Schaeffer."

Chapter 30

PALM BEACH 1954

Rebecca and Jacob could not loosen their physical bond for even a moment, as if in doing so they would be lost to each other forever, again. As the committee moved to retreat to the foyer, they were unable to completely process what they had witnessed, but somehow, they were all still envious of the romance before them. As the pair left the room, the Jack Schaeffer they had met had literally swept Rebecca off her feet and was carrying her away, with her belongings, as if she were as light as a pillow. Rebecca wanted to say something to Eleanor, whose eyes, like all the others', were glued on her and Jacob. Rebecca could not withdraw her one hand from its position locked at the hip of this no longer elusive man. But with her other hand, she pointed to him and mouthed to Eleanor, "This is him – this is Jacob Schaevitz," as if it were even possible that Eleanor did not already realize that.

After leaving the library, Jacob set Rebecca down, and like the prince in Cinderella, he placed her second shoe easily on her foot. He reached for her hand and began to run with her out of the synagogue, to the curb.

Rebecca was astonished for the second time that morning, when Jacob opened the passenger door to a striking showpiece vehicle, and he helped Rebecca to get seated. She remembered being attracted to the car when she saw it parked in front of the building, before she entered, never anticipating that soon after that her attraction would take a whole new direction.

As they sat in a cobalt blue Cadillac convertible, with a vanilla leather interior, a special design created for the fiftieth anniversary of the automobile company, not a car passed by without slowing down for a look.

"Why are we sitting in here? Do you know whose car this is?" she said, cautiously, turning her head this way and that, as if fearing a "Get out of there, now" would be sent her way at any moment, by an outraged owner.

"Do you like the car?" Jacob asked softly, calmly.

When she looked at him, she could hardly believe that despite the passage of years and his sophisticated appearance, she still saw every reflection of the driven and daring and mischievous boy that she knew. "Well, of course, I like the car. It's spectacular, I guess," she answered, and then she paused. "But please," she begged him. She was not a rule breaker. "Whose car is this? We are not children anymore. We can't play games." She started to open the door to leave.

"Rebecca, how can I make you believe that this is my car?"

"Car," she repeated, laughing at the word. "The last time I saw you, you had a cart. She exaggerated the "t" sound at the end of the word. "You had a wooden cart with wooden wheels, not whitewall tires."

He wanted them to stop talking, although with this dialogue, he thought, fondly, of their teasing banter all those years ago. But now, he only wanted to drive his car to somewhere away from here, somewhere private. He knew there was so much they needed to understand about what had happened to each of them over the lost years, but his immediate wish was to kiss her and hug her and love her in any way she would accept. He could not spend ten more minutes sitting in the open, talking to her. "I need to take you somewhere. I need to be alone with you," he pleaded. He softly traced the back of his hand along her jawline and continued to the arch of her high cheekbone. When his hand touched her neck behind her ear, she experienced a wave of desire and begged him to move this car that he said was his, and to drive her away from the building. With his impish grin resurfacing, he dangled the keys in front of her. He turned on the car and drove for about four blocks, parking along a neighboring street.

He was working up his courage to ask something. "Rebecca," he said, shyly, "Could we please find somewhere we could go? You may see this as forward. You may think this is out of line, inappropriate after decades of no communication. But you need to understand. In my mind, in my fantasies, I have had you with me so many times. But those dreams always ended too soon. And then I always awakened to the same nightmare. We are separated and I can't find you."

She brought her hand to rest over her heart and she took a deep breath, like a Victorian-age sigh. She found it hard to believe. He had just described her own restless nights.

She was not answering him, but she had not said no, so he just continued. He took his hand off the steering wheel and turned to her. "If you don't like the car. I'll return it. Suddenly, I don't care about it, anyway. I never knew, I never dreamed, or I always dreamed, but I never knew . . . that I would actually have you beside me again. I just craved something beautiful that I loved to accompany me once more."

He wove his hand through her chestnut waves. "I know, you have so many questions, and so do I. Let me start at the end, so I can just tell you how I came to be in this place at this time. And then you will tell me the same. I need you to know how my travels have led me to this city. During World War II, I was stationed on the Aleutian Islands, off the coast of Alaska, where America was on the alert for another Japanese attack, this time at our northernmost territory. You can imagine the weather could be brutal, although the mountain landscapes were beautiful. There was a group of airmen who had received their flight training in this very area of Florida, and they loved telling about their time on the Palm Beach coast, before they were sent into action. As we sat around talking, our puffs of breath visible either from the cold air or our cigarette smoke, they said that their fond memories of Florida were what they would hold on to while on their combat missions—the desire to return to Florida, to vacation or maybe even raise families where the sun was always shining and the weather was warm."

"So last month, when I saw an article about beautiful Palm Beach homes and this exclusive resort, called The Breakers Hotel, I was reminded of those wartime conversations. You probably know the place. It's rather large." She didn't answer him, but covertly smiled to herself. "I felt that I had earned a vacation and it was time that I took one. I'm a few days into a stay at the resort. I've been exploring the area to see if it's right for me. I was looking at some real estate, and as I always do, I sought out a synagogue. After the Shabbas service last Saturday, I told them I would like to join the congregation. Even if I did not move to the area, it was a contribution I would like to make. I've done this before, in blessed memory of my family. I think if you have success, then *tzedakah*, our giving of charity, is important." He was suddenly overcome with a feeling of contentment, having someone to share these thoughts with who really knew his family. He saw that a few stray strands of hair were bothering Rebecca, and he gently whisked them away from her eye and wrapped them behind her ear. Jacob could not yet understand what that simple gesture meant to her, and he continued talking. "You know how welcoming the temple ladies can be. They put me to work shelving books as soon as they saw me walk in today," he laughed out. Then he took her hand again and brought it to his lips. "Rebecca, would you come with me to the hotel? I have a beautiful suite there."

Rebecca shifted uncomfortably in her seat. "Jacob, please. I don't live far from here. Please let's just go to my home so we can talk."

"But your husband, what will he think? How will you explain who I am?" He paused, and then he admitted what he tried to ignore. "I should be ashamed, I did see it, but not before it was too late to control myself. I saw the ring on your finger."

Rebecca shook her head and offered a slight laugh. "Jacob, it's okay. I have been a widow now for four years." He finally realized that although he had been talking, although he had been captured in reminiscing with her, he had been holding his breath in between, and now he felt like he had been given a tank of oxygen.

It was not far to her bungalow. She directed him turn by turn, but he could hardly concentrate on the road. He knew he could never sell the vehicle, for the joy of having her in it. Even at this slow speed, with her hair blowing only slightly in the wind, her sunglasses added to her glamorous appeal. She could be mistaken for a movie star.

Before they left the car and they went into the house, Rebecca needed to understand something.

"Please just explain this," she said. "How is this possible?" she asked, gesturing around the car.

"And you think I don't have a million questions about you?" he echoed, struggling to make sense of it all. He thought for a moment, as he tried to decide where was the best place to start. "Perhaps the easiest answer is about the car," he finally said. "Isn't a luxurious car part of the American dream? Apparently, the years have brought many changes for each of us. But you knew this about me. You said it before I even knew it myself. Do you remember when I spoke to you about having a store instead of a stall? Do you remember?"

She whispered a "yes" back to him. "I said that next, you will be talking about going to America, where they say the streets are paved in gold." His spirits were elevating by the moment. He now knew, like him, that she had a recording in her head of every one of their conversations.

He finished this one for her, "And then you warned me to keep my voice down, and not let the Soviets hear me."

With that terrible word, "Soviets," her stomach lurched, and she fought a wave of nausea.

Her mouth angled down into a frown. "They took him. Oh Jacob, the Soviets took him. They took them all, my father and his friends. Most likely, they killed them all."

"Rebecca, what are you saying?" he now cried out himself. "Please don't say that was what happened to your wonderful father, Abraham."

She started with a few tears and then the sobbing continued in intensity. Jacob wrapped his arms around her, and they cried together. She closed her eyes, and she was in New York City again, having just read the letter from Mrs. Gorshen, telling her of her father's fate. She tried to regain control. Jacob walked around to open her car door, and he escorted Rebecca up the walk to her front door, with his arms firmly around her shoulders.

At the house, Rebecca prepared a pot of hot tea for them to share. She placed an assortment of her own freshly baked cupcakes on a plate. Sitting at the kitchen table, Jacob noticed the beautiful tablecloth and napkin set. He tried to lighten the moment. "Quite impressive," he said, as if it were all those years ago and he wanted to purchase her decorative linens. She smiled at the comment and then looked into his eyes with an almost searing need. Jacob set the linen pieces aside and took her hands in his. "How did you come to be here?" he asked. There was an intensity of caring in his voice, that was levels beyond sheer curiosity. "I don't mean here in this city or here in this house. I mean here, in America. After I arrived, I was desperately working to earn money to send for you. But, it's . . . it's so complicated." He shook his head in frustration. How could he possibly make her understand and believe what the memory of their time together had meant to him through all these years?

"When I arrived in New York, things were not as I expected. I don't even know how to explain it." He told her about his voyage to America, and how, in third class, he met the group of young adults like himself, Jews who were fleeing Eastern Europe, looking for opportunities, and not just a society with freedom of religion, but also a freedom from the strict religious guidelines of their ancestors. "We all embraced Judaism; we were like-minded. We all just wanted a more modern way to be Jews, like you were in St. Petersburg. But when my uncle saw me on the dock waving to him, at first he did not even recognize me." He paused to give her space to digest the power of his next words. "And then he shunned me. Without my beard, my curled *payas*, or my *tallit katan* with my *tzitzis* showing under my clothes, with a modern cap over my *kepa*, instead of my wide-brimmed Hasidic black hat, he accused me of leaving the faith, of wanting to be an American gentile. He spit on the ground, showing his disdain for me. You have to believe . . ." Again, he paused so that Rebecca could absorb the images of his humiliation. "I tried thanking him for the passage, explaining that I had not left our faith. Though he dismissed me, I followed him to his apartment." Jacob cupped his hands at his forehead and continued to shake his head in frustration. "I found my belongings set outside when I woke the next morning.

"I had to live on the streets for months, finding ways to pay him back and then ways to earn more money so I could get you and then my family here. And I did pay him back quickly when I had made the money. I wrote to you and my father constantly but received no letters in return. When I understood my uncle would not show me any letters even if they came, I used another return address. A nice butcher who lived several blocks away was sympathetic, and he knew my uncle as a stern and unyielding man. But still, it was like everyone I cared about had disappeared. I was desperately sad."

"Oh Jacob," she cried into his chest. "I never believed what your uncle told me. I knew you would never have disrespected him."

Jacob did not understand what she meant. He had no idea she had any interaction with his uncle. And then she told him things he had never known, how the uncle had written that he was held in quarantine. "My father understood that I needed to try to be with you and I would be safer in the United States. He gave me the passage to go to America, to find the uncle and to find you. He wanted me to join you, because he feared for my safety if he was targeted by the Soviets. Once I arrived, I found that you were not held in quarantine. Your uncle lied to your father and to me. I told him I knew you would not give up Judaism, that you just looked for a more modern observance. When I challenged your uncle, he said awful things to me. And so, I left his place and settled in a boarding house, although I stopped by weekly for months to see if you had returned or letters from my father had arrived. I left information with your aunt, as to where I would be, but that poor woman, I knew, was too paralyzed to follow her own conscience.

"Eventually, I learned English, as a kind gentleman from London that I met on the passenger liner to America had advised me to do. I stayed in New York for a few years and worked my way up from a seamstress to a salesperson at Bloomingdale's Department Store."

Jacob was overwhelmed by Rebecca's strength. What an amazing girl he had planned to have as his bride. "Just explain to me, Rebecca, I know I am not the same observant Jew that I was raised to be, but I swear, I did not forsake God, no matter what my uncle said. Each time I traveled to a new city, I searched for any kind of *shul* to attend. I pleaded with God to believe I did not abandon him. So, tell me. Why did God abandon me?"

"My darling," Rebecca began, as she reached to surround Jacob's hands with hers and looked lovingly into his eyes. "God did not abandon you," she insisted. "At the right time, he led you here to me."

For a while, they just stood together, clinging to each other, kissing each other's cheeks as tears accumulated.

"How about your father, your sisters? Do you know anything?"

He tried to answer, but he could only weep out the first words, until he collected himself. "I finally did find out, and only in the last few years. I located a friend of the family and learned, just as you said, that my uncle sent letters detailing how I had abandoned my religion, been disrespectful to him, and even stolen money. And these terrible lies drove my father near to madness. He grieved from the heartache and humiliation of it all. So, he packed up the family's belongings and moved in the wrong direction, to a place he felt could withstand the pull of assimilation. He took the girls back to Motele, our hometown in the Pale of Settlement, and their fate was sealed. Eyewitness accounts by the small group of those who lived through it, who ran into the woods and were aided by partisans, confirmed that my father and my sisters were viciously murdered." With the last two words, he began sobbing, his body wracked by unfathomable images of brutality, of complicity with the Nazis by the Poles, that had been described to him, that he could not bear to repeat.

Once more, Rebecca wrapped her arms around Jacob, and they cried together. Then she led him to her bedroom, and they stood in front of the bed, just studying each other's faces, mesmerized as they looked at their reflections in the mirror. It validated that they were finally together again. When Rebecca sat on the bed, she pulled him to join her. She laid her head on the pillow. For a full minute, he could not stop staring at her face, but then he began to carefully release each button of her blouse and she sat up and tossed it to the floor. He unhooked her bra, as she raised her arms, and then that garment was flung on the carpet. "You are so exquisite. You are twenty years old," he said. He touched and tasted her beautiful breasts, until he could no longer control his hunger. He unzipped her skirt and maneuvered it completely off her body. She raised her hips, helping him to undress her. And then he threw off his own clothes. Slowly, he explored the contours of her still exquisite body, until she begged him for the final act of desire. They made love slowly the first time, and then with an uncontrollable intensity, until the hunger for each of them was satiated. They laughed and cried together the next morning, waking up in each other's arms, marveling at the miracle that had literally made each of their dreams come true.

Chapter 31

PALM BEACH 1954

For breakfast, Rebecca created a cheese soufflé and offered
fresh orange juice and biscuits. Jacob grabbed her around the
waist, as she used mitts to withdraw the casserole from the
oven. "What are you doing?" she scolded, "the soufflé is delicate. It might deflate before I serve it. Are you crazy?"

"Yes, to that question," Jacob teased back. "I am crazy,
crazy in love with you." He took the dish from her, using a
towel as a hot pad. She went to the table and poured him a cup

of freshly brewed coffee and she added a fair amount of cream. "You remembered how I like things," he smiled.

"That was an easy one. Now I know how you like a lot of things," she returned, coyly.

With those words, Jacob could hardly think of anything except holding her again, but he knew how happy she was to have prepared the breakfast for him. "I'm thinking of plans for later today, but I know we should continue catching up now. I want to hear about you, and then my turn can be over lunch or dinner. "So, how did you meet your husband?" he asked first, pointing to a silver framed wedding picture, resting on a coffee table between two fashionable black and white patterned chairs. Can you tell me about the photograph? I'm betting that is your daughter as the bride. She is beautiful. She reminds me of you."

Then he pointed to the man next to Rebecca in the picture. "Tell me about him."

"Yes, that man was my husband, Harrison Abelman. Remember, I mentioned the man on the ship who told me how important it was to learn the language of the country to secure a better position in any field of work."

"A shipboard romance? And on the way to come meet me, supposedly," Jacob said, suspiciously.

"No, not a romance, just a friendship. She explained how Harrison was recruited from the Savoy Hotel in London to be an Assistant Manager at The Breakers Hotel in Palm Beach. She told him about the slip of paper Harrison had given her before they disembarked, detailing how to reach him if her plans did not work out. And she said that is what led her to Florida, at her lowest point in New York, when she learned the fate of her father. "So in answer to your question from yesterday, yes, I am familiar with The Breakers. It was my elegant, glorious home until Harrison passed away a few years ago. We lived there with our daughter, Addie, in a manager's apartment suite."

Harrison could not hide his astonishment. "You lived at The Breakers . . . in that magnificent setting?"

"It was a most privileged life," Rebecca answered, modestly. "We were working people, although we spent our years among the elite of society and the captains of industry."

For a moment, Jacob digested what he had been told. "Did you love each other very much, you and Harrison?"

"He was a good man, a good provider and a dedicated worker."

"You haven't answered the question."

"There was comfort; there were good times and responsibilities on both our parts. We were blessed with the most wonderful daughter, and a circle of friends from the hotel and the neighborhood and from the temple you were just at. Addie's marriage is to Nathan Bernstein. His mother, Eleanor, was the woman who just introduced me to you."

"But . . ." he interjected, knowing there was more and wanting to hear it.

"But," she sighed out, uneasily, "however I tried to mold Harrison into someone physically and emotionally loving, he was not that type of person. Perhaps the fault was mine, in not accepting him for who he was. And so . . . no, our marriage was never what I imagined it could have been with you." Jacob took in a deep breath, trying to stifle an emerging sob. No words could have meant more to Jacob to help erase the pain of the lost years.

Later, he told her he wanted to go on a drive. This time, she prepared herself with a scarf to keep her hair away from her face while it played in the wind. "I want this to be a special day," he said. He had obviously researched the area before he arrived. "Can we start on Ocean Boulevard?"

As they toured, Rebecca pointed out the homes of her friends, like the Evington's estate, and those of famous people, like Marjorie Merriweather Post, who was using her property, Mar-a-Lago, often for charity functions, most notably the Red Cross Ball. Next, he wanted directions to Worth Avenue. He knew she would resist him, but he insisted she shop for a negligee and a new dress. "Anything you want, and, yes, I imagine you have made yourself the most beautiful clothes, but please give me this pleasure. I have money, and a lot of time to make up for." He opened her purse and put an envelope with cash inside. While she went shopping, he stopped at a few stores himself, and he made a lunch reservation at Ta-boo, where she had been told to meet him at one o'clock.

At the restaurant, she was greeted warmly by the host and many of the patrons, who looked at the couple curiously, wondering who was this handsome gentleman with their lovely Rebecca.

"Will you show me your shopping bags?" Jacob asked.

She was shy to open the packages. "Certainly, not here, not now, but anyway, you promised it would be your turn to tell me about your journey."

He was ready and eager to share his story with her, and he began as their first drinks were served, barely finishing the narrative by the dessert. He told her how he had remained in Manhattan for a few months, beginning as a pushcart vendor, hawking goods on the lower East side but quickly moving on, realizing there was no sense in poor people selling to each other. He then began accumulating merchandise, from clothing and accessories to household items. He would drive to increasingly distant towns and then cities. He had a salesman's personality, an engaging manner, and quality products. Store owners found his goods quickly leaving their shelves. They were anxious for his next deliveries. After a while, he added men's and women's specialty health and beauty products to his inventory. Eventually, he became tired of moving from town to town, where there might be one clothing store, a few barber shops and beauty parlors, and just one general store. He became tired of being a *schlepper*, dragging his goods around, although he was successful in his job. In these years, with his exposure to quality goods, he became more fastidious in his own dress and appearance.

"I took my job so seriously, that I became critical of the way my items, and even those of other vendors, were displayed in the stores. Tabletops that were neatly stacked with pricey apparel would fall prey to customers' ill-mannered shopping habits and would become haphazard messes partway through the day. Nice, modern stores sometimes looked worse than our old outdoor bazaars, with merchandise cluttered and in disarray. In servicing my accounts, I would go over and straighten my customers' product displays, and often, when I entered a building, the call would go out, 'Hey, bring some cakes, Jack is back, and he'll straighten us up.' Then I started to think. Could I turn my proclivity for neatness into a marketable skill? What is it that I could sell to every type of store? What is it that every store needs? And I realized they needed organization – tables and racks, and shelving, dedicated to their particular specialty. Along the way, I befriended most of the owners from all cultures, and so many were immigrant Jews, like myself. They had established small stores, many growing those stores into large family businesses, selling everything from groceries to pharmaceutical needs, to shoes and clothing. In the forested areas of the Carolinas, I met manufacturers of lumber goods. Eventually, I partnered with a production firm and made a catalogue of retail shop necessities, even shelving specific to restaurants or bakeries, for instance.

"I was so proud to be in this country that had afforded me opportunities. I was so proud to be an American, to have served my country in World War II. At first, I named my company American Store Supply, until someone pointed out the initials read ASS. Quickly, I realized the name should be United States Store Supply. My card read, and my advertising said, "For all of your retail store needs, Come to Us – USSS, United States Store Supply." He took out his card and gave it to her. "I would make my appointments and mail the stores our catalogue, and then I would travel to the shops to take some measurements and make some sketches to help them decide what they needed. I was traveling then in a car with only a catalogue and some samples of our quality work. But that is already so long ago. We had a good start, slowed down in the Depression, but grew beyond my dreams with the post-war boom. We sell to mom and pop stores and giant ones, too. Our materials go from woods to metals and there are new synthetics on the pipeline.

Initially, Rebecca didn't know what to say, until she beamed for him. "I'm so proud of you. And you do this all yourself?"

"Rebecca, honey. Over five hundred people work for me now. And that's only because I'm not ready to expand past the Mississippi, but that might happen. I have design and installation teams that go to do our sketching and measurements. I only travel to our biggest, long-time, accounts, like Stein Mart, and Federated Department Stores, for example, to make sure everyone is happy and feels assured that Jack Schaeffer, who they know and trust, is still in charge.

"And no *schlepping*," she added, laughing. "Hence the beautiful car." He fed her a bite of a luscious chocolate layer cake that the waiter had just presented, and he kissed off the buttercream frosting from her lips.

"I've traveled to so many places around the country, building my business," he continued and then he took her hand, looking directly into her eyes. "But along the way, everywhere, in every place, I was always looking for you, often running up to women I thought were you, only to be disappointed. From New York to Cleveland to Chicago to Atlanta, I searched through phone books in every city. Of course, it made no sense, I didn't even know you were in America, but, you see, it didn't matter. Continuing my search kept my hopes alive. "Yes, I went on dates, had a few relationships, but I never married." He stopped to shake his head and give her time to react to what he had said. "It wouldn't have been fair to a wife, to have a husband in her bed with someone else in his head." He did not say it to make her feel bad, as if she had betrayed him. "I'm glad you did, though. I'm glad you married. It is too hard for a woman to be alone, even someone as accomplished as you. And now, my only regret is having had no children, especially since we have learned how many Hitler has taken from us." He dabbed his eyes with his handkerchief, the color of the linen, as would be expected, a perfect complement to his shirt and tie. "Okay, we're done with the catch up and the sadness, so now we go forward." She smiled and nodded at him in agreement.

"But as far as The Breakers, my suite is incredible. Will you do it? I hope you won't feel awkward. Will you join me there tonight?" he asked, but when her face turned frozen, contemplating the propriety of it, he understood. "Let's just leave it at this. I'll pick you up at seven p.m. Just be sure to bring your packages to show me, and we'll at least enjoy dinner in the elegant dining room. Certainly, an exquisite widow is allowed a date night with a . . ." Jacob paused for her to interject a phrase, and she played along.

"With a handsome gentleman," she offered.

"Yes, an old friend who has come into town," he continued.

"It would only be polite," they said in unison.

"One more thing." He paused, and she saw that playful grin again. "I may have another small package for you."

The meal that evening was delicious. Billed as a five-course affair, after the seafood appetizer and the rack of lamb entree, they asked if the dinner could be abbreviated to just three courses, apologizing that the wine and bread had filled them up. One after another, familiar guests and people from the hotel meandered by their table to say hello to Rebecca and get a closer look at the man with her. When he introduced himself to them as Jack Schaeffer, Rebecca smiled and nodded at him, indicating she would try to embrace his new name, at least in public. Standing in corners together, the staff pretended to be at their tasks, but were all covertly gossiping about the pair, until a manager quietly clapped his hands in their direction. He understood their fascination; he felt the same. The dining team knew to allow privacy to celebrities and dignitaries, often filling their tables, but this was their Rebecca with a princely figure. They had often seen Rebecca look as beautiful, but her demeanor as a regal empress had now softened into that of a princess in love.

When they were interrupted again by a well-meaning couple, Jacob motioned to the waiter and politely requested that the dessert be brought to his room. When Jacob looked to Rebecca for concurrence, she shyly nodded and smiled.

Once in the suite, they danced to the music on the radio, fulfilling one of Jacob's ever-persistent dreams, the dream of waltzing together with Rebecca in his arms. She was wearing the lavender dress she had bought that afternoon. She looked breathtaking. But when she changed into the red negligee, Jacob went out of his mind. He wanted her to keep it on as they made love.

In the morning, Jacob had arranged that the bellman leave their breakfast cart outside the door. When they were ready, Jacob rolled in the tray. In the center of a plate enhanced with rose petals, he placed a small gift he had purchased from a Worth Avenue jewelry store while she had been shopping the previous day. He went down on one knee. "Rebecca," he said, "over thirty years ago I asked for and received your father's permission for your hand in marriage once I was settled in America and could afford to send for you. I never was able to ask you the question, directly. But now I cannot wait another hour, another day in fear that some unforeseen twist of fate would keep us apart once more. I know, before we proceed to be husband and wife, I will need to meet your daughter and her husband to convince them I am an honorable man with good intentions. So now I will ask you. Rebecca, my first and forever sweetheart, with apologies for the longest pre-engagement period in history, will you marry me?"

The day after his proposal, Jacob arranged for train tickets for them to meet her daughter, Addie, and son-in-law, Dr. Nate Bernstein, in New York. First, though, Rebecca had a long, emotional conversation with Addie on the phone, and she finally told her about her first love and the full story of her last years in St. Petersburg and her journey to America. Rebecca was sensitive to the fact that Addie might be unable to embrace this shocking turn of events, just several years after the loss of her father. And she would not blame her. Yet, she would not proceed to marriage until Addie was comfortable with the decision and gave her blessing. But, as it turned out, Addie was Rebecca's daughter to the core, having the same romantic heart as her mother. So much of this helped her understand her parents' relationship over the years, something she viewed as almost platonic. Rebecca and Addie cried, once again, over the loss of Harrison, feeling lucky to have had him in their lives. "But now, I'm so happy for you," Addie said over the phone. "I do remember, Mom, even though you may think I didn't hear it, when we spoke after my own engagement. When I asked you about my marrying Nathan, the only boy I ever dated, when you agreed that you truly believed that your first love can be your true and only love, there was something in the way you said it that made me wonder."

Of course, when Addie and Nate met Jacob at dinner at the Waldorf Astoria in Manhattan, they were immediately captured by him. He was so handsome, so well dressed, so well mannered. His slight accent, like Rebecca's, gave him the air of a foreign dignitary, although they came to realize that he was an everyman, the embodiment of the American spirit. They loved hearing his stories, the small steps that chronicled his successes. But he was not full of himself. Rather, he tried to steer the conversation toward their accomplishments. And mostly, they loved the way that Rebecca and Jacob looked at each other. For the entire meal, Jacob kept one arm around Rebecca. It was obvious. He could not bear to let her go.

• • •

Three months after they were finally reunited, Rebecca and Jacob became Mr. and Mrs. Jack Schaeffer at Temple Israel. When they returned from a European honeymoon, Jacob surprised his bride with a beautiful new home. It was one of the iconic beachfront "cottages," the three-story vintage houses of fourteen to fifteen rooms on Breakers' Row that flanked the magnificent hotel to the north and south. Jacob had tied a large red bow to the veranda railing, and he carried Rebecca over the threshold. Although initially she thought he was crazy, when she toured the interior of the house, she began hugging him and sobbing in astonishment and appreciation. She was beginning to understand. No matter what she said, this man was going to spend the remainder of his life making up to her for lost time.

Although Rebecca had questioned why they would need such a place, it was easily filled. There was a constant flow of friends for drinks and dinner, lounging at the beach and playing croquet on the lawn. When they were in town, Natalie and Will Whitney came often with Trey. The little boy who had told his "Aunt Rebecca" that he needed to fulfill his legacy had grown into an impressive young man, going on to Exeter and then his grandfather's university alma mater. There was Edward Evington and his lovely new wife, Mary Elizabeth, and so many friends from the temple and the hotel. Streams of out-of-towners, whom Jacob had befriended in his traveling years, came for extended weekends. And, most important, there was the family. After Nate finished his medical training, he and Addie built a new home in West Palm Beach, and he set up his practice. Addie and Nate would always call Jacob by the name of Jack, as most people did. But with the birth of their children, they made him understand he would be their grandfather, their Papa, as much as Rebecca was their grandmother, their Nana. And to further show their love for their family heritage, Addie and Nate's firstborn, a son, was named Benjamin Hershel, in memory of Nate's brother and Addie's father. When twin girls arrived two years later, Jacob could not stop his outright sobbing on learning that the names of his two sisters who had perished in the Holocaust, Hannah and Sarah, would come to life once more.

Chapter 32

PALM BEACH 1975

Ten years after Jacob purchased their Breakers Row house, the March 31, 1964, the *Miami Herald* ran a story headlined "Joy of Living in an Anachronism."

Although the article stated, "The cottages of Breakers Row have not only withstood but have disdained the changes of time and tide," that had not proven to be true with the passage of one more decade. Then, the *Miami Herald* headline in the Homes Section read, "Beachfront Cottages for Sale But

Cost of Moving Deters Most." It was the era of modernization and high-rise opulent living. "The 20-room, Newport-style homes, termed 'cottages' in typical Palm Beach understatement," the article read, "have to be moved to make room for planned construction of 96 apartments and townhouses just north and south of the hotel. The cottages are no longer economically suitable for The Breakers, according to a Flagler Systems spokesperson."

In truth, Jacob and Rebecca were fine with this decision. They began looking forward to their next move to a beautiful luxury apartment building along Ocean Boulevard.

• • •

Kathryn Morgan and her daughter, Beth, had had their suite at The Breakers for over a month, although some of that time Kathryn had still spent in the hospital, with Beth a dedicated visitor.

After two weeks at JFK Memorial, Kathryn was released. Dr. Nate felt she was well enough to return to her room at the hotel. His initial diagnosis seemed to hold up. She had a TIA, a transient ischemic attack, a mini-stroke, that left her with no marked disabilities. Her blood pressure was being controlled and now was within the acceptable range. The scare of it all had soured her taste for cigarettes, and she promised to restrict herself to only one glass of wine a day. But Nate knew it would be a struggle to maintain her new regimen. When he suggested she try chewing gum to help her with the withdrawal process, her answer was emphatic. "Dr. Nate, a lady does not chew gum in public." He had known her only for a brief time, but he identified her answer as "classic Kathryn." He encouraged her to remain in the area for at least another month, perhaps more. The beautiful weather would be good for her, and she would not feel trapped in her Manhattan townhome, having to stay inside most of the still-cold days up north. He did not want her focusing only on what she could not do, when she could enjoy a new lifestyle of healthy eating and exercise In Palm Beach. Medically, he felt he was giving sound advice that would be best for her. He did not tell her that Bear had begged him to find a way to keep her daughter Beth in Palm Beach for as long as possible. Addie and Nate had known since their first dinner together with the pair that Bear was in love with Beth. And within a short time, they recognized the feelings were quite mutual.

At home in New York, the Morgan housekeeper, Marie, was so extremely worried about her lady that Kathryn and Beth came up with the same idea. They would fly Marie down to Florida as a treat for her, and to be a companion for Kathryn during the recuperation period. Marie could accompany Mrs. Morgan on Worth Avenue shopping trips and be at her side enjoying the beautiful new Breakers' Beach Club that had recently replaced the old Beach Casino on the property.

Beth was appreciative of the free time this new arrangement afforded her. She was busy working on the interior design project from her Manhattan firm, but still, she could not wait to do something very special for Addie. Beth treated her to an art exhibition luncheon at the marvelous Norton Museum of Art on Olive Avenue in West Palm Beach as a way of expressing to this woman, her new friend Addie, just how grateful she was to her. She was responsible for discovering the root of and orchestrating the resolution of her mother's anxiety. Beth could not imagine how her mother could have carried that burden of guilt all those years. She had taken to calling Addie "angel." And then she appeared to her as an angel once more. When Beth told her that it was the Huntington estate that she would be working on through her firm up north, Addie called her acquaintance, "Honey" Huntington, and received high praises for the work that firm had previously done with Honey's Manhattan residence. Addie's mother and her stepfather, Rebecca and Jack Schaeffer, were planning to move into one of the fabulous new apartment buildings that were under construction on Flagler System property. With this connection, Beth was able to secure the interior decorating commission for that project. Again, one of the senior consultants would fly down and work with Beth and the client on the initial architectural and design concept, but Beth's bosses had already sent her a bouquet of flowers with a note saying they saw great potential with her at the firm.

Beth knew of the revered Rebecca through the correspondence between Addie and Natalie from thirty years ago, and she was excited to have this opportunity to meet her. Once again, as Rebecca herself had prophesied during the war years, Addie's role had been as a listener, the one to make connections.

As they spent time on decorating plans, Rebecca told Beth about reuniting with her long-lost Russian love after Addie's father had passed away in the 1950s. She learned of her early years helping to dress the tsarina and her daughters in St. Petersburg, and her career as a courtier dress and fabric designer in America. Oftentimes, Beth felt that she actually learned more about style from working with Rebecca than she helped Rebecca to make selections.

Chapter 33

PALM BEACH 1975

At The Breakers' residence of Kathryn and Beth Morgan, a new arrangement was made when their housekeeper arrived. Marie shared the suite with her employer, sleeping in the smaller bedroom, and Beth moved to a room of her own on the floor below. Having Marie as her mother's companion also gave Beth precious time to spend alone with Bear. But "alone" was hardly the correct term. His warm and affable style drew people to him wherever they went. Walking the corridors of the hotel, eating or drinking in the lounges, strolling along the beach. Even her mother, once ever-critical of Beth's choices, would say, "There's something about that young man that I like," and then she would reach for her purse and hand Beth some bills. "Take that young man to dinner on me." Along Clematis in the downtown area, he was always recognized and sought out for a "Hey, Bear, join us tonight at the Grille?" or "How long you in town for this time, Bear?" When Beth would say he seemed quite popular, he would make light of it. "Don't be silly. Just bigger, easier to spot than most."

During Bear's docent hours, sometimes Beth tagged along as he led groups on the hotel tour. She saw the young women practically swooning over him. They would think of one more question to ask in order to secure a place closer to where he was, up front. With Bear's height, he could easily spot Beth holding back at the rear of the crowd, and he gave her a wink, which each of the women on his tour thought was meant for her.

One afternoon in her room at the hotel, Beth was slow to answer the continually ringing phone and missed the call. She had just returned from swimming laps in the pool and had come back to change for dinner. She had simply dozed off while engrossed in a book. When finally she awoke to an increasing blast of knocks on her door, she feared something more had happened to her mother while she was napping. As she opened the door, only slightly, she saw it was Bear. She had a look of dread on her face. "Is everything okay?" she asked, fearfully.

"Well, yes, except that I called from the lobby, and you didn't answer. I couldn't wait until dinner to tell you something." He paused, and realized he should add, "Something good. Don't worry, everything is okay." When he saw she was in her swimsuit, he said, "Except, well, you're not even dressed and it's . . . well, it's kind of time to go." He started to turn away to give her a chance to change, but she opened the door wider.

"I guess I fell asleep," she said, rubbing her eyes like a toddler awakening from a nap. "So sorry. Give me a few minutes. I'll change quickly."

Since the beginning, they each knew their attraction was undeniable. They devoured each other often in kisses. But Bear was the cautious one, not wanting to rush her into a hasty rebound relationship when she had just come off a broken engagement. But that was then, and this is now, he thought.

"This is now, wow," he whispered aloud, in a dreamlike state. She was intoxicating. "Well, wait a minute. Could you, could you maybe stay in your swimsuit," he stammered out. He looked at her enticing figure, defined by the tight contours of the black and gold vertical stripes of the suit. In her sleepy state, her hair was still somewhat damp and messy. Beth had not realized that one of her breasts was partially escaping the fitted cup of her plunging neckline. Bear had never seen her so sensually, imperfectly . . . perfect. He couldn't stop looking at her. He couldn't stop wanting her. He was in her bedroom and she was in her swimsuit . . . that is, somewhat in her swimsuit.

With no further hesitation, he accepted her offer to come inside. And then she was not in her swimsuit for much longer. For both of them, emotionally and physically, there was no past. There was only the present . . . and the future.

When they awoke together, hours later, clasped in each other's arms, they looked around at the room and at the mirror. Their hair was a mess, their clothes were strewn about, the elegant, plush linens, pillows, and duvet of the bed lay in a twisted wrinkled pile. Bear began to laugh. "What?" Beth giggled back, inquisitively.

"I feel like the squire of the manor house who has just ravished the peasant girl in the barn haystack," he said.

"The Breakers? Not quite a barn," Beth smiled back.

"Not quite a peasant girl," Bear corrected himself.

"Not quite against her will," Beth said.

"Oh no," he agreed, "definitely a mutual lustful act."

Suddenly, Bear shook his head, as if he were struggling to remember something. "Wait, I came here for a reason. I had something important to tell you."

"That's right, somehow that got lost in the . . ." she struggled for the next words.

"In the sheets," Bear said, once again, finishing her sentence. "I want to take you to my place. I have some news to share."

"What is it? Can you tell me now?" and then she thought about it. "Wait, I didn't know you had a place you wanted to take me to. You always made it sound like you lived above a garage, so I never pressed."

He laughed to himself at what she must have imagined. "I'm going to try to smooth out my clothes enough to make it through the beach exit and to my car. I'll be back in one hour. Look beautiful, but not too sexy, please, or we'll never get out of here, again." He thought it over. "Maybe I better just call you from the lobby and you can come down."

His garage apartment was the impressive coach house of a grand beachfront estate about eight blocks from the hotel. "So, you're a historian, a docent and a caretaker, too?" she asked.

"Well, not quite, but I do have a third vocation." He grabbed her hand and quickly brought her up the stairs to his enormous and handsomely decorated living space. He escorted her to a seat on a small curved sofa. "I received this today. I could only think that I wanted to share this news with you." He opened a large manilla envelope and withdrew a set of papers. "This came from my agent. A New York publisher has offered me a substantial advance on my book based on my dissertation: 'Flagler's Florida Vision.'"

Beth threw her arms around his neck, planting kisses on his face and lips, and then she just broke away, smiling. "So, you are a historian, a docent, a caretaker, and a writer," she said, emphasizing the last word.

"But not a caretaker," he corrected her. "In fact," he said, shyly, almost embarrassed. "I have a caretaker." She looked skeptical as she scanned the room and saw unkempt stacks of enormous books from a variety of historical periods. There were some piles of paper next to the typewriter on his desk, and others spread randomly across the floor. "He just knows not to touch any of my research." Beth was trying to digest all of this. "You see, this is my grandfather's estate. The coach house is for me whenever I'm in the area," Bear explained.

"But don't worry," he continued, "We don't have to live here. We can live anywhere you want. Nate told you I've had university job offers in various places. I promise, I'll let you decide."

"Wait, Bear, um, I'm just wondering why I would be deciding or why I would be living here."

"Oh, I guess I forgot one part. Did you see the movie *The Absent-Minded Professor*?" She nodded, smiling, almost laughing. "I guess I forgot to tell you that I love you and to ask you if you would marry me." He barely paused for breath, "but this is not the official asking, not in this mess. Will you give me another chance to do it better, in a beautiful place? And maybe I should ask your mother first."

Tears were forming in her eyes. "Yes, Bear, yes to everything you just said," she answered softly.

"But before we leave," he said cautiously, "maybe we should discuss one more thing I just found out."

Chapter 34

PALM BEACH 1975

Over the years, Addie had always remained in close contact with her great friend, Natalie, no matter where each of them resided. But in the last weeks, their phone conversations were an endless stream of priceless memories. They loved the intimacy of hearing each other's voices and the convenience of phone calls, but they acknowledged that the almost lost art of letter writing should be credited for giving everyone closure to this chapter of personal history that had allowed Addie to weave the story of their lives into Kathryn Morgan's world.

In a brief phone conversation arranged by Addie, Natalie assured Kathryn that what Addie had told her was correct. She never blamed her for not passing on the letter. Natalie acknowledged that it was her place to approach Theo's parents if she had wanted; Kathryn would only be needed to corroborate the story. Natalie said she could tell that Kathryn had a good heart. As Kathryn listened to Natalie, she felt grateful for her words, but she remained nervous, overwhelmed by so many emotions that she found it hard to speak. Finally, Kathryn said that she was sincerely delighted to hear that Natalie had eventually married and was incredibly happy. But she was still cautious to ask about meeting Trey. When she finally did, Natalie said he would be coming to a Palm Beach get together that Addie had arranged for the next weekend. Natalie added that she could not wait to meet Kathryn, so the two women would have a chance to talk. She hoped to share memories of the Theo they each loved, one as a brother, one as a boyfriend. They were the same words Kathryn would have said, if she could have found her voice.

• • •

The formal table in a private area of the new Venetian dining room at The Breakers was a beautifully set large oval. As the group entered pair by pair, Addie directed the guests to their chairs while making any necessary introductions. Addie and Nate Bernstein sat across from Kathryn, with Rebecca and Jacob next to them. Kathryn knew it was Natalie the minute she entered. She was certainly the woman who had set flowers on her brother's grave so many years ago. She had the same stately carriage and beauty. The years had been kind to her.

Although she had obviously aged, she could still be a runway model for the Palm Beach set. Immediately, Natalie walked over to Kathryn and gave her a sincere hug, which a teary-eyed Kathryn returned with the same warmth. Natalie's husband, Will, by her side, was a perfect match for her. He did not look at all like Theo might have looked now, had he been given the gift of years of life, but even within minutes of meeting him, Kathryn saw he had the same bright and warm appeal. Finally, Beth walked in and took the seat next to her mother, with Bear on her other side. Natalie nodded to each of them, knowing they would talk more later. Suddenly, Kathryn, her face targeting the entrance to the room, appeared disappointed and gave a concerned look to Beth, who took her hand and patted it. Kathryn was apprehensive to say what she was thinking, but she found the courage. "Natalie, dear. I was hoping that I would be able to meet your son, Trey. I know I don't deserve to. And it's okay if you felt he shouldn't come. Perhaps, you don't want him confused with an aunt he never knew."

"You do know, Kathryn," Natalie said, smiling and almost laughing in a comforting, not condescending way, as she went over to her and put a hand on her shoulder, "Trey is not a boy anymore. He is a grown man."

Natalie paused for a moment as Kathryn processed that and shook her head and said, "Of course."

"Nevertheless," Natalie continued, "ever since he was old enough to understand, Trey has known the circumstances of his birth, that I was pregnant when his father died in combat. For his early years, he embraced my father, his grandfather, as his male role model, and I guess I would have to say, his bond with his grandfather has never diminished. But when I married Will, he wanted Trey to know that he would be his dad, and he insisted on adopting him. But Will would never want him to lose the heritage connected to what he refers to as Trey's huge given name, Theodore Edward Evington III. He wanted us to be a real family, especially because we hoped to add to that family one day." There was a long pause, and Natalie continued with great pride, reaching for her husband's hand. "And we did," she said, with a jubilant voice, "We have a daughter. Trey has a sister, Julia, who is in college near the Bernstein girls." Natalie sent a smile to Addie and Nate as she said this.

"So, I will meet him?" Kathryn said, her hopes elevated.

"But Kathryn, you know Trey already. In fact, you know him well, I understand," Natalie said to her. And then she repeated a story as it was told to her. "You see, when Trey went to school at Exeter, although he envisioned himself as more a scholar than an athlete, the school coach saw him at orientation and recruited him to come out for the first practice of the football team. He was taller and bigger than most of the other players. The coach looked at the tryout roster on his clipboard and just shook his head. One by one, he called the names and it seemed like a full third of them were Theodores. Just like so many of their fathers, they were named after the twenty-sixth US president, the beloved Theodore Roosevelt. 'I'll tell you what,' the coach said to the group, 'I just can't have one more Theo, Ted, or Teddy on the team. You guys will never even figure out who I am yelling at half of the time. So, you, Mr. Theodore Edward Evington III, I don't know what you like to be called, but let's just call you who you are. Not Theo, Ted or Teddy, but Bear. And I want to see you living up to that name on defense.'"

At first, Kathryn sat silent in her chair, with an open mouth and a glazed look on her face. "Oh my God," she said loud enough that people at neighboring tables glanced in her direction. Suddenly, her facial expression turned into a broad smile and her eyes almost lit up. She turned to Beth in astonishment, "Can you believe this? Did you know this?"

Beth stood up and walked behind her mother's chair, directing her answer to Kathryn, but allowing the group to also hear what she had to say. "I had no idea until two days ago when Bear told me that his mother, Natalie, would be coming into town. You see, before then, Bear only knew the beginning of the story, the background I had told him and Addie and Nate when we went to dinner at Ta-boo, one of the first evenings you were in the hospital. I told them you seemed really disturbed about something, especially when you heard about the babies born at The Breakers. I thought that had to do with me, since I've always known I was adopted. But I was too young to have been one of the babies. Bear never really knew about the letters and the connection until his mother just called and told him the whole story of why she was coming to town to see Kathryn Morgan, and that he would meet his real aunt."

On Kathryn's right side, Bear had crouched down to talk to her. He hugged her and kissed her lightly on the cheek. "I need to take over the story," he said, so they all could hear. "On the very night that Beth and I knew how serious we were about each other, I came to realize that she is my first cousin. I was stunned and a little nervous while processing that. But then I remembered, like she just said, Beth had told us she was adopted." He smiled broadly. "And I could breathe again. And so, with your permission, I hope soon to ask Beth, who is my cousin, but not genetically, to be my wife." He sent a wink to Beth, and then turned back to Kathryn. "And I would ask to call you Aunt Kathryn if I may, for now, that is, until I hope to call you Mother."

"Oh, Bear, you would do that, even after you learned from your mom how I threw away the letter, how I denied you of your birthright?"

"Aunt Kathryn, my mother doesn't just forgive you, but she understands why you did it. We talked about it. You did more than most people would do. More than once, even when you didn't know there was a baby for sure, you came to find me. And I'm grateful for that . . . and grateful because this time you brought Beth to me when you came."

Kathryn took Bear's face in her hands and really looked at him. "You have Theo's cowlick, I see." Tears swelled in her eyes, and she started to sniffle. "Something about you, from the beginning, just felt comfortable and familiar to me. It's not as much your looks. I think it's your confidence and your caring manner." Beth was touched by the new, softer version of Kathryn that had been emerging.

Rebecca was the first to stand up. "Let's toast to this evening, to this reunion, and to Beth and Bear, soon to be engaged."

Jacob stood, as all the others did the same. "My advice, Bear," he said, lifting his cup high, "is proceed with the engagement and the wedding with your beautiful Beth as soon as possible." Everyone laughed, knowing how long it took for their storybook ending to come about.

"A toast to Addie," Kathryn said next. "Thank you for everything."

"To Addie," they all echoed.

Next, Beth was clinking her crystal goblet to gain everyone's attention. "We have one more thing to celebrate." She looked proudly at the man she loved. "To Bear, who has just received a publishing contract for his book," she announced. They all put down their glasses and began applauding.

Humbly, Bear motioned for them to stop. He reached for his drink with one hand and pulled Beth closer to him with the other. He smiled down to her and kissed her forehead. And then he raised his glass as he scanned the group. "To Henry Morrison Flagler," he boomed out, "the subject of my book, the man who developed Florida into a vacation destination, the founder of our beautiful Breakers. I thank him for his passion for the grande dame hotel that has touched all of our lives and brought us to this day."

The End

AUTHOR'S NOTES AND ACKNOWLEDGMENTS

Researching and writing a novel involving The Breakers of Palm Beach has been a true labor of love for me over the past several years. The hotel was a most fertile setting for my own personal passion: reading and writing historical fiction. Spending an increasing amount of time in Florida, I have continually been drawn to the allure of the property, with its rich history and historical significance from the Gilded Age through so many decades of the twentieth century. Once I discovered the incredible vision of Henry Morrison Flagler in developing The Breakers, and then learned of the hotel's devastation and rebirth through fires and its supportive role in

WWII, I was hooked. I started to picture fictional characters to weave through the timeline.

And, yes—all my main characters (those around the dining table as the novel ends) are my own creations. But I do try to design their stories to reflect the universal human experience of the eras. And there will be times when they will interact with actual figures from the past.

For that ability, I give great thanks to the Historical Society of Palm Beach, where I had the privilege of spending days in their research room. The staff was most helpful in pulling an abundance of requested newspaper gfr articles from their archives. Clippings from 1926 and 1927 stories in the *Palm Beach Post* and the *Palm Beach Independent* afforded me the opportunity to have actual witnesses tell Rebecca their stories in their own words of the night of The Breakers' fire.

References in the novel to well-known personalities, historical figures who have been guests of the hotel, are also documented through research, although any dialogue is conjecture.

I was sensitive to offer an accurate portrayal of Palm Beach Jewish life in my novel, as I envisioned Jacob and then Rebecca coming to the area. In my research on this point, I was especially drawn to an article from *The New York Social Diary* titled *Best Friends: Jewish Society in Old Palm Beach*. At Rebecca's first dinner with Jacob and the temple group, I tried to introduce the revolving history of antisemitism in the area, where affluent Jews were sometimes accepted, sometimes restricted from clubs and venues.

Although there have been rumors that Jewish people were never allowed at The Breakers, that is not true. Since the early 1900s, there have been Jewish guests at the hotel. Many of the most prominent and successful Jewish families enjoyed weeks or seasons at the resort. In March of 1965, however, the Anti-Defamation League, a division of B'nai B'rith, one of the largest Jewish organizations, filed a complaint against The Breakers, and the federal government targeted the hotel for a test case of the recently enacted Civil Rights Act. When written hotel reservation requests for those with traditionally Jewish surnames were denied and similar requests from those with recognizably gentile names were accepted, the ADL presented their evidence to the Department of Justice. While denying the charges, The Breakers did agree to adhere to the Civil Rights Act. The owners said if there may have been a covert practice of selective discrimination over the years, that practice would end.

I would also like to give credit to the following publications for providing a wealth of information that helped my characters live out their stories in their historical framework.

Images of America, Palm Beach County During World War II
    by Susan Gillis, Richard A. Marconi, and Debi Murray

Flagler Museum, An Illustrated Guide

The Breakers, A Century of Grand Traditions

Jews of Florida, Centuries of Stories, by Marcia Jo Zerivitz

Countless news stories, many of them retrospectives from the *Palm Beach Post*, the *Post-Times*, the *Daily News*, the *Christian Science Monitor*, and the *Miami Herald* helped me to re-create a portrait of the times.

Many thanks to the editorial and design professionals, whose guidance and encouragement brought the book to life: Alyssa Matesic, Laura Boyle, and Skye Loyd.

ABOUT THE AUTHOR

Deby Eisenberg is a former high school teacher and journalist who has a master's degree in English education from the University of Chicago. With her first novels, book club favorites *PICTURES OF THE PAST* and *PROTECTING PAIGE*, she enjoyed touring as a Jewish Book Council author. Deby and her husband Michael, an obstetrician-gynecologist, live in Florida and the Chicago suburbs. They have three children and nine grandchildren.